conditions
of a
heart

ALSO BY BETHANY MANGLE

Prepped
All the Right Reasons

conditions
of a
heart

BETHANY MANGLE

Margaret K. McElderry Books

New York   London   Toronto   Sydney   New Delhi

MARGARET K. McELDERRY BOOKS

An imprint of Simon & Schuster Children's Publishing Division

1230 Avenue of the Americas, New York, New York 10020

MARGARET K. McELDERRY BOOKS is a trademark of Simon & Schuster, LLC.

Simon & Schuster: Celebrating 100 Years of Publishing in 2024

For information about special discounts for bulk purchases, please contact Simon & Schuster Special Sales at 1-866-506-1949 or business@simonandschuster.com.

The Simon & Schuster Speakers Bureau can bring authors to your live event. For more information or to book an event, contact the Simon & Schuster Speakers Bureau at 1-866-248-3049 or visit our website at www.simonspeakers.com.

Interior design by Irene Metaxatos

The text for this book was set in Sabon LT Std.

Manufactured in the United States of America

First Edition

10 9 8 7 6 5 4 3 2 1

Library of Congress Cataloging-in-Publication Data

Names: Mangle, Bethany, author. Title: Conditions of a heart / Bethany Mangle. Description: First edition. | New York : Margaret K. McElderry Books, 2024. | Audience: Ages 14 up. | Audience: Grades 10-12. | Summary: After an incident leads to her suspension, eighteen-year-old Brynn's high school persona that hides her secret disability is shattered, and she begins embracing her true self on her journey to self-acceptance. | Identifiers: LCCN 2023017361 (print) | LCCN 2023017362 (ebook) | ISBN 9781665937634 (hardcover) | ISBN 9781665937641 (paperback) | ISBN 9781665937689 (ebook) | Subjects: CYAC: Self-acceptance—Fiction. | Health—Fiction | Ehlers-Danlos syndrome—Fiction. | High schools—Fiction. | Schools—Fiction. | LCGFT: Novels. Classification: LCC PZ7.1.M364675 Co 2024 (print) | LCC PZ7.1.M364675 (ebook) | DDC [Fic]—dc23

LC record available at https://lccn.loc.gov/2023017361

LC ebook record available at https://lccn.loc.gov/2023017362

For anyone who has ever
fought themselves from
the inside out

AUTHOR'S NOTE

This book considers what the world might have been like several years after quarantine if COVID-19 were no longer a threat. I made this choice deliberately to show that even if COVID-19 is eventually eradicated, it doesn't mean that life returns to normal for the disabled, chronically ill, or vulnerable people who were treated as expendable. We learned hard lessons about who society deems worthy. This is not meant to minimize that experience in any way.

Additionally, Brynn's story reflects my personal experiences with one subtype of Ehlers-Danlos syndrome and other disorders. It's not meant to be fully representative of these conditions since there are many distinct forms and presentations.

One

I'm just like other girls, and I'll throat-punch anyone who says I'm not.

Every time I turn around, someone is making fun of Basic White Girls. Well, I'm a Basic Yellow Girl, then. I live for yoga pants and bath bombs and pumpkin spice lattes. I have a designated seat in detention and last year's junior prom crown on the doorknob of my closet. Go ahead. Tell me I'm so predictable. Uninspired. Ordinary.

Tell me I'm like everyone else. Please.

I keep my eyes trained on the football field as my hand massages away a dull pulsing in my knee that worsens with every shiver. Between the storm looming on the horizon and the slow creep of time, I know that the pain will only get worse. I can feel the first whisper of winter in my bones, a deep ache lurking beneath flawless makeup and the kind of well-rehearsed smile that hurts if held too long.

My armor.

"Why are we still here again?" Francesca asks off to my right, clutching the sides of her jacket around herself, a broken zipper dangling in between. "It's freezing. We could leave and they'd never know."

The cheerleaders finish up their act and scatter, opening the field for the marching band to parade through in an ornate formation. "My sister's skit is up next. You don't have to stay."

Her face falls, and I search for a quick way to shore up our friendship, if that's what you want to call spending inordinate amounts of time together without so much as making a dent on each other. We're like two refrigerator magnets who would repel each other if only we ever got close enough in the first place. A prolonged acquaintance.

"Thanks for coming, though." I jerk my chin toward the pep rally, where the rest of our prolonged acquaintances are holding instruments or hovering on the sidelines in various sports attire. "It's nice to have company."

She perks up again and shifts closer to me, just an inch.

I lift my phone and start filming as Eliza and the

varsity crew team spread out onto the field. Even at a distance, I can tell that she's nervous from the way she's gripping her fake oar as they pretend to row their plywood boat past the fifty-yard line.

I don't know why she worries so much. With the universe's most tragic quarterback and swimmers who apparently can't swim, we all know the crew team is our school's only chance of winning anything more athletic than hopscotch. "Let's hear it for the Pineland Prep Women's Crew!" the announcer shouts. "First up, the rowers in the women's varsity four: Romano, Lopez, Edelstein, Kwan! Led by Coxswain Jones!"

I scream extra loud for Eliza, who towers over Amy Jones as she shouts into her fake bullhorn. Just as they finish introducing the men's varsity, a dubstep remix of "Row, Row, Row Your Boat" blasts from the stadium speakers, and the junior varsity teams rush out onto the field in full-sized goldfish onesies with blue fins on the backs of their hoods. The last person out is dressed in the Sammy the Shark mascot costume, the torso naked where it usually sports a football jersey in the fall and a lacrosse outfit in the spring.

"No way!" Francesca giggles, clapping a hand over her mouth as she watches Brandon get a bit too frisky during the team dance. "I'm telling Kayla that Brandon is cheating on her with Sammy."

I look around for Kayla's notable height even among the boys, but I don't see her. "I think she *is* Sammy."

I never thought I'd be recording a video of a goldfish gyrating on our school mascot while my sister spanked them with an oar *to show to my parents*. Still, the crowd loves it, and it's clear from Eliza's relieved expression that she wasn't sure people would laugh.

I stop recording as they reach the sidelines and wriggle out of the straps that held up the plywood boat.

"I wonder if I could snag that for comedy club," Francesca muses.

"Why do you need a boat for that?"

She shrugs. "I don't, but it never hurts to have more props for improv. I feel like we *always* have to build every single thing from scratch."

"I'll ask my sister and text you. And if she says no, I'll just ask Kayla because she definitely won't care."

The cringeworthy Pineland Prep anthem cycles back on as our outgoing homecoming court takes the field again to close out the pep rally by giving wreaths to all the team captains. For some reason Pineland has a tradition of only electing jocks as our homecoming royalty, a fact that doesn't bother me as long as they don't encroach on prom.

"I cannot believe we elected Pat Zeller and Lisa Baker-Grant as our prince and princess," Francesca mutters as we watch Pat try to stuff an extra flower into the homecoming queen's cleavage. "I have lost faith in humanity."

"Don't even get me started."

"Are we allowed to go now?" Francesca asks, searching for a signal from one of the chaperones. "I don't think there are any teams left."

"I have to pee, so I'm leaving." I descend the bleachers with care, waving to TJ, the co-chair of the student council, to signal that I can talk since he's been relentlessly blowing up my phone for the past fifteen minutes.

Francesca follows, head swiveling to see if we'll get caught. We're technically leaving a bit early, but none of the teachers seem to be policing the formal dismissal time. With only a half day of classes and the rest spent on the athletic fields, they're probably tired of keeping us corralled.

I pause at the corner of the bleachers to wait for TJ. Ethan, the senior class vice president, isn't far behind. "Pretzel sales are down," TJ laments in his most dejected co-chair voice, cupping both of his hands into a megaphone and leaning so close to my ear that the bill of his hat pecks against the side of my head. "I don't know if we're going to have enough for the Community Costume Closet *and* the Boo-Boo Blood Drive."

I shake my head at TJ's obsession with alliterative

names and run a few quick numbers on my phone, mentally pulling up the spreadsheet with our projections for costumes, blood-drive snacks, and decorations. "We might be able to scrap some of the decorations or send out a notice that we're accepting costume donations for charity."

"We could donate some cash from the senior-class fund," Ethan proposes, shamelessly eavesdropping over TJ's shoulder as he herds us away from the noise of other students chatting while they wait to be released.

I glower at Ethan, old arguments fresh to my tongue. "You can't keep giving away all our prom money just because you're friends with everyone." I let the declaration sink in for a moment as we round the corner and leave the field behind us. "I know you snuck money to the freshmen."

"But they're so tiny and sad and bad at fundraising," TJ points out, pressing a freckled hand to his heart. "We have to save them from their terrible bake sales."

"You're both such suckers."

"Ice queen," Ethan stages-whispers to TJ.

I shove his arm and almost push myself over in the process. Damn swimmer biceps. "At least I'm not a bleeding heart."

"Party pooper."

"Tool bag."

"Scrooge."

TJ lets his hand fall and shakes off a pretend burn, hissing through his teeth. "You're making me glad I'm a junior. This senior class is too intense." He leans his neck back to catch a glimpse of Francesca. "Except you, Franny. You're the bestest art-class buddy ever."

"Anytime?" she offers, laughing. Her laugh trails off as we circle around the bleachers and into the parking lot, where the crew team is facing off with a group of red-faced lacrosse players. Of course the instigator is Pat, fresh off the field with last year's sash for homecoming prince still wrapped around him.

My heart jolts when I spot Oliver De Luca a few steps away, wearing a matching expression of curiosity and distaste as he watches the argument become more animated. Or maybe that repulsed look is for me. We lock eyes for a moment, and I tilt my hand in a half wave that he doesn't reciprocate.

Francesca tugs on my sleeve. "Did you just wave at Oliver? Are you getting back together? We can go on double dates now!" She practically vibrates with excitement, her loose curls springing in every direction from under her Pineland Prep beanie.

"Hardly." Though whenever I see him in person, my conviction to not beg for him back wavers somewhat. I run my eyes over his tanned skin, his hair long and mussed by the breeze. He's even wearing the school polo I shrank by accident in the wash, the one that shows every muscle of his torso. I'm staring. I'm staring. *Stop it, you useless eyeballs. Look somewhere else.* "I'm just being nice."

"But. But. I just don't get how you can go through"— Francesca lowers her voice and looks over both shoulders for imaginary eavesdroppers—"*freshman year* and then break up now."

"We don't talk about the F-year," I mutter. "No one wants to talk about the F-year."

There was no point in talking anyway. When the worst of the virus was over, everyone was so burned-out by illness that they just wanted to forget. People took off their masks, if they'd bothered to wear them at all, and swapped stories about how virtue or eating pool cleaner—not science and luck—had kept them safe.

And those lifelines that we'd so desperately clung to together, the remote medical appointments and free testing and permission to just be sick without having to apologize for it? It turns out those had an expiration date, and even whispering about the coronavirus that wiped out seven million souls made you the new buzzkill. Healthy is always in vogue, after all.

"I didn't mind getting to stay home," Francesca reflects, almost like it was an optional break instead of a narrowly dodged doomsday. She turns her attention back to the scene before us. "At least I didn't have to deal with Pat."

The situation between the two teams is clearly escalating, at least judging by the rise in voices and the fact that Brandon's shoulders are so high that they count as hackles. Pat is the opposite, slouching his weight back on one foot, pausing his verbal tirade long enough only to let his cronies add in their live laugh track. "Yeah . . . about that . . ."

"Should we do something or just go?" Francesca asks, pausing far enough away that we could scurry in the other direction without anyone noticing.

I sigh, choosing the former option but only because Eliza would want me to stick up for her teammates. "You don't have to come with me." I know that Francesca doesn't have a confrontational bone in her body, but that's okay because I'm a Scorpio, so I've got 206 of them.

The shouting and profanity become easier to hear as I approach. It's not so much a dispute as a one-sided attack. The issue seems to be the theft of the Sammy the Shark costume from the athletic storage room. I was wondering how the crew team managed to convince the lacrosse coach to lend them the mascot.

Brandon, still dressed as a goldfish, takes the costume

from Kayla and tries to return it. "Here. Sorry. We didn't think it was a big deal."

"We don't want it now that you've rubbed your fucking fish dick on it, man."

Francesca leans against me, whispering, "What do we do?"

"This is so petty." I don't how much more of a toxic, homophobic asshole Pat Zeller can be before he actually grows a second anus on his forehead or something. I've never forgiven him for "Fran-chest-a"—the seventh-grade nickname that still makes Francesca walk everywhere with her arms folded, her fingers tucked under the straps of her backpack.

I put on my cheeriest smile and step between the two groups before this escalates even more than it already has. I don't like to get involved in stuff like this, but most people listen when I talk, if only to avoid my revenge when they want something changed in the yearbook. "You know you're not all going to be able to play this season if you get in a fight, so let's just leave it."

I feel the creep of eyes and glance over, registering that Oliver is still there, still watching me. I wish he would just go home already. Go work on his screenplay and bake with his grandmother and bond with his rescue animals. And be perfect.

And forget how I blew through his life like a tempest,

an unwitting tribute to the line he whispered in my ear that idyllic morning, with dying junior prom flowers on the bedside and my dress shed just inside the threshold. *Awake, dear heart, awake.*

The linemen back away a bit now that I've inserted myself into their spat, but Pat doesn't budge. "We'll get the costume dry-cleaned or take it to a fish-dick exorcist or something," I say. "Everybody good with that?"

Pat takes a deep breath. His shoulders rise and drop. "Okay. Fine." He shifts to my right and extends his hand to Brandon. "Shake on it?"

As Brandon moves to reciprocate, Pat lashes out with a quick jab and punches him in the face. Brandon stumbles, blood spraying from his nose, and I scramble to catch him before he can fall on the rough asphalt. But Pat isn't finished. His next blow, this time from his left, is midswing by the time I notice. I've stepped straight into it.

Seeing stars is an understatement; I discover new galaxies in the microseconds it takes my brain to process the shock of impact. The momentum. Gravity.

On instinct I throw out one arm toward the ground and wrap the other around my head. My left arm buckles under the combined weight of me, Brandon, and the shark costume, sending spikes of pain bursting through my shoulder. I lie there, gasping, feeling the warmth of blood trickling from the side of my mouth.

Beyond the throbbing in my ears, I hear one of the lacrosse players screaming while Francesca pulls Brandon off of me. "What did you do? You! Punched! Brynn! Kwan!"

He punched Brynn Kwan.

Two

I try not to flinch as I take inventory of my body like a computer running a virus scan. My hip is partially popped out—*subluxated* if I want to be medical and fancy about it—and my cheek is swelling around the imprint of my teeth. But the worst damage is to my shoulder, which I can feel hanging out of socket, the pain pulsing intermittently with the white-hot burning of my elbow, the numbness in my fingers that almost tickles.

I attempt to move, but all that happens is a slight tensing of my muscles. Like troubleshooting the knotted skein of wires balled up behind the entertainment stand, I become aware of the commotion around me one sense at a time.

The pain subsides enough to become touch, the pressure of hands on my neck, my face.

My ears tune in next. "Your breathing and heart rate seem fine." Instead of panicking, Eliza's voice is the same leaden, almost gravelly tone I associate with her lecturing me for leaving the bathroom dirty. Like I'm a chore. A responsibility. "Brynn? Can you hear me?"

There's a brief intermission as I blink, my eyelids barely lifting enough to see Eliza pawing through my stuff. She wasn't here just a second ago, was she? I scan my limited field of view, realizing from the chaos that they must have dismissed the first set of bleachers.

Prescription pill bottles, a pulse oximeter, and my purple pill organizer are lying beside me, half-spilled from the open mouth of my tote bag. The shock wave of panic that slams through my system is like a hard reboot. I flail upright, my ankles twisting free of TJ's grip as my hip slides back into joint with a mix of agony and relief. Before any of my classmates get the chance to scrutinize the contents of my bag, I shove Eliza away and start stuffing pill bottles and medical crap back inside like some timed carnival game.

"Oh my God, Brynn, would you stop?" Eliza tries to grab my arm. "No one cares!"

But she doesn't get it. After an entire childhood of pills and stitches, wobbling around in braces and slings,

I know that once you're The Disabled Girl, you can't be anything else. People stop seeing you, but they *never* stop looking. Judging. Helping. Imposing.

Isn't it so much easier to just pretend? Pretend Brynn gets a few colds a year, and she's a little self-conscious about the dimpled scar on the side of her chin from toddling into the coffee table, but really, it's almost kind of cute. Pretend Brynn doesn't resemble an exhausted bridge troll that needs fifteen pills a day just to feel totally worthless anyway.

With the last of my strength, I tag that Brynn into the ring, basking in the rush of her confidence as I let out an effortless laugh. "Calm down," I drawl, batting away Eliza's hand. "I got knocked down, not hit by a bus."

A few people manage to chuckle. I sit up on my knees, wobbling as Oliver helps me stand. I didn't even see him come over here. I almost topple over again before he catches me around the waist. "Are you okay?"

I feel the performance stall a moment as I wonder how much he saw, but I never forget my next line: "I'm fine." I wrench my arm free before his touch can singe my flesh. He steps back, eyes averted, and I want to throw myself against him and kiss him until some uptight teacher pulls us apart, as if we don't all still have lost time from lockdown in our ledgers. But Oliver and I don't belong to each other anymore, if we ever did at all. "Pat's got a weak left hook."

He points to the corner of his own mouth. "You're bleeding."

"I just need a paper towel." I heave myself through space in jerky, lurching stumbles as security guards and administrators descend on the two teams. My hip and shoulder ignore the demands of my threadbare nerves, my body an unmanned vehicle, a hostage crisis.

And always that question—

"Are you okay?" TJ asks in the horror-stricken tone of someone who can only be serious three times a year, and this is one of them.

Ethan holds out a tentative hand, not quite making contact on my forearm. "Hey, you should sit down. The nurse is probably still here."

I swing my gaze in lolling arcs across the crowd, seeing my friends seeing me for the first time. The smog of their compassion envelops me. *What happened?* Suddenly I'm in first grade again, realizing from my teacher's bloodless, nauseated expression that I was *not* supposed to pull out four baby teeth during the story about the tooth fairy just because I'd discovered I could.

I stand up as straight as I can, affecting a slight lean onto my back leg that I hope is close to nonchalance. "I'm good. You might want to check on Brandon, though." I limp away before I can attract any more attention. Some mobs carry torches and pitchforks; others bludgeon you with pity, a death of a thousand wishes well.

At last I reach the sanctuary of the bathroom. Beads of sweat form along my hairline and trace rivulets around the curves of my nose as I shut myself into the first stall. I lean against the door, the cool metal nothing but a raindrop on a wildfire. It hurts to breathe. I can feel the interconnectedness of it all, how one sip of air is the difference between relief and agony.

I mash my shoulder joint and attempt to force my humerus back into place. *Come on, Left Shoulder.* Somehow, narrating all of my body parts like they're a bunch of inconsiderate houseguests has always made the pain easier to bear. *I thought we were friends.*

LEFT SHOULDER
You let the doctors poke me with scalpels
too many times for us to be friends.

ME
I hate you.

LEFT SHOULDER
Wow, that's very hurtful.

I hear footsteps smacking against the floor and jam a knuckle in between my teeth to avoid letting a whimper escape as I release my grip on my shoulder socket. "Hey, uh, Brynn?" Francesca calls out. "You still in here?"

"Yeah," I say, a little sharper than intended. Where else would I be? I didn't open an interstellar portal in the toilet.

I bite harder against my knuckle until I can taste the salt on my skin, the grime of the asphalt. I pull air through my nose in a slow drag. *Don't become a pain monster.* It's not Francesca's fault. She's trying to help.

"Brandon's nose might be broken. Did you find some ice for your face?" she asks. I can see the tips of her fat sneakers through the gap at the bottom of the stall door, a trend I unwittingly started when I needed enormous clown shoes to house my arch supports. In a private school with uniforms, we're all desperate to break the mold just a bit. "I'm supposed to meet Amber for our one-month anniversary, but I don't want to leave you like this. She probably won't care if I cancel. I could stay."

I press the tips of my fingers against my throat to steady my voice. "That's okay. Thanks. I'll catch up with you later." When she doesn't move, I add, "Oliver helped me out." That'll distract her.

I hear a shuffling noise and see the end of Francesca's hair hovering under the door. "Is he in there with you?" she hisses, sounding half-impressed and half-scandalized.

"What? No!" I would facepalm if my busted face wasn't already well acquainted with the human hand. "I'm just saying that I'm good. Eliza's going to want to get home soon anyway. Say hi to Amber for me."

"I will," she says, still sounding hesitant. "Feel better."

"Thanks."

I listen to her leave. The sound of her footsteps grows louder as she transitions onto the concrete, then disappears once she's in the strip of grass that divides the restrooms from the parking lot.

I peck out a text to Eliza with one thumb—the only time I've ever been thankful for autocorrect—and arrange to rendezvous out back.

Eliza [2:32 P.M.]: WHERE ARE YOU?

Brynn [2:32 P.M.]: Bathroom by
the concession stand.

Eliza [2:33 P.M.]: You ran away!

Brynn [2:33 P.M.]: Just meet me
in the parking lot.

"You can drive," I say in greeting as Eliza comes jogging around the corner.

Don't let her see how bad it is. I grit my teeth and curl my toes inside my shoes. *Don't ruin her pep rally. It's her day.*

My purse, though abused, is still slung across my chest. I retrieve my car keys and dangle them from the pinky of my good arm.

RIGHT ARM
Am I the good arm?

ME
Yes, you're the good arm. Shut up.

Eliza looks at me like I just offered her a bottle rocket instead of asking her to use the learner's permit I know she has in her wallet. "I'm not allowed to drive with only you in the car. How's your shoulder?"

My laugh is more of a wheezing grunt. I toss my whole lanyard at her, counting on her reflexes to kick in. She snatches it from the air. "You know how to drive," I point out. "Just do the speed limit and no one will notice."

"Did you even check your blood pressure?" she demands.

"I can take care of myself. It's not as bad as it looks."

I hate the tinge of desperation souring my voice. Eliza

is like an auditory bloodhound, her ears attuned to the slightest inflections of pain. She plants both feet and lofts a single brow, a pose she absorbed from Dad. "It looks pretty significant."

"It's nothing." I cast around us for something else to talk about. My eyes land on the fake oar jutting out of her backpack. "Your skit was funny. I recorded it for Mom and Dad, but I was kind of far away, so it's not the best quality."

Eliza ignores me and starts rattling off random guesses. "Knee? Elbow? Heart rate? Seriously, what is it?" When I open my mouth to speak, she holds up her index finger in a challenge. "Don't even try to change the subject."

"My shoulder's still out," I mumble, kicking at a crack in the pavement where two clumps of weeds are fighting for a sliver of space. "Everything else mushed back in already."

"Can you put it back in?"

I shake my head, swallowing as a wave of dizziness passes over me at the motion. "I tried. You'll have to do it for me. I can show you on YouTube. It's easy."

"I'm not going to let a *YouTube video* teach me how to do a medical procedure."

I rotate my wrist to check the time, and shooting pain lances through my arm. I tug on the passenger-side door handle of my trusty Chevy Spark. "At least unlock it and let me sit down. I don't want to be vertical anymore."

Eliza clicks the button on the fob, her teeth scraping her bottom lip as she weighs her options. I open the door and melt into the seat, curling onto my side to alleviate the worst of the nausea roiling through my stomach. I hear the clunk of her bag getting tossed in the trunk.

I call Dad on speaker, balancing my phone on my thigh and stabbing at it with one hand. He picks up on the third ring. "Hey, I'm with a student. Can I call you back?" I hear a high-pitched caterwauling in the background that is either small animals being thrown into a woodchipper or an extremely new clarinet player.

"My shoulder is out and it's doing that thing where it's kind of stuck, you know?" It's a relief to have Dad on the line, the only other person who speaks my body's weird language. "My hip slid out a little too, but it was on my non-op side. I don't think it disturbed any of the breaks or screws." When my hip-dysplasia surgeon told me I could start moving more after reassembling half of my pelvis over the summer, I don't think getting a hay-maker to the face is what he meant by "high-impact activities."

"What happened?" Dad asks.

"I got punched in the face by accident—I'll tell you later—and I fell on my arm."

Eliza climbs into the driver's seat and shuts the door. She quirks her head as the clarinet gives off another shriek.

Dad makes a *hrmm* sound low in his throat. "You should go to the ortho or the hospital to get an X-ray and make sure you didn't fracture anything." His voice is muffled for a moment, the receiver scratchy as he gives some instruction or another to his student. "Our deductible is met," he adds a moment later, though I'm not sure if that's him talking to himself or talking to me.

I try to recall the numbers on the last insurance document I snooped when no one was paying attention. "What about the out-of-pocket max?"

"Let me worry about that. I'll come by as soon as I can, okay? Just text me where you end up."

I roll my eyes so far up in my head that I'm surprised I can't see my own frontal lobe. "Fine. I'll see you later. Love you."

"Love you too."

I hang up and groan, half from pain and half from the anticipated *mental* pain of having to deal with the hospital. "Actually, wait," I say to Eliza, as if she's in a huge hurry to illegally chauffeur me around. "Let me see if the ortho can squeeze me in." Literally. But after calling and navigating the infuriating automated phone tree, the receptionist tells me that they have a packed schedule.

"No dice?" Eliza asks.

"Hospital it is."

Eliza rises up in her seat to see better, peering down at my hunched form. "Here's the deal." She adjusts her seat to a rigid ninety degrees and grasps the steering wheel at the precise points denoted in the driving manual. "I'll drive, but next time you need to ask one of your friends who actually has a license. I could lose my permit for this."

Yelling would require me to breathe, which actually hurts more than I want to admit, so I stay silent. Eliza doesn't understand. All it takes is one person finding out that I'm disabled and my whole life will unravel, just like it did when the non-disabled members of Dad's extended family learned I was diagnosed before I'd even found out the truth about Santa. My cousin Tori never made a spectacle of me, but one voice isn't enough to negate a whole ensemble at family reunions and holidays.

Oh, it's so awful. Did you hear that Brynn has it too?

Or the weird celebration when Eliza wasn't.

Thank the Lord that both *of Jason's kids didn't get it. Can you imagine?*

I don't want to spend my senior year having everyone question whether I can do whatever activity, whether I need to take a break, take a pill. Calling me inspirational for eating a sandwich or scratching my butt. The scrunched, beaming faces people make when they refer to me as *special* or ask to borrow my handicapped-parking placard to go to a concert.

Eliza slows at a yellow light, stopping just in front of the crosswalk.

I knock the edge of my hand against the dashboard. "I know it's farther away, but take me to Four Towers. I'll die before I go back to University."

She opens the GPS and pauses with her finger hovering over the touchscreen. "What's the real name of Four Towers? I always forget."

"Deaconess Medical Center."

"I thought Dad doesn't like that one," she says, hesitating.

"I'm not Dad."

A few minutes later I see the four towers that give the hospital its unofficial namesake stretching above the treetops. Eliza accidentally drives into the ambulance entrance and has to turn around. I chuckle under my breath, realizing that she doesn't frequent these buildings like I do. "Main ER entrance is on the ground floor of the east tower." I point in the general direction. "You can just drop me off."

Eliza scoffs. "I'm not going to leave you by yourself."

"Yes, you are." The last thing I need is her hovering over me, asking me if I'm okay every six seconds while

I drain my phone battery in the waiting room reading about every possible complication that could occur. "Unless you want to miss your SAT tutor."

She groans. Checkmate. "Maybe I could reschedule."

"I'm going to tell the doctor not to let you come back with me, so you might as well go make your enormous brain even bigger, nerd."

After another few minutes of arguing and cajoling and calling Dad for reinforcement, Eliza agrees to go home. "But if you need anything, I'm coming right back."

"I'm fine."

"Just make sure you keep me posted!" she insists, sounding exactly like Mom in pitch and tone.

We have a brief standoff while she's waiting for me to go inside and I'm waiting for her to leave. I cave first and check in at the desk, passing over my identification and grabbing a stack of intake forms. I fill them out in as little detail as possible, since no one ever reads them anyway except for the billing and insurance ones. I reluctantly write in *Jenna Kwan* as my emergency contact but only because Mom always answers her phone, while Dad's gets drowned on a regular basis by screaming piccolos and sonic blasts from the business end of a tuba.

A triage nurse brings me into a separate room and

asks me the same questions, eyeing my shoulder without touching. She rates me as a four, which means that I'm doomed to sit in the waiting room for all eternity, maybe even until the gross vending-machine food starts looking appetizing.

Dad [3:06 P.M.]: Hey, you hanging in there?

Brynn [3:08 P.M.]: Arm is literally hanging. I'm at Four Towers.

Dad [3:08 P.M.]: Sorry. I'll head over as soon as I can.

Brynn [3:09 P.M.]: No hurry. They rated me a 4 in triage.

Dad [3:09 P.M.]: In that case, I'll take a nap first.

Brynn [3:10 P.M.]: My phone's dying. Tell Mom.

Just as my phone further protests its lack of charge, a different nurse leads me into another wing and takes my vitals in one of the narrow, cubby-like exam rooms. I need to remove my jacket to accommodate the blood-pressure cuff, which takes both of us and a fair amount of moaning to accomplish.

When she's done, I flail my arm at my purse and accidentally knock it to the ground, not even caring that it's my favorite bag and I'll never get the smudges and scuffs out of the leather. "There's a . . . a paper in there." It's the short version of the enormous medical binder I keep at home, an abstract to a dissertation. "Here, give it to me, please." I realize belatedly how sharp my tone is, but it's like the pain makes me into a different person.

The nurse passes it over and I dump the contents onto my lap, sorting one-handed through the mound of old receipts and Q-tips, loose pills and scarred coins. I open my EpiPen carrying case with my teeth and fish out the paper. I waggle it at her. "This has anything you might want to know."

She gives it a quick scan. "I'll give this to the doctor. He'll be by in a minute."

A real minute or a hospital minute?

"Thanks."

She slips out through the gap at the edge of the curtain where it doesn't quite meet the wall. There's no television, so I sit in silence and appraise the room around me, my gaze drifting over the biohazard container and the cheap chair in the corner. I wonder if hospitals have a decorating committee where a bunch of designers sit around choosing the blandest color palette in existence.

The doctor's introduction is so short that he forgets to tell me his name, and I can't quite read it off the embroidery above his pocket. He has my medical sheet in his hand.

I point to the unnatural, throbbing lump that I assume is my bone. "It's dislocated."

He tilts his head a bit with a saccharine smile that drips with condescension and the wafting smell of wintergreen gum. "Well, a lot of people use the word 'dislocated' to mean 'slipping slightly out of joint.' That's not the same thing. But let's have a look."

I unbutton my shirt and pull down the collar, pivoting on the bed to show him the worst of it. He startles. "Oh, it *is* dislocated."

"Told you so," I singsong through gritted teeth, my fist twisting braids into the thin sheet beneath me. They always sound like it's such mind-blowing news. *Call the press! Girl with condition that makes you dislocate everything dislocates everything!*

"Have you ever dislocated anything before?" he asks, squinting at me with newfound interest, the way a child might stare at an exotic frog at the zoo.

I nod, almost shrugging before the pain reminds me to keep still.

"When was that?"

I think back. I popped my thumb out trying to open a bottle of chocolate syrup to make sundaes with Dad. It was so ridiculous that we laughed for ten minutes. "Last Tuesday."

"I'm being serious."

I lock eyes with him. "So am I. Did you read the notes?" I gesture to the paper he still has clutched in one hand. I can tell it's my notes from the thick creases and a splotch on the back where I set it down on a drop of vanilla pudding the last time I was stuck in the ER during dinnertime.

"Ehlers-Danlos syndrome." He sounds out each syllable like a first grader with phonics homework. "What's that?"

"It's a connective-tissue disorder. I also have its two comor—its two best friends, mast cell activation syndrome and POTS. The heart thing." It's always a battle to sound like I'm informed enough to not get gaslighted without upsetting some white coat's ego by wanting to use actual medical terminology.

"Oh, is this the thing all those girls are diagnosing themselves with on the internet?" He squints at me over the top of the page. "What makes you think you have, uh, Evers-Damos?"

This is going well. "My board-certified geneticist told me so, but maybe he just spends too much time on TikTok."

The doctor's face becomes an abstract of whites, pinks, and reds as all the blood drains into his cheeks. "I'm going to send you off for an X-ray to confirm the dislocation and get a look at the bones to rule out fractures. While you're there, I'll do some more research to see if there's anything specific to this"—he looks down at the paper—"Enlers . . . Ehlers-Danlos syndrome that I should know about."

That means he's going to look it up on the internet. *Paging Dr. Google.*

"Sounds good."

"I'll have someone take you down to radiology. It's a bit of a walk, and I don't want to risk you falling."

He's not going to get any arguments from me. I've already tested the theory of gravity with my face once today. I'm not looking for a repeat.

As I watch the doctor leave, I contemplate the question of what happens in medical school to make certain physicians this jaded. Maybe it's because so few people on this side of the sickbed can make it through the rigors of training and residency. I still fantasize about it sometimes, that there will be some breakthrough that fixes it all and makes it possible for me to dilute some of the toxicity in medicine with a firsthand perspective.

But deep down, I know those aspirations were cemented into idle daydreams as EDS took one ligament after another, a joint here, a bone there. There's no way I'll be able to clock sixty-five-hour weeks or stay up all night cramming for complicated exams. I can barely go four days without accidentally stabbing myself in the face with a fork or almost shoving chopsticks up my nostril because I missed my own mouth.

RIGHT CHEEK
Someone give that girl a scalpel!

"Goodbye, bad thoughts. You don't live in my brain anymore," I mutter, parroting one of Dad's little verbal cues to snap himself out of a doom spiral.

Instead I check my phone, which seems to have conveniently turned off since I didn't have the foresight to charge it in the car. I groan, berating myself for not moving my charger from my backpack last night when I decided that I could manage an abbreviated class schedule and a pep rally with just this tote.

The curtain to my room opens, its metal rings screeching across the bar. I keep poking at the screen in my futile attempt to see if it'll power on at all. "Sorry. Give me one second."

And just because this day hasn't been awful enough already, I look up to see the last person I ever expected to be here, still dressed in his school uniform with a white-and-green pep-rally ribbon pinned to one lapel: Oliver De Luca.

Three

Why is it so hard for this boy to just forget my existence?

"What are you doing here?" I ask, my voice shrieking into the same octave as dog whistles, paranormal activity, and bad clarinet players.

"Eliza said you weren't answering her texts and asked if I could check on you."

"She did what?" I run a hand through my hair, frowning at the flakes of blood that break off and fall into my lap. I don't know if it's my blood or Brandon's, and I don't know if it's more disgusting if it's my blood or Brandon's. "Uh, I, uh. Dead phone."

Oliver does that thing where he forces himself to maintain eye contact even though I know he wants to stare at my shoulder or ask about the darkening bruises on my face. Whenever people do that, they forget to blink. "Anyway, you ready to go?"

"Go?" I repeat, horrified. My left arm is still doing its best impersonation of a pool noodle.

"To radiology? There's someone with a wheelchair out here for you."

I smack my palm against my forehead and hold it there. "Right! To radiology. You don't, uh, you don't have to stay. I'm fine." I go to gesture to my body to show how fine I am and scream as I accidentally move my dislocated shoulder. Panting, I swipe the tears away with my other hand. "I'm fine adjacent."

His mouth literally hangs open for five entire seconds. "I don't feel right leaving. I can just wait with you."

Hooray. Witnesses.

But I don't have the energy to argue. "O." The other letter sticks in my throat and comes out as more of a click than a sound. "K."

The porter is clearly oblivious to the tension as Oliver robot-marches down the hallway beside me, typing furiously into his phone. I hope he's giving Eliza an earful for thinking this was a good idea.

I'm glad that he doesn't seem to expect me to talk. I can't think of anything except for the slow decay of our relationship, the wrenching defeat of realizing that I'd trapped him into loving a form of me that only existed from homeroom to the final bell.

It was a fade of months as I unraveled my love a stitch at a time, tugging at the seams until there were only holes remaining in the fabric of us. And when it was our turn to write poems and present them in Creative Writing class, he wasn't afraid to show me—and all of our classmates— the pain I'd wrought.

> *Her love is a storm,*
> *The hopeless run for cover—*
> *The devastation.*

The porter bumps the button for the automatic door-opener with his hip and pushes me into a secondary waiting area. I know better than to expect to go in immediately, so I lean back in the wheelchair as I try to figure out what Eliza was thinking.

Oliver sits in the chair beside me and folds one leg over the other. I stare at the black screen of my phone just to have a place to look. "Some of the teachers jumped in after you left," Oliver mentions. "I think Pat is in serious trouble."

"It won't matter," I mutter. "He'll find some way to weasel out of it."

Oliver makes an *urrggh* sound in the back of his

throat. "I like to think I get along with most people, but Pat is just . . . a brute."

"That's a nice way of putting it."

"I'm sorry," he says, vaguely, as though our breakup or my throbbing face is in any way his fault. "I wouldn't have bothered you, but Eliza thought it might help."

"Thank you for coming, though," I say to a discolored splotch on the carpet where a plant used to be. "Eliza worries too much." She also assumes too much. Imposes too much. Eliza *is* too much, at least when it comes to scheming and meddling and nagging until I just want to strangle her.

BRAIN

Now, Brynn, you can't actually kill her.

(A.) You'd be short a little sister.

(B.) It's premeditated homicide, and we try to avoid that at all times.

(C.) In a fistfight, you'd probably lose. Let's be honest. Eliza is ripped.

She just doesn't understand that even injuries that seem huge to her are almost nothing to me. I make injuries like these as neat and compact as possible, always leaving space for one more or else I'll burst.

Thankfully, a technician emerges from around the

37

corner a moment later, riffling through a batch of paperwork on her clipboard. "Brynn Kwan. Shoulder."

The way she barely pauses between the words makes me feel awesome, like one of those famous people or superheroes with three-part names. Helena Bonham Carter. George Washington Carver. Obi-Wan Kenobi. *Brynn Kwan Shoulder.* "Yeah, that's me."

"We can take you back now."

Oliver hops to his feet and reaches for my wheelchair, but I can't stomach the thought of being around him for another second. It's only a matter of time before his polite façade devolves into fussing, and I can't bear having him look at me the way that TJ did earlier.

"I've got it." I attempt to stand on my own, but Right Ankle isn't quite cooperating and rolls so far that the knot of bone on the side hits against the footrest of the wheelchair. I wind up elbowing the lamp and falling over the end table in a flailing mass of limbs and hair. A magenta streak runs across my upper arm where my lipstick smeared across it.

RIGHT ANKLE
I'm sorry. I couldn't help it.

ME
You're dead to me.

Waving Oliver away, I laugh, but it's too shrill to be natural. He only shakes his head at my usual gracefulness and says, "I'll rescue the lamp."

I follow the technician while I try not to literally die of embarrassment, though I'm sure there's a billing code for that. I still remember the day I turned eighteen and Dad had to give me what he called "The Other Talk," a two-hour crash course in ICD codes, in-network doctors, and how not to accidentally bankrupt us.

The X-ray is quick, a reminder to stand up straight and hold my breath. Minute adjustments of my body positioning. Confirming three times that I'm not pregnant. Before I leave, I ask for a copy of the images to add to the growing pile of CDs at home with names like *Jason Kwan, L. Hip Arthrogram* and *Brynn Kwan, Neck, Flexion/Extension.*

The technician helps me into the wheelchair and rolls me out into the hallway, where Oliver is leaning against the wall, humming, the bottom of one sneaker pressed almost flush against the wall. "All done?" he asks, fake-smiling at the technician until she leaves.

"Yup." From this angle, his hair hangs in an unruly mess, the last sun-bleached layers of summer blending into the deeper browns beneath. As he turns to face me, keen eyes glinting in the too-bright hospital lighting, I can see why everyone was shocked that I let him go. As if I had a choice.

I feel a slight shift as the porter steps behind my wheelchair. I hope that one of my parents has arrived by now. I can't just sit here and pretend. It's not just Oliver's nearness that bothers me. It's the sandalwood scent from the cologne I bought him last year, the timbre of his voice that I got to know so well when we were freshmen, all of us suddenly sent home one Tuesday with tiny laptops and cheap earbuds and foolish, foolish goodbye kisses fresh on our lips. And then there was a year of just that voice on the other end of the line, a crumb of goodness in the dark. Our fears blended into one until we were nothing but echoes of each other:

What if they never find a cure?

I miss your face. I miss everything.

I never even heard of a coronavirus before this.

I can't believe it's been two three four five months.

Did you ever think that something like this could happen?

Is this some kind of punishment? Do you believe in God?

But that love forged in terror and loneliness couldn't survive the dawn of a resolute world hell-bent on moving on. The last secret Oliver shared with me was such an offhand comment, a throwaway blight. *I'm so glad none of us got sick. I can't imagine living like that.*

But I don't have a choice, and I can't drag him down with me.

"Does it still hurt a lot?" he asks, mistaking my silence for pain. "Did they say whether it's broken?"

"They don't read the images in there. I'm sure it'll be fine." I mean that more as a command to my body than a platitude. My shoulder has been wedged out of its socket so long that my fingers are simultaneously numb and on fire. A headache looms over the crown of my head.

I wish that he would just go; I wouldn't run away faster from the Devil himself.

I almost scream when Oliver pulls back the curtain to my room and I see Dad sitting in a chair, his legs propped up on the rails of the bed. "Surprise!" He shakes an enormous grease-stained bag at me. "I come bearing many, many deep-fried things. I didn't know what you wanted, so I just grabbed one of everything."

"God, I love you."

Dad looks up with a minute jerk of one shoulder. "Hey! Oliver!" His eyes widen to the point of absurdity. "What are you doing here? After-school job?"

"Mr. K!" Oliver's face breaks into the smile that he couldn't manage for me. "No, I'm just checking on Brynn. Eliza was worried."

There's not one bit of weirdness even though Dad knows exactly what transpired between us. They're all grins and puns. It's like watching two golden retrievers unite at a dog park, just thankfully without the butt-sniffing.

I stare at my records that the nurse must have returned while I was gone. It's all there, carefully typed out to convey everything that matters in case I'm hurt at school or in a car crash or I get punched in the face defending the honor of a fish costume.

Beside me, Dad pesters Oliver about his senior year so far, his head nodding along with each answer. Oliver slouches against the wall, his finger ticking back and forth like a metronome as he recounts how busy he's been between school and work. They laugh the same way, heads thrown back, the sound too loud in the confines of the triage room.

From the grocery store cashier to random strangers, it's like Dad is everyone's long-lost best friend. We'll go to the gas station on the corner for a jar of mayonnaise and leave with six people's secrets. Why couldn't I have inherited *that* from Dad?

I fold up my records and stick them back in my purse. *Ehlers-Danlos syndrome. Postural orthostatic tachycardia syndrome. Allergies to the entire solar system. Too much deficit and not enough attention. The hips of a LEGO figurine.*

Instead of this?

Four

In medical school, one of the little sayings they teach is "When you hear hoofbeats, think horses, not zebras." It's supposed to be a cutesy reminder to avoid looking for rare diseases for no reason, but what it really means is that those of us who are zebras end up placing last in the horse race. "I can't believe that doctor. Aren't zebras endangered?" I ask Dad as we pull into the driveway. "Can't I complain to the United Nations or something?"

"I wish," he replies, parking and reaching into the back seat for his crutches.

I follow Dad inside the house, leaving my shoes on the mat by the door and hanging my keys on the hook. "Wait," I say, pausing. "How are we getting my car home?"

Dad's face scrunches as though I've caught him off guard with my question. He wrestles free of his bags and sets his favorite six-string acoustic by the stairs. "I could have your mother come with me later to pick it up."

"Sorry. I kind of forgot about it."

"It's fine. You shouldn't be driving right now anyway." He shakes the bag of prescription painkillers and anti-inflammatory meds we picked up on the way home.

I throw away the paper bags and leave the bottles on the counter while I stash my backpack in the formal dining room that Mom insists on having even though we never use it. By the time I get back the pills are already put away. "I was going to get that."

"It's okay," Mom says, kissing my check. "How are you feeling?"

Always the same questions. "I'm fine. Arm hasn't fallen off yet." At least the itchy sling makes a convenient holder for my phone.

I open the fridge to grab a bottle of iced tea, careful not to upset the ever-present packets of paper stuck to the fridge with magnetic metal binder clips. When I close the door, I scrutinize the first page of each to see if Mom's left me a dissertation about how my room is too dirty. One is her latest patent-law quiz—a B+ that she's been using to remind herself of her "failure"—and the rest are various bills, notes for Dad, and to-do lists.

Mom stirs one of the four pots on the stove while she thumbs through an environmental textbook for her night class. "Dinner should be ready in about five minutes." Even with the delay for the X-ray, she must have rushed to beat us home and be this far into dinner. She hasn't even taken off her Smart Cart manager polo with the perfectly straight name tag that I swear she measures.

Dad and I exchange guilty looks, though neither of us will ever confess to eating fast food when we knew Mom would have dinner. "I don't know how hungry I'll be. The meds and all." I stick my tongue out at Dad, patting my stomach where a cheeseburger the size of my head is sitting like a boulder.

"Way to leave me hanging," he mutters as I plop into my spot at the square, counter-height table situated in the tiled, neutral ground between the kitchen and the living room. He takes the seat to my left, leaving me to contemplate the empty space where Eliza will be.

Maybe she won't freak out. Maybe she'll be able to respect why I'm upset. But even as I think it, I know it's doubtful. Eliza can only be the microscope, never the specimen. I wince as she appears through the other doorway, texting and shuffling along in mismatched socks. "Oh, you're back."

I try not to hear an accusation in her tone for not

45

telling her that we were on the way. "Yeah. We just got here."

"How's your arm feeling?"

"It's fine. I'm fine."

I offer my limited, one-handed services to drop utensils onto the appropriate places while Mom and Eliza shuttle dishes and trivets back and forth. I'm relieved when they finally sit down; with so much medicine dulling everything, their pace is dizzying.

We wait for Dad to finish his prayers before we dive in, passing bowls around the table and reaching over one another. Meanwhile, Mom tells us her daily horror story about interacting with the general public, an evening ritual that makes me ponder whether I want to be part of the human species anymore. "One more semester," she chants, her motto of the past year. "And then I won't have to listen to one more person go on some seven-minute rampage about their expired coupon ever again."

"Yes, I'm sure there will be much more reasonable people involved in the legal system," Dad mutters, his eyes flitting to his right to look at Mom's reaction. "Just wait until she tries her first coupon lawsuit."

Mom's smile is just a twitch at the corners of her lips, a blip that only Dad can earn these days. "Yeah, but at least then I'll be making good money. I just have to pass the bar first." She sighs, then adds, "This is the part where you tell me I'm very beautiful and smart and will obviously pass it with flying colors."

Dad shrugs. "Eh, I guess you're okay."

The way they talk to each other reminds me of the good times with Oliver, the moments when our pretenses fell away and we could just *be*. And none of those resulted from Eliza's meddling. I spear each one of my green beans individually, mashing them in my mouth like a bored cow as I think about how I want to bring up everything from today.

Mom makes the opening I've been waiting for. "So Eliza told me the gist of things, but what happened with this fight at the pep rally? I've been waiting for the school to call to talk about it, but no one's reached out yet."

I fill her in on the rough details, not wanting to delve too much into the particulars of the fish costume. Before Mom can come up with another question, I wait a beat, then add, "And, to be honest, Eliza . . . I'm kind of pissed that you asked Oliver to check on me. I mean, you knew I was fine."

Eliza tilts her head. It's less of a cutesy Dorothy-from-Oz motion and more *Jurassic World* velociraptor. "If you would answer your phone in a timely manner, I wouldn't have to make assumptions about your status during a crisis."

"Okay, please, I can't handle your Middle-Aged Secretary Voice right now."

Dad chokes on his food and emergency-ejects a half-chewed glob of mashed potatoes onto his plate, sputtering as he tries not to laugh any harder.

"You don't need to make this about me," she replies, as if that negates my point entirely. When I try to say something else she holds her hand in the air, palm out. "I took a rational action based on your unresponsiveness."

I look to Dad for help, but he pretends that I've suddenly become invisible. "You know that I haven't told Oliver that I'm busted. Why would you send him to the hospital? It's none of his business. We're not together."

"I don't know why you won't just talk about it. You'd feel better if you talked about it."

"Yeah, maybe that's easy for you to say. What about Alexis?" Silence crashes over the table so suddenly that you'd think I invoked the name of some ancient demon. It's an apt comparison. "Twelve years of friendship out the window because I'm not *fun anymore*. I can't go ice-skating anymore. All I do is talk about doctors *for attention*. It's *so sad*."

Eliza turns to Mom, her face slack with this righteous confusion that makes me wonder why I even bothered bringing this up. "Well," she says, folding her arms, "I just don't feel like you're considerate of other people's opinions." She pauses, her voice dropping lower. "Caregiver burnout is a real thing."

"You're not a caregiver!" I jump to my feet, knocking over my glass with such force that the resulting puddle spans half the table. "I don't ask you for shit."

"You don't need to cuss at me!" she shouts back, grabbing a handful of napkins and dabbing at the water. "And look at this mess you're making."

"Girls," Mom pleads, leaving Dad to continue eating his pork chop, his eyes bulging as he dunks a piece in applesauce. "Don't fight with each other. Come on."

I smack my chest with my palm. "I had to let it out, or I was going to explode. Why am I in trouble when Eliza is the one putting my personal business all over the place?"

"I didn't put your business 'all over the place.' It was just to Oliver! Have you ever stopped to think that maybe this is hard on me, too, and I'm doing my best to help?"

"By running your mouth about my secrets? You have no idea how people look at you when you're different. I let you talk me into that acceptance crap once, and then I was just the pity invite to every party and the sad loser with no friends. At least now I'm popular! I'm normal! I'm so *fucking* normal that everyone wants to be just like me, and you can't stand it because it's the one thing I have that you don't!"

"You know what?" Eliza snaps as she draws herself up to her full height, fists planted on her hips. "Maybe Alexis was right. Maybe all you do care about is attention."

Dad slides off his chair, grabbing my hem in one hand and Eliza's shirtsleeve in the other. He locks eyes with Eliza, his nostrils flaring with each breath. "You're out of line."

"I'm not apologizing until she apologizes." She attempts to turn away, but Dad still has a grip on her shirt. "I always have to be the mature one, and I'm done extending olive branches."

I pinch the fabric of my hem and twist it free of Dad's grip. "Whatever. I don't want your apology anyway, you self-righteous, unmutated bitch."

I pace circles in the garage, which is basically just a 150-square-foot reminder that Dad and I have bodies held together with questionable collagen, screws, hope, and donor tissue. The shelves are packed with extra braces and special pillows wrapped in plastic. Medical debris that we hope we'll never need again but continue to keep because we know deep down that we will.

"I know that was heavy back there," Dad says, "but you cannot call your sister a 'self-righteous, unmutated bitch.'"

"Where is the lie, Dad?" I kick around a physical-therapy ball before plopping onto the foam flooring we installed in the half of the space not occupied by Mom's SUV. I should do my hip exercises, but I can't bring myself to even literally go through the motions.

My eyes land on the box labeled *keepsakes* that Mom refuses to throw away no matter how many times I beg. It has the license plate from Dad's beloved muscle car, sacrificed when his leg became too unsteady to work a clutch. The jersey from the last time I could still play a sport like Eliza does, like "normal" eleven-year-old kids. Softball, shortstop, a pocketful of sunflower seeds—the vague memory of my coach sprinting to second base where I rolled around in the orange dirt, screeching, my fingers dug around my obliterated knee ligament. My first surgery. *Keepsake.*

"Do you want to talk about it?" Dad asks, side-stepping across the garage with a blue exercise band tied around his ankles, his arms held out for balance like some absurd crab.

I don't even lift my head. "Eliza was messed up, right?"

Dad sighs the unique heave of displeasure he makes when I'm forcing him to mediate. "It was wrong of her to ask Oliver without your permission, but you can't act like this doesn't affect her too. Eliza can't possibly understand what you're going through. That doesn't mean you should make the same mistake by assuming you know everything she's feeling either."

I know what he's saying makes sense, but there's a certain level of sameness in sickness that no one else on the outside will ever unravel from looking in. "I just wish that we could, like, switch bodies for a day."

"Maybe this is her way of trying to get you to talk to Oliver," Dad suggests, taking a seat to do his leg raises. "I'm not saying that you have to get back together, but maybe talking would give you some closure."

"I don't want to talk to him about it. The more we talk, the more he knows."

"And maybe Eliza has a point there." Dad scoots to face me. "It's your decision about whether you want anyone to know about your health. I'm not going to make you. But it's no way to live, and I'm sure that Oliver would have been there for you over the summer."

I blow out a long breath. "I didn't want him to see me like that." As if I had a choice to tell Oliver the truth without showing him that I'm merely a tourist who's only welcome as long as I can fake it.

It's been years since COVID-19 locked down the world, but I still remember what it was like to watch a ripple become a swell become a tidal wave. And as that tide finally receded and my friends returned to summers in the sun, the healthy toppled the bridges behind them, sank the lifeboats, and decreed that the sickness was over. The rest of us would have to swim— or drown.

Oliver had so many plans for us. After all the restrictions of quarantine, how was I supposed to tell him that I couldn't hike to mountainside picnics or drive to glamorous New York City stages because I'd be stuck in bed for weeks after surgery, barely able to move? *Sorry, I can't go on any of these amazing dates with you. I have to go to Philadelphia so that a doctor with two first names can hack my pelvis apart and screw it back together like bad IKEA furniture.*

PELVIS

Is it my fault?

ME

Yes, it's your fault. Asshole.

ANUS

I take offense to that.

53

I wrap an exercise band around one hand over and over. "It was just easier to tell Oliver that we went to Korea to see family."

"You really think he'd look at you differently just because of a hip surgery?"

"It's not just a hip surgery. It's everything. What am I supposed to do when he gets me a 'Get Well' balloon? Write 'No' on the other side?"

Dad doesn't judge me, not the way that others might. "I get what you're saying. I do."

"I'm just tired of everyone trying to make us get back together when he doesn't want to be with me anymore." For too long Oliver and I were always just there, a pair that people cheered for at first and then demanded later. But sometimes all that pushing hardens you the way that diamonds are formed from the pressure, the heat, the crush of a world. And although everyone expected us to sparkle, we could cut too.

It's not that I don't love you, he said on that drafty summer night he left me barely standing on my front doorstep, broken and bereft. *But you vanished. For weeks. You couldn't have called back one time? Didn't you miss me?* He kissed me then, a chaste kiss—a goodbye kiss that would bear no repeating. *I guess you did me a favor. By making me live without you, I finally realized that I could.*

Dad picks at the plastic piece on the end of one shoe-lace as Mom comes out with the recycling bin. "I'll drop it. But if you ever want to talk, I'm here. I just don't want you to regret this later. If me and your mom broke up every time we had a fight, you wouldn't be here."

"You never fight."

"We had our rough patches."

"Like what?" I feel like every story I know is about them frolicking through a magical forest on a path of rose petals with a unicorn playing bridal music in the background.

Mom carefully checks the bottom of each bottle of sports drink to ensure it's been rinsed. She tosses them into the overstuffed recycling bin and bops the lid, earning a metallic shudder from its contents. "Just disagreements here and there. How we wanted our lives to go. Money. Kids." A muscle in her jaw wriggles, a wrinkle disappearing from her cheek as her face shrinks back into neutrality.

My head is throbbing, and I can't decide if it's from my swollen eye or the weirdness of this evening. "I might go to bed early," I say, suddenly overwhelmed with the events of this horrible day that won't end. "I just can't anymore."

"Okay," Dad says, exchanging a look with Mom

that I could study for ten years and still not understand. "Sleep tight."

I head upstairs and veer right into my room, my mind still buzzing too much to spare a single thought for schoolwork. I pick up the backpack that Eliza left just inside the door and chuck it unceremoniously in the direction of my desk to deal with in the morning. It lands with a *thud*, and Eliza comes sprinting down the hallway a moment later, a pen still clutched in one hand. "You good?"

"Yes?"

"Okay, I was just checking on you because there was a loud noise. You don't have to give me an attitude *all the time*."

"Maybe if you weren't in my face all the time, I wouldn't have to give you an attitude."

"Fine. Don't go crying to me the next time you fall over something." She spins on her heel, ranting all the way back to her bedroom. I only catch every fifth or sixth word. ". . . unbelievable . . . trying . . . no . . . fault . . . *witch* . . . day . . ." There's the creak of her computer chair and then her voice, louder and clearer. "Sorry, I'm back. I had to ask my sister something. Did you already go over question six?"

Once upon a time I would have texted Oliver to vent

about her. He was the only one who saw the behind-the-scenes footage of Eliza Kwan, the price of her brand of perfect. I'm always going to be more popular, but I'm no future valedictorian, nationally ranked varsity champion with a 4.0 GPA. Hell, when Pineland Prep scouted Eliza from her middle-school rowing club, they threw in free tuition for me to sweeten the deal. I'm the add-on item to get free shipping.

But there's a difference between being priceless and being worth nothing at all unless I can keep up in this rat race.

I just wish I knew how Dad managed it all—a job he loves, the girl of his dreams. What if you really do only get one soulmate, and they don't want some broken, ruined, literal genetic mutant weighing them down forever? In these vows there's no health to my sickness, no better to this body that is always worse and worse and worse.

Dad always jokes that Mom is one of a kind—and I've never been so terrified in my life that maybe he's right.

I scan the bookshelf below my desk for Oliver's last gift to me. It's there, tucked in the corner with ticket stubs and corsage petals hidden between its pages: *Romeo and Juliet*. My eyes glance past the orthopedic-medicine text

I bought at the library sale as a preteen wishful thinker, back when I naively believed a surgeon could fix my right hand enough to ever stand in an OR of my own. That maybe, if I could hold myself together long enough, I could fix Dad's leg one day.

THUMB CARPOMETACARPAL
LIGAMENTS
What, scalpel drawn, and talk of peace?

ME
I bite my thumb at you, sir.

I pull one of the books free, my fingers feeling every notch and once-familiar crease. I cradle it to my chest, soothed by the coldness of its spine, and carry it to bed like a fairy tale or a lover or a small comfort in the lonely dark.

Five

I wake up to the feeling of a lightning storm thundering in my skull. I let out a cross between a moo and a moan in response. *Mraaah*. I'm usually excited for Friday and the promise of the weekend, but today I'd rather stay in bed.

Mom is always talking about the importance of breaking things down into manageable pieces, but I'm not sure that's possible when every nerve ending in my face has decided to greet the dawn by firing all systems go, go, go. I start by turning off my alarm, then waiting to see which of my joints I've rolled slightly out of socket in my sleep.

I spot myself in the mirror as I set my jaw with a *snap*, click my thumbs into a normal figuration, and flail my leg until my hips are happy. It's very attractive. And Dad wonders why I'm not in a hurry to shout to Oliver, the boy who doesn't even have bad breath in the morning, that I'm a poorly assembled string puppet.

"How do I want to do this?" I mumble to myself, swiveling to inspect the open space next to my bed with my unswollen eye. Thanks to my postural orthostatic tachycardia syndrome—medical terms are such a mouthful sometimes, so I prefer *heart-did-not-understand-the-assignment syndrome*—my heart rate skyrockets whenever I stand up, making my morning routine an adventure even on days when I haven't been recently punched in the face.

I like to think of it as introducing my heart to the concept of gravity eight hundred times a day. I climb out of bed with my uninjured arm, then carefully walk on top of the foam matting that Dad arranged to make sure I don't hit my head too hard if I pass out. My heart rate monitor hasn't alarmed yet, so it's better than some mornings.

I stare at myself in the yellow glow of the cheap bulbs in the bathroom fixtures, my fingers picking apart the layers of my hair. My roots are growing in coal black, and I can't tell if it's obvious against the dark chestnut and lighter hazelnut layers. I don't think the stylist really understood what I meant by milk-tea hair.

After throwing on my uniform I descend the stairs

slowly, listening for one click or two as I hear Dad getting his lunch together. Two clicks. "Rough morning?" I ask in greeting, nodding to his forearm crutches.

He jerks his chin toward the collapsible cane on the counter. "Just saving energy. Have two upright bass lessons later, so I'd rather stand on my own then."

"I can put your wheelchair in the car."

Dad stabs a butter knife into the top of his sandwich. "No. I'll never fit it around the store. I tried the other day."

I open the cabinet next to the stove and pluck out the prescriptions with the blue and red stickers on top. I sort the red ones to the side for Dad, counting aloud to make sure we haven't forgotten to pick up a refill. "You want a Big T?" I reach into the back row for Dad's emergency pain pills. "You look like you're not doing so hot."

He takes the bottle and shakes the tiny, white pills into his hand, counting with a shaky index finger. Finally, he sighs and grabs the store-brand Tylenol knockoff. "Little T is fine. I don't want to run out in case I need the serious stuff."

We invented this code when I was younger to make sure we could communicate in public without people staring at us. It turns out that strangers frown upon fathers asking their fourteen-year-old daughters if they want any tramadol at the grocery store. Go figure.

"I thought you got more," I say, my tone heavy with suspicion as Dad screws the lid back on, wincing as he rearranges his crutches.

"No, they said my pain wasn't bad enough." He waves around half of his sandwich, frowning. "Chronic care. Blah, blah."

"Addiction risk."

"Rising tolerance."

I pat him on the shoulder. "Pain is a mental construct, Dad."

"We should just try yoga," he croaks.

"And lavender essential oils."

"I hear they work extra great if you rub them on your butt with a moonstone."

Eliza must still be cranky about our argument because she hardly speaks as she buzzes around us, throwing snacks into her crew bag and pouring herself a mug of coffee. Thinking of our routine, I turn toward Dad. "Did you go get my car last night?"

"Crap. I'm sorry." He motions at his head. "Brain is bees."

I sigh. "Can I take Mom's?"

"Can you take my what?" she asks as she rushes in with a towel twisted on top of her head like a giant ice-cream cone, her blond hair peeking out from the edges. "Ugh, this is so irritating. John called out *again*, so I have to go open."

I pause to admire the bizarre dance of Eliza and Mom flitting around each other, elbows grazing as they just miss a collision. People-pinball.

"Sorry, you were asking if you could have something?" Mom says as she shoves bits of dried cereal into her mouth by the handful straight out of the vacuum-sealing container.

"I need a ride to school."

Mom pours a travel mug of coffee and smacks two Splenda packets together with a few flicks of her wrist. "I can drop you off on my way to the store."

"That works." Eliza's teammates pick her up most mornings, but I don't want to deal with the awkwardness of asking to join them. Mom is the better choice. "It sucks that you have to go into work early."

"It really does," she says, sighing. "I'm going to have to rewrite my entire planner. Plus I have so much homework to do. I guess I'll have to take it with me and do it on my break."

"Oh. I'm ready a little early, so I can get your books. Where's your bag?"

Mom shakes her head. "Just worry about you, okay?" She says it gently, but it feels too much like a snub, especially since she asks Eliza for help all the time. "How are you feeling?"

"I'm fine." I chew on the inside of my cheek and breathe until I don't want to snap at her, too. I'm not so fragile that I can't carry in a couple of grocery bags or bring the laundry upstairs. I make it through the next fifteen minutes and the walk to the car. I make it through Mom forgetting her bag after all and having to drive back for it.

Mom almost tries to broach a new subject, but we're already turning into the horseshoe-shaped car-rider lane out front. I wave a hand to tell her to just forget it. She doesn't understand. Eliza doesn't understand. Even Dad, with his *I don't want you to regret this* speech, doesn't understand. He got over twenty years before the ghosts of Ehlers and Danlos showed up to collect their due, protected by muscle mass and testosterone.

And they wonder why I want school to just be for me. I know it's a fucking fairy tale, but even Hansel got to eat some cake before the witch tried to cook him. Tears prick my eyes as I think of graduating and losing this last safe haven, the only place that I can think in dances and yearbook deadlines instead of prescription refills and annual follow-ups.

After spending so many years hiding various injuries and braces, it seems surreal to walk into school with my sling and swollen eye. This time there's an acceptable explanation to the question I'm so sick of answering: *What happened?*

Francesca and Amber rush up as soon as they spot me. "Oh my gosh," Francesca says, her hands hovering over my arm. "Are you okay? Your face. Like, not to be rude."

"Is it that bad? I tried this new concealer, but it doesn't look anything like the picture. It's too pink."

"Right?" Amber rubs a fingertip across her brown skin, tracing the contour of her cheekbone. "It always looks different online, but they never have anything in the store that matches."

"My mom is white, so I'm doomed borrowing anything from her." I remember belatedly that they've met Mom before; I'm just so used to having to explain. With my coppery skin and black hair that took two rounds of bleach to dye, EDS isn't the only way I seem to have inherited more of Dad's genes.

"I'll just have to make a new fashion statement." I attempt a smile, but it hurts my eye. "Inspired by, uh, who's that boxer you like who looks like she could punch through a cinder block?" It's amazing the details you accumulate about people when you're with them the first time they get reliable cell-phone service all day. The yearbook room almost feels enchanted in that regard.

"Claressa Shields." Amber giggles and holds her hands over her heart. "I'm *also* inspired by her."

"Shameless," Francesca jokes.

"Okay, maybe, but have you *seen* her? Come on." Francesca pauses, staring off into space with her lips pursed in a convincing impression of indignation. "I don't personally get it. She's not my type."

They both turn to me and I laugh, which is worth it despite the spike of pain through my shoulder. "I am way too heterosexual to break this tie. I'm sorry."

They continue to debate as we make our way to my locker. Everyone around us is buzzing about Pat punching me in the face, but I tune it out, focusing on my friends as their conversation veers into discussing the math homework I'm not going to turn in.

"Last math class you ever have to pass," Francesca says, her eyes darting to Amber as their lamenting loses steam. "Um, and then it's summer! And college! Yay!"

I love her so much for trying to distract me, but the tension reaches a breaking point as I see Pat pushing Marissa Lopez, the bow-seat rower in Eliza's boat, as she gestures to me. A few others leap to my defense, and I track them, noting that I'm apparently popular with the entire photography club for some inexplicable reason. Maybe we've bonded during yearbook assembly more than I thought.

"What?" he yells, shoving through them. "I'm not apologizing to some snoopy slut who can't mind her own damn business."

Amber scoffs and sidles in between us, blocking my view of Pat. "Don't listen to him. He's just jealous that you had something real."

I think about that morning after junior prom again, the way the pink-and-orange ombré of dawn gleamed against Oliver's flawless skin. I slipped out of bed and dressed quickly to hide the marks of staples and stitches, the ugly truths he hadn't been able to see in the dark. "That would imply that he even knows I slept with Oliver. He doesn't. He just thinks we're all sluts."

"That's Pat for you," Francesca mumbles. "May he step on a broken LEGO with the squishy part of his foot."

There were only a handful of people sleeping at Francesca's that night. I trust all of them to protect this secret at least. "And even if he does know, who cares?"

Francesca unsubtly steers me away toward my homeroom. "That's the spirit. Just . . . focus on happy thoughts like . . ."

"Claressa Shields?" Amber volunteers.

"Oh my God." Francesca leans her head back, eyes rolling. "You are the worst. It's like you don't even love me."

I pull open the door to my homeroom-slash-first-class,

holding it with the tip of my sneaker. "I'm going to leave before you start smushing faces," I tease, watching Francesca playfully shove Amber before they begin the thirty-part process of saying goodbye until our fifth-period lunch.

When I turn back, Oliver is there, his hand resting on the door above my head.

"I've got it," I insist, ducking back unintentionally.

"After you."

It is a little difficult to maneuver in the sling, so I give in and step closer. The top of my arm brushes against his chest as I squeeze by.

"Are you feeling better today?" he whispers, almost against the curtain of my hair, his voice-smell-body-existence too close, too everywhere.

"Yeah, I'm fine," I manage to reply, ignoring the fact that if I turned my head, his lips would be right there. It would be so simple, unlike the elaborate gesture of our first kiss when Oliver took my hands in the park and held me, swaying. *He knew that when he kissed this girl, and forever wed his unutterable visions to her perishable breath, his mind would never romp again like the mind of God. So he waited, listening for a moment longer to the tuning fork that had been struck upon a star. Then he kissed her . . . if she didn't think he was an insufferable loser for spending all of English class memorizing these lines.*

I know that I shouldn't keep replaying these moments, but it seems impossible to avoid as I sit through morning announcements and pretend that I am not eleven feet, nine inches away from Oliver De Luca. It would help if our first class wasn't so horrendously boring now that Mr. Waller has made Francesca sit in the back so that we stop the "side conversations." It isn't our fault that his lessons aren't exactly enthralling.

At some point the school decided that we should all pass a Life Skills class to learn about stuff like taxes and nutrition. Here's a life skill for you: try not to fall in love or get punched in the face, but if you have to choose one over the other, at least the pain of a punch is fleeting.

"Okay. Let's get this party started," Mr. Waller says, clapping his hands as soon as the bell rings. He's in a weird formal-wear phase that has nothing to do with his crush on our recently divorced English teacher, so we waste a few minutes while he attempts to pull down a second projector screen next to the SMART Board without untucking his shirt in the back.

He finally gives up and stands on a chair, the shoulders of his suit jacket bunching around his ears. "I'm getting too old for this," he mutters, stepping down to ground level with a good-natured wave. "Go ahead and laugh."

That alone earns a few giggles, and in retrospect

I'm happy that at least this mind-numbing first class of the day is taught by someone like Mr. Waller. So many of my classes nowadays are led by rotating substitutes who can't even remember our names. We hear a lot about burnout and some ominous thing called the Great Resignation—which I've gleaned is a ton of teachers getting so fed up with nonsense after the lockdown that *they* dropped out of high school—but I do miss how it used to be. Back then. Before the panic.

"If you couldn't tell by the second screen," Mr. Waller begins, "we're moving on to the fall-semester project." He raises his voice slightly to talk over the smattering of groans from throughout the classroom. "It's creative, so don't start crying yet. Here are the instructions." He drops a stack on each desk. "Take one and pass it back. You know the drill."

When I get my copy, I skip over the rubric and skim the instructions to see how much worse this could possibly be than writing an essay about credit-card offers last month. I hear murmurs of approval as we all digest the details: a collage and a presentation. "No PowerPoint?" someone mutters off to my left. "Sold."

Mr. Waller smacks a remote against his palm and sighs. After jabbing the power button a few more times, the SMART Board and the ancient projector on the ceiling whir to life to show pictures of previous students' projects and what appears to be an accounting sheet of some kind.

"As you've probably read by now, the project is to make a collage about your life ten years from now. You have to come up with a plan to manage your fake household and explain it to us in a ten-minute verbal presentation. Here's what good looks like." Mr. Waller points to a picture of a colorful poster board. "As you can see, these are real pictures or real estate listings, et cetera. Don't just cut up some magazines or download stock photos. That's cheating.

"I've uploaded everything you need into your folders on the cloud. You have to pick your career, a city, a place to live, and then tell us about how you're affording everything based on the average salary of your, uh, fake job here." He pretends to wipe sweat from his forehead. "Hopefully, none of you are Life Skills teachers in Pineland, New Jersey."

From the front row Brandon responds with a respectful laugh and then presses the heel of his hand against his swollen nose, air hissing through his teeth. When he glances at me in his peripheral vision, I point to my purple eye in solidarity, curl my fingers into the shape of a heart, and hold it to my chest. I hope his nose isn't broken, but it's hard to believe it isn't when it's still eighteen different shades of black and purple.

"There's only one thing missing."

It hits me at the last minute. In every sample picture, there are two people standing by each collage. I go back to the rubric, the heat rising in my cheeks as I scan for the two worst words in the English language—

"Group project!" Mr. Waller exclaims, waving with unreciprocated enthusiasm. "Part of life is learning to work with other people, so you're each getting a roommate to make you compromise on running your fake household. Now, I've been doing this long enough to know that exactly zero of you are going to be happy if I pair you up. For self-preservation purposes, I'm going to leave this up to chance."

He pulls a canvas tote bag out from behind his desk and steps up to the first row. "I'm sure there's an app for this, but this is how us old people assign partners." He shakes the bag by both handles. "Columns one and two, you're in the hot seats. Pick a name."

Everyone on my side of the room immediately looks over to check where their friends are, but I'm too busy counting people, counting odds. Because Oliver is over there, just a few seconds away from his turn. There are only fourteen possibilities. I turn around in my seat to lock eyes with Francesca, sending telepathic vibes into the universe to just pair us together.

"You can pair up for the rest of the period to get started early," Mr. Waller calls over one shoulder. "If you're going online, keep your tablets on topic, please."

I watch Oliver pick a slip of paper and read it without reacting. There was no smile, no frown. It can't be me then. I relax a bit, sitting back in my chair and thinking about where I'm supposed to find authentic pictures that represent me instead of just butchering a few magazines.

My classmates start to pair off, and my boxing partner must be hurting more than I thought since Oliver has to volunteer to carry Brandon's desk over to Maria's. "Thanks, man," Brandon says, offering him something between a clap and a handshake. "I'm not s'posed to really do anything 'cause of the whole mashed-potato face."

"Yeah, no problem," Oliver says, stepping around Maria's chair and squeezing by with his back pressed to the white-painted bricks. He pauses in front of my desk, pressing his index finger onto the rounded corner. "Well, what do you want to be when you grow up, Brynn Kwan?"

"What?" I look up at him, nauseous dread snaking through my guts like chilled water or poison or the awful homemade iced lattes a lovesick girl will drink by the dozen to avoid hurting her boyfriend's feelings.

Oliver unravels a crumpled slip of paper, pinching it taut between both hands like a tiny banner with my name printed on it. "We're roomies."

Six

I stare at a single letter of my name, the *K* in *Kwan*, and can't seem to look away. It's like my entire body is suddenly occupied as my brain fills with static. I swear that I can hear the lightbulbs humming along to the same faint buzz of open air.

"Are you all right?" Oliver asks, presumably because I haven't moved or blinked or breathed in . . . one, two, seven, twelve seconds.

Part of me wants to just go sign myself out, walk over to the football field to get my car, and drive home. That single, concentrated thought is enough to break through the almost silence in my skull, and my feet twitch at the thought, my heels hovering above the ground as the tips of my toes grind harder against the floor.

PREFRONTAL CORTEX

Impulse control is what sets humans apart from animals.

ME

Technically, I'm a zebra, remember? This is my safari. Shut up.

HIPPOCAMPUS

You forgot your car keys at home.

ME

I forgot? Aren't you supposed to be doing the remembering here?

Oliver drags over an empty desk and turns it until it's almost touching mine. He doesn't sit, though. "Brynn?"

"Yeah." I don't know which question I'm answering or if I'm just reacting. I push the assignment sheet around on my desk with my good hand. "I was just thinking about something else. I didn't realize we were partners."

He shrugs. "Luck of the draw?" There are two kinds of luck, but I can't tell which he's talking about. "At least we know the basics." Sweat speckles his forehead, and his thin smile reminds me of a child opening an unimpressive gift. I'm the socks and underwear in this pile of presents.

Before I can so much as pick up my pen, I hear the intercom kick on. It's too early for the bell and too late for announcements about a late-arriving bus. We both unconsciously glance at the speaker on the wall.

"Will Pat Zeller, Brynn Kwan, Francesca Hill, Kayla Rivera, and Brandon Mosley all report to the principal's office immediately?" The office administrator's upbeat voice rings out, the hard consonants crackling on her microphone.

I feel every eyeball in the room pointing at me like a laser. "Three guesses what this is about," Brandon announces loudly as he stands, drawing the attention away. "Somehow I'm gonna be the asshole in all this."

"Oh, I'm sure it'll be a horrifying nightmare," I reply at the same volume as I attempt to pack up my supplies. I appreciate Brandon trying to focus the heat on himself, but it's a moot point when we're all about to be burned at the same stake.

Oliver immediately takes my bag and finishes cleaning up for me. He must see some annoyance in my face because he returns it at arm's length. "Sorry."

"Thanks. We'll just deal with this project thing later, okay?"

"Mrs. Nguyen didn't sound like it was bad."

"That's because she's so nice." On the first day of school, you could barely see her over the piles of candy she brought back from her family reunion in Vietnam, insisting I try one of each kind even though I was just there to drop off a doctor's note about my epinephrine injector. "She always sounds like that." But when she summons you because you're in trouble, it's sort of like having Tinker Bell invite you to your doom.

Brandon loosely knocks his elbow against Francesca's arm as we head for the door. "You good? You look like you're gonna puke."

She takes a long sip from the straw of her water bottle, her face waxy and pale. "I seriously might."

I don't know how much the faculty has heard about the fight, but Mr. Waller gives us a solemn nod as we pass. "Good luck."

I drag my feet on the way to the office as we rendezvous with Kayla halfway. "Let's get this over with," she mumbles, the only words we exchange between the four of us. "Can't wait to hear all about how the rich, white kid is so innocent."

I don't bother hoping for anything better. When it comes to students like us, the ones who aren't wealthy and white and straight, there's a whole different rule book.

Somehow Pat is already at the office when we arrive, kicked back on a short bench with his feet on the edge of Mrs. Nguyen's trash can. She spares me a genuine smile before her face settles back into pointed indifference, nudging a picture of her grandchildren a few inches to the left to block her view of Pat's feet.

He nods to each of us, his gaze lingering on Francesca's blouse. "Lookin' good there, Fran-chest-a."

Kayla has to launch herself onto Brandon's backpack like a distressed baby sloth to keep him from slugging Pat in the mouth. Francesca ignores him like the classy, classy person she is, though she's trembling slightly as I reach out to steady her.

Mr. Dombrowski opens the door and ushers us inside. My stomach lurches as I see Pat's parents packing up their matching embossed portfolios. They stand off to the side with Pat, wearing blank expressions worthy of mannequins or poker players. I'm curious to know how many different lawsuits they threatened, even though I'm the one with the black eye. Unbidden, the ridiculous *Zeller & Zeller, lit-i-ga-tors* jingle plays in my head from their commercial.

I take a seat when no one else moves to do so. Francesca stands behind me like the second in a duel, her fingers wrapped around the back of the hard, wooden chair.

"I've called you in here to discuss the altercation that happened yesterday," Mr. Dombrowski says in a weak voice that suggests he's questioning whichever life choices led to this meeting. "Pat Zeller gave us a statement already alleging that the four of you were involved."

For the next five minutes we're forced to listen to a very creative retelling of what transpired. Pat confronted us over the team's disrespectful use of the Sammy the Shark costume. He was standing up for righteousness and justice. We mauled him when all he wanted to do was go back and turn in his homecoming regalia. Poor Pat. Cry for Pat.

Meanwhile, no one even offers us the opportunity to call our parents. Not that I would anyway, but it's just more evidence that we're already damned. "Brandon didn't even touch him," Kayla retorts when there's finally a lull.

Mr. Dombrowski consults a document on thick, ivory paper that's so long he has to lift his arms slightly to keep it from dragging across his desk. "According to Pat's statement, Brandon 'reached for him aggressively,' which made him fear for his personal and bodily safety."

Behind her back, Kayla pinches Brandon's arm when he opens his mouth to speak. She stands up to her impressive full height, and I swear that I see Dombrowski shrink slightly in his seat. "It was a handshake!" she insists.

My heart melts at her fervent attempts to protect him. Kayla hasn't figured out that this isn't a trial; it's a sentencing.

"I don't know what a handshake looks like in Mexico—" Pat says before his mother silences him with a stern glare and a sharp tap against his bicep with the back of her hand.

"I'm Dominican," Kayla snaps back.

"There are several other witnesses who confirm that you instigated the fight," Mr. Dombrowski pronounces to the group of us, speaking louder and louder as though reciting from a script. When the paper catches the light, I notice the names of several of Pat's cronies, as well as his simpering girlfriend, Lisa Baker-Grant, who would testify that Pat cured cancer with a pineapple and a traffic cone if he asked her to do it. "Ms. Hill, Ms. Rivera, and Mr. Mosley, since you weren't as directly involved, you'll receive three days of in-school suspension each with a week of counseling to follow."

"Me?" Brandon gestures to his face, the bruising even worse with the sunlight from the window contrasting the light yellows and greens against his fading summer tan. "But—"

I whip my head around, fixing him with an urgent look. I mouth, *SAVE YOURSELF.* After all, I should have seen this coming. Kayla and Brandon are on scholarship, but they're still nationally ranked varsity athletes. My entire house could fit in Francesca's bathtub. I'm the only one here who's completely expendable.

Kayla continues to argue until Mr. Dombrowski beats her into submission with another day of in-school suspension for "talking back." She gives me the gentlest of hugs and taps the Pineland Prep logo on my shirt. "That's why it says PP on everything," she hisses in my ear. "Because this place is run by dicks."

Reluctantly, everyone else shuffles out, leaving me alone with just the principal and the Zellers. This is my surprised face.

I take a deep breath, forcing myself to remain as aloof as possible. The only thing more humiliating than this is to show that I'm upset in front of Pat. Mr. Dombrowski scribbles a few notes onto a legal pad, then addresses me. "Ms. Kwan, your situation is a bit different since you physically put hands on Mr. Zeller."

Excuse me as I scrape my eyebrows off the ceiling and paste them back on my face. "What? I didn't touch him."

"Lying isn't going to help," Pat says, pulling aside his shirt to reveal a long line of scratches deep into his chest. My mouth flops open like a broken nutcracker. I wonder how long it took Lisa to do that.

"I'm not lying, and you know it!" I almost reach out and hold my palm up to his skin. None of them know that Ehlers-Danlos syndrome has given me exceptionally long, unstable fingers that bend in odd directions. If I scratched Pat, he'd look like he got attacked by a broken rake.

"We should press charges," Mrs. Zeller says to the empty space in front of me, "but we don't want to completely derail the life of a young person. However misguided she may be."

I stare at Mr. Dombrowski, still slack-jawed. The heat rises in my cheeks, and I lean against the arm of the chair as a wave of dizziness sweeps over me. "That's not true. I didn't do that. I mean, he punched me in the face! That's indisputable!" I mentally reach out for Pretend Brynn, trying to channel her diplomacy and calm, but it's like she decided to take a day off without telling me.

"I'm sorry," Mr. Dombrowski says, not sounding sorry at all. "We have a zero-tolerance policy for violence. You also have an extensive history of violating the dress code, skipping physical education, and showing up late. In light of those many, many infractions, you're out-of-school suspended for next week, and I'm barring you from all senior activities for the remainder of the year."

"You can't do that! That's not . . . That's ridiculous! He's lying!"

"Zero-tolerance policy, Ms. Kwan. Don't make me revisit this because you're out of line."

"You see how emotional she gets," Pat drawls.

I snatch the paperwork that Mr. Dombrowski holds out to me, his bottom lip wilting into a pout that I think is supposed to be an apology. I don't want to hear it. I storm out of the office and head for my locker just to have a destination. How the hell am I supposed to get home when I don't even have my car keys and Mom's on day shift?

Brandon, Kayla, and Francesca must be back in class already. This concrete structure has no cell service to speak of, and I assume our school tablets are monitored, so I'll have to tell Francesca later if I don't want to risk people spying on us. As I walk through the empty hallway, it begins to sink in. No senior activities.

That means no more senior yearbook committee shenanigans with Amber. No student council meetings with TJ. No arguments with Ethan about the senior field trip. Prom. If Mr. Dombrowski seriously enforces his ban, I technically won't be able to chip in backstage during senior improv nights if Francesca is shorthanded. Will I even be able to walk at graduation?

I deflate onto the nearest bench, staring at a poster with my picture on it as I help advertise the senior class calendar. My breathing quickens until I can't breathe at all. It can't be gone. This was all I had left. "It's not fair," I mutter, crushing my hands into fists until I can feel my brittle nails bending, the sharp ends biting into the thin skin of my palms.

Everyone else in that office is going to have a whole life after this. They don't have to worry about making all their memories in the few years before they're too broken and ill and exhausted to make more. They can fall in love and run marathons and be beautiful and have adventures and friends for decades after we toss our caps. But for me there's no guarantee. I need this now. I can only count on right now.

When first period ends and students flood the hallway, I stand among them, wondering again how life can be so fickle. I crumple my suspension notice into a ball, a tear leaking past the swollen orb of my purpling eye. It all hits me at once, the grief of having everything I've ever wanted torn away by lies.

I feel naked without my titles, stripped of the positions that keep me from being just . . . me. I turn in a slow circle, the shame scorching across my cheeks and smoldering in my eyes. I can't be *just* me. Just Brynn.

I don't want to be that girl. There's something wrong with her. She's a mutant. She's a time bomb. That's not me. I'm junior prom queen. I'm class president. I'm co-chair of the student council.

I'm . . .

I'm no one.

But after dreading it for so long, maybe this is my reality check. I should just embrace it after years of hobbies becoming too hard, of winter breaks getting sewn and stapled back together. If my body is a temple, then this illness has made it a ruin. It chips away at the best parts of me until I'm sculpted into a stranger. And with one stroke of his pen, Mr. Dombrowski has set it into stone.

I'm reminded yet again of that long-ago freshman summer when the healthy declared that the worst was over and it was time to stop living in fear. Thus ended their strange foray into sickness, and we the forgotten donned well-worn masks of a different kind to return to their world for as long as we could.

Seven

As my toes point in the direction of my Algebra II class, it hits me that Mr. Dombrowski didn't even tell me whether I'm supposed to leave or finish out the school day. He probably meant to send me to the in-school suspension area, but I don't blame him for being distracted with Pat's whole family staring him down. They built the Zeller Athletic Complex; I'm only here because Eliza took "Row, Row, Row Your Boat" too seriously as a child.

I need to get as far away from here as possible before I start screaming. I belatedly realize that I left my backpack halfway down the hallway where I dropped it onto the floor by the bench, trusting the tablet inside to the fickleness of gravity and protective cases. I should have remembered that it was in there. Should have been more responsible. Should have thought about the consequences.

Should have. Should have. Should have.

I walk all the way to the other side of the school in search of cell-phone service, but I can barely get a couple of texts out to the family chat. I don't even register how long I've been wandering until the bell rings yet again. This time I can tell immediately that the rumors have started spreading. People surge toward me, offering platitudes and support as I attempt to get away.

Eliza's voice rings out, her arm chopping in between two juniors and shoving them aside. "You got suspended?" she bellows as she pushes closer. "Are you kidding me?"

I know better than to interpret her comment as indignation. "I don't need your preachy shit right now, Eliza."

"What did Mom and Dad say? This is going to be terrible for your college applications."

"I don't care about any of that. I just want to go home, but I forgot my keys." My arm brushes against the bank of lockers, and I'm cornered now, stuck between the open door to my right, the mob on my left, and Eliza front and center, just the way she likes it. My voice is a rasping mewl as I shrink away, overwhelmed.

Eliza leans her head beside mine, whispering, "Did

the principal say anything about me? I'm not in trouble, right?"

"Not everything is about you," I snap, attempting to extricate myself, which only results in banging my skull against the door behind me. "I thought you'd be happy. Another chance for you to be the perfect sister."

I don't even look up as I hear the slap of flat soles against the tile. I assume it's security until I see fingers curl around Eliza's sleeve and pull her back. "Hey," she exclaims, batting at Oliver. "Get off of me."

He glowers at her, stepping in between us and rolling his shoulders out of their usual slouch. "Oh, is it upsetting to have people touching you without permission? Getting in your face?" His voice rises as the crowd grows quiet. "Yelling at you?"

"We're family." Eliza tosses her head, her ponytail inadvertently smacking a random student who's gawking over her shoulder. "It's different."

"It should be different, but it isn't."

Panic ripples through the group as a teacher begins investigating the commotion. I can't tell if it's someone I know or a substitute, and I don't want to risk getting sent to in-school suspension. I seize the chance to slide around the open door and slip into the adjoining wing just as the bell rings.

I whirl around when I sense someone behind me, but

it's only Oliver, his thumbs hooked into the pockets of his uniform-approved khakis. "You're going to be late to gym," I admonish, accidentally revealing that I have his schedule memorized. "But, um, thanks. For dealing with Eliza."

"I like Eliza, but she's out of control sometimes." He stands there, arms hovering a few inches from his sides like a confused penguin in a polo shirt. Before I can respond, he blurts, "Doyouneedahug?"

I nod, pure will keeping the scream building inside me from escaping the echo chamber of my throat. Oliver folds me into a bear hug that I wish felt more familiar than it does. I bury my face against his chest, my forearm blocking the light like a boxer waiting for the blows to stop.

"What can I do?" he whispers, swaying us gently as if we're in a ballroom and not the middle of the hallway. "You're okay. You're okay."

"Will you just take me home? Please?" I don't really want to go home, but I can't think of any alternative. "If you won't get in trouble?"

Oliver brushes the side of his cheek against the top of my hair, and it's so close to the kisses he used to press against my temple that I almost pull away. "Sure. I just have to go to the office. My parents won't care. They won't even notice." He shrugs. "Did you sign out already?"

I reluctantly pull away and produce the crinkled

suspension notice from my pocket, smoothing over the tear where my fingernail punched through the paper earlier. "I don't think I really have to. I'm suspended. Like, *suspended* suspended."

"Oh." His brows crease, eyes narrowing. "Wait, what? They suspended *you*? Did Pat get in trouble too?"

"What do you think?" I hum the jingle for his parents' law firm under my breath. Between their overkill radio campaign and local television ads, I know he'll get the reference.

Pink splotches explode across Oliver's cheeks. "That's ridiculous."

I realize in retrospect that I never did hear Pat's punishment, if there even is one. He'll probably pick up trash in a park for three minutes and graduate with a squeaky-clean record that only shows some community service. Convenient.

I take a step forward, and Oliver spins on his heel to follow. "I swear that this is the worst school I've ever gone to," he mutters.

"That's saying something since you went to, what, like, forty-nine middle schools?"

He pretends to count on both hands, waggling his fingers. "Seven actually. But none of them were this . . . toxic. They have so much money, and for what?" Oliver jerks his thumb at a cabinet of old trophies, the glossy finish of the polished cherry and spotless glass. "A place like this can do whatever they want, but they're still making us bow to big donors, eat Styrofoam lunches, and put on productions of *Our Town*. Where's the imagination? The justice?"

I slap a locker with the flat of my hand as we pass. "It doesn't exist."

We don't speak to each other as we head back to retrieve my belongings, both of us digesting what's just happened in our little school stratosphere. Oliver insists on carrying my bag no matter how much I protest, and I tell myself that it's foolish to want to lift things when I'm already in pain.

I hide around the corner from the office while Oliver goes to sign himself out. It occurs to me once he's inside that he still has my very distinct peach-colored, quilted backpack over his shoulder, but I doubt anyone will really put two and two together. After all, it's not like we're together. We're just two . . . somethings, two not-nothings.

"Walk faster," Oliver manages through gritted teeth, both hands ushering me urgently toward the front door.

LEFT HIP
I don't think I like your tone, good sir. I'm
doing my best.

91

But I make it outside before anyone sees, fighting the urge to limp and cling to the railing with both hands. Oliver blows out a short puff of air. "Principal Dudebrowski was right behind me."

I snort, wondering if Oliver remembers it was my dad who coined that now famous nickname. "Honestly, though, what's he going to do? Suspend me again?"

"Let's not find out," he says with a last look at the closing double doors. "I'm parked over by the road."

It's not difficult to spot Oliver's car, a squat, navy blue SUV with a Louisiana plate and rusty splotches around the wheel wells. The back windshield is covered with faded stickers, evidence of his mom's old parking permits for oil refineries and processing plants. I climb inside and buckle my seat belt with my good arm, moving slightly to let Oliver set our belongings in the back.

"The other door still broken?" I ask, nodding at the rear driver's side door.

"My mom keeps insisting that it works, but I'm afraid it'll fall off if I pull too hard." He perches on the side of the seat as he sheds his uniform polo and trades his hideous brown suede uniform shoes for plain black sneakers. "She slid out in a snowstorm when we lived in Pittsburgh. The roads are 'paved' with . . . I've seen better infrastructure in Minecraft maps." He

92

starts the car and pulls out onto the road as the *Chicago* soundtrack filters through the speakers.

"Aren't you sick of this yet?" I swear that he's been listening to the same playlist since we broke up months ago. But maybe I'm wrong to doubt his patience given that he's ignored the same pinging dashboard light since sophomore year.

Oliver laughs at my exasperation, and it almost hurts how much I miss that sound. He's different in school, where there are always people watching, waiting to pick you apart the moment they can find a place to peck. "It's a great performance."

"Great enough to listen to a thousand times?"

He holds up a finger in warning. "Ten thousand times. That's Chita Rivera."

"You're talking to the wrong Kwan here. The music genes skipped straight over me." Just not all the other genes unfortunately. "Though who knows? Maybe I'll finally let my dad teach me an instrument now that I'm going to have so much time on my hands." I let my head fall back against the seat and close my eyes, lamenting the day I agreed to jump ship from public school.

"What do you mean?" He turns his head to look at me for a moment before peering past me, watching a minivan approach and then pass before we turn onto the street. "How long is your suspension?"

"All of next week, but there's more than that." I squeeze the squarish pin that locks the door, pull until it pops open, then push it back into place with the tip of my finger. I forget that I'm halfway through an explanation until the third or fourth time. Pop. Push. "I'm not allowed to be in any senior activities anymore." Pop. Push. My throat tightens around the burning knot in the back of my throat. "Like, any of them."

I watch Oliver's face mold and meld into disbelief, then anger, then a soft sadness that seems to start in his eyes and wash across his features like the swell of a tide. "I'm so sorry. Is there anything you can do?"

I shake my head, soundlessly mouthing the word *no*. When I move to reach for the locking mechanism on the door again, Oliver hits the control panel on his side first, popping the pin before I can do it myself. "Too slow," he whispers.

It's so silly, so Oliver, that I choke on a cough that isn't a laugh and isn't a cry. Tears I didn't know were there burst free, and I fumble with the glove box for a moment, instinctively holding my knee in just the right spot to catch it as the broken compartment flops open, nearly spilling paperwork and a couple of napkins onto the floor.

I grab one of the rumpled napkins to dry my eyes. "Sorry. It's just a lot." My makeup runs in streams of cream concealer and green color corrector, staining the napkin everywhere it touches. I flip open the mirror on the visor to smooth the edges by my eyes, but it's too late—the purple and blue of my bruises are already showing through, seeping through the patina that couldn't really hide them anyway.

"Oh my God." Oliver gasps, jerking the wheel straight again as we inadvertently drift too far onto the shoulder. "Your eye is that bad?" He smacks a hand so hard over his mouth that I hear the band of his new class ring click against his front teeth. "Brynn, what the f—"

"It's fine," I say, turning away and slamming the visor closed. It's only half a lie. With a condition that makes me bruise worse than other people, it really does look worse than what it is.

"It doesn't look fine."

"Why do you have to do that?" I snap, shifting in my seat to stare at his profile until his eyes flick over for just a moment before returning to the road. "I said I'm fine. Why can't anyone just believe me when I say that I'm fine?"

RIGHT EYEBALL

Clearly, we have different definitions of fine.
And don't you even think about rolling your
eyes at me.

Oliver sits at the stop sign at the entrance to my neighborhood. He reaches for my knee, then curls his hand into a fist and slowly brings it back to rest on his own. "Because . . . Brynn, you're not fine." He says it like they're the most obvious words in the world. "You're hurt. And I know Pat didn't mean to punch you, but that's not the point."

"If it wasn't one thing, it would just be another." This is my destiny after all, isn't it? I was knocked out in round one, when I was nothing but a new life fighting the Hydra of the human genome. Somewhere along the way there was a blip in my DNA, a stuck key, an ink smudge.

"What do you mean?"

"You know how it is." I stare at the side-view mirror, willing someone to pull in behind us and force Oliver to keep driving. "Every time it seems like things are getting better, they're just getting different instead. And that's not the same thing."

The muscles of his jaw tighten and loosen, as though he's chewing my words. "I know what you mean." He waves a hand at the windshield and the plain suburban landscape before us. "My mom used to go through this whole thing whenever she found out she was getting transferred to another state. 'It'll be better there. It'll be new. Their maintenance department is *so* good. I'll have so much more time at home.'" He squints a bit, his index finger tapping in a depression in the steering wheel where the foam is missing. "But it wasn't better, and she wasn't home early, and there's a point where too much new gets old."

A hot-pink Toyota honks from behind us, and Oliver rolls onto my street, putting on his blinker as he slows to a stop in front of my house. "Oh, sorry, I forgot about the mud pit." He throws the car back into gear and pulls into the driveway, sparing me the worst of the mud that takes over the front yard any time it rains. "Do you, uh, want me to hang out with you for a while?"

"That's okay." While I climb out one side, Oliver steps out of the other. "My dad'll be home soon. He works a weird schedule now."

He comes around the front of the car with my backpack, then continues up to the driveway to set it on the front step. "He's not still teaching at that guitar place?"

"He's at a music store now." I unlock the door, unable to escape the needling feeling that we're drifting into small talk. It's all too pleasant, too unfamiliar, the kind of not knowing that can only creep in with someone you've loved.

Oliver looks at the darkened windows. "You sure you'll be all right by yourself?"

If he were anyone else, I'd think it was just a ploy to get invited inside when we're clearly alone. But I suspect that he's asking more to soothe his own guilt than any-thing. "Yeah, I'll be fine. Thanks for taking me home."

"It's the least I can do after all that shit with Pat."

"I owe you a ride the next time your radiator blows up." I stare at the point of his white V-neck undershirt, knowing that if I lift my eyes even an inch, I'll never be able to stop myself from hooking my fingers inside his collar and pulling him close. "Guess I'll see you when I'm unsuspended."

Oliver rolls his weight back onto his heels, the tips of his fraying canvas sneakers rising for a moment. "Sure. I'll see you." He shakes his keys in farewell, walking away with his head down, his fingers sorting one key after another along the ring.

And like I've done day after day, week after week—I let him leave me behind.

Eight

Being home alone is almost eerie. I'm so used to the background noise of three other people, the sound of Eliza clomping down the stairs in her gigantic house slippers or the scratching of pencils when Dad's hyperfixation cycles back to coloring books. I turn around more than once, unable to shake the feeling that someone is standing just outside my peripheral vision.

I click on the television as a mindless distraction and plop onto the couch to wait for the wave of fatigue to pass. But the longer I sit, the more the fog settles in, making everything too loud, too bright.

BRAIN
There is definitely a kraken hiding in the dishwasher.

It's time to take a nap.

I don't fuss with setting an alarm, hoping that maybe I'll just sleep until I feel as well rested as it's possible to feel when your autonomic nervous system is made of three drunk carrier pigeons in a trench coat. I make it forty minutes before I snap awake, my shoulder demanding a heating pad and a harder surface that keeps my joint more stable.

I splay out on the kitchen floor and try not to drop my phone on my own face as I scroll through my feeds online. I'm morbidly curious about the rumors that must be spreading by now, but I don't see anything yet. I count down the minutes until lunch begins and hope that one of my friends can pick up a cell signal in the outdoor courtyard attached to the cafeteria. Francesca's first message comes through almost immediately, and it wouldn't surprise me if she sent Amber on a mission to buy her lunch so that she could get outside as quickly as possible.

Francesca [10:52 A.M.]: IS IT TRUE

Brynn [10:53 A.M.]: Which part?

Francesca [10:54 A.M.]: UM, ALL OF IT??? You never came back to class!

Did you really get suspended? For
a whole week?

> Brynn [10:55 A.M.]: Yeah. Pat
> said I scratched him, so it was
> self-defense to hit Brandon
> and then punch me in the
> face. Makes sense.

Francesca [10:55 A.M.]: I HATE IT
HERE.

The rest is a long string of emojis that somehow translates perfectly in my mind: *Angry face. Brain explosion. School building. Middle finger. Pile of poop. Middle finger. Middle finger.*

We text back and forth a few more times before I suspect that she's lost service. The suspension part of my sentence didn't seem so harsh earlier, but when I do the math in my head, it's even bleaker than I thought. Five days of out-of-school suspension and weekends on either end mean that I'm stuck at home for nine days.

The panic sets in again every time I spot a reminder of what I've lost, like the way Dad's jaw tightens when there's a motorcycle or a muscle car in some action movie. I peel myself off the floor, incensed by the calendar for the senior yearbook committee mocking me from where it's stuck to the side of the fridge with a Frostbite Regatta magnet.

I tear it free and shove it into the trash. Don't need that anymore. Everywhere I look there's another symbol of senior-class fundraisers and student council events. I tear up as I hold one of the little pumpkin-shaped stress balls we ordered for the Boo-Boo Blood Drive. I didn't even want to be that involved before, and now I can't.

The real gut punch comes when I head upstairs and spot the gaudy, rhinestone-encrusted tiara I've held on to since junior prom, hoping to win the senior crown and make something of the pair. It doesn't matter now, but even after sitting for five minutes with my thumbs pressed so hard against the plastic that I can feel the fake gems imprinting into my skin, I can't bring myself to break it. I set it back where it was before, dangling precariously from the wooden knob of my closet, forever half a dream.

It doesn't even occur to me to worry about what Mom and Dad will say until I hear a car pull into the driveway. It must be Dad and Eliza coming home from crew practice since the upstairs shower kicks on shortly after.

I debate whether it's better to hide in my room with Eliza on the same floor or if I should run while she's distracted. I choose the latter, padding down the hallway in my socks and slinking away to the relative safety of the ground floor before Eliza can emerge from the bathroom.

As soon as I round the corner, Dad lobs a paper airplane in my direction. It catches the air and seems to hover for a beat before spiraling to the floor to crash-land in front of my foot. "I was hoping that Eliza exaggerated some of what went on this morning, but it appears not."

"I literally didn't even do one single thing to that guy, and they kicked me out of everything."

"I know." He points to the paper airplane. "That's what I think of your principal's disciplinary letter, by the way. He's a real winner."

"They called you?"

Dad nods and shakes his cell phone in the air. "After they decided to suspend you, of course. But you're lucky they called me and not your mother. She would have gone thermonuclear in there."

The mental image isn't pretty. "Just forget it. We'll never win against Pat's parents. And if we make a big deal out of it, they could start screwing with Eliza too."

"It's not that I don't believe you," Dad stresses. "I want to fight for you. I want to drive down there tomorrow and cane every single one of those administrators in the shins. But we don't have any kind of advantage. We're lucky they didn't bring up your scholarship. And the Zellers could make a lot of trouble for your mom in law school."

"I get it." If there's one thing I've learned from having to repeatedly pay for some jerk in a white coat to diagnose me with female hysteria and prescribe yoga, it's that people in charge will double down the moment you make a peep.

"I'll smooth it over with your mother if she's upset," Dad promises. "I asked Eliza not to say anything to her yet. And I'm sorry about the dances and stuff."

My throat tightens, transforming my words into a weak rasp. "It's more than that."

Our conversation fizzles out when the door to the garage opens to reveal Mom, the handle of a canvas grocery tote twisted around her wrist. "Who left the garage open?"

"Was that me?" Dad's eyebrows rise as he thinks, then fall as he winces. "Yeah. My bad. There's a lot going on."

Even though she wants to become a personal injury lawyer—personal injury is kind of a family specialty, after all—Mom has all the personal mannerisms of a hammy Hollywood prosecutor. She can't stand in one place to have a conversation, instead flitting from the refrigerator to the sink to staring out the sliding door onto the deck.

I slowly retreat into the living room to eavesdrop. It's amazing how it seems like there's an invisible force field between the kitchen and living room despite the lack of a physical wall. There's just something about the lightness of the kitchen and the dark furniture of the living room that makes one place seem to vanish when you're in the other.

Dad catches Mom's attention, his voice taking on a certain urgency. "Hey, Jenna? I just remembered that we have to go get Brynn's car from the high school. Why don't you come with me, and we'll talk on the way?"

"Now?" Mom asks, clearly caught off guard as she shucks her work polo and shoots it into the laundry basket on top of the washing machine. "I just got home."

I can only see the back of Dad's head, but I know that he must be making some kind of face because a moment later Mom says, "Okay. Okay."

He shoos her down the hallway, and I love him for just buying me a few more minutes of peace before this has to become a whole family affair again. "We're not making real dinner!" he shouts up the stairs to Eliza. "There are potpies in the freezer!"

When they get back, Mom's face is so red that she looks like a toddler left unattended with a palette of blush. Dad's lost whatever color she gained, his skin gleaming with a pale, nervous sheen. He catches my eye and toggles

105

his hand in the air. That means there's a fifty-fifty chance that Mom's going to freak out, try to fix it tomorrow, and probably end up getting me expelled and ruining her future legal career in this town in one fell swoop.

But she's calmed down somewhat by the time she takes up her usual spot on the couch, a glass of red wine in one hand and a grimace that says she hasn't completely ruled out committing a felony tomorrow.

I prefer not to leave these types of things to interpretation, so I finally just ask point-blank, "Are you mad at me?"

"I have no right to be," she replies, and it's not lost on me that it isn't a real answer.

"I didn't stand a chance in that meeting." The protection afforded by being the sister of a star athlete only extends so far. I don't have the right name or face or connections to stand my ground.

"Maybe this is a silver lining," Mom says after two hearty gulps of wine. "If you're not fussing with yearbook and staying so late at school, then maybe you can get more sleep and you won't feel so worn down all the time."

"I'm not holding my breath." She just doesn't understand that sleep and fatigue have nothing to do with each other. It's like pouring water into a bucket with no bottom.

Mom quirks a brow suddenly. "If your car was still at school, how'd you get home?"

"I asked Oliver to drop me off."

"Oh, that was nice of him." She exchanges a loaded look with Dad. "He's really been going out of his way for you lately."

"We're just friends," I mumble. I'm "just friends" with Oliver the same way that eggplant is technically a fruit. It's the truth, but it still doesn't make sense. He's certainly not my enemy, but shouldn't there be a third category of not-*not*-friend?

Enough time passes to feel awkward, but I'm not sure if we all notice or it's just me. "Well, you'll have a lot of availability to get that shoulder looked at," Mom says. "How's it feeling today?"

"I'm fine. I would tell you if I wasn't fine. You know I hate it when you do that." My voice trails off, ending in an even heavier silence. I don't know why there always has to be a bright side or a pep talk. When something bad happens, Mom's the first one leaping up to find sugar and a lemonade pitcher, but sometimes when life gives you lemons, you're just stuck under a pile of rotting citrus fruits, and it's kind of bullshit.

Mom looks up from her phone, either from the group text she has with her friends from law school or Eliza messaging something she doesn't want to say in front of me. "Do what?"

"Nothing." The squashy recliner does its best to suck

me into its depths, but I manage to rock forward hard enough to roll myself onto my feet. "I think I'm just going to sleep."

There's a slight delay as she finishes typing a response. "Don't forget to take your pills."

"I won't. I'm not in kindergarten."

"I don't need the attitude," she calls after me.

"I don't either!" Even if I did forget to take my meds, she or Eliza would inevitably check and then wake me up for a midnight snack of allergy pills and enough high-dose vitamin C to glow in the dark.

I count out an oval pill, a square pill, and four of the yellow tablets. When I get upstairs I crawl into bed still wearing my uniform, feeling like some banished medieval traitor in the wrong livery. I burrow under the blankets, squirming against the surgical screws dotting the top of my hip crest, the taste of lemons melting across my tongue.

Nine

Even though it's the weekend, it doesn't fully sink in that I'm suspended until I wake up on Saturday without the weight of homework or clubs hanging over me. Unfortunately, it also seems to be sinking in for everyone else.

> TJ [9:12 A.M.]: I can't do Boo-Boo
> Blood Drive without you! Who will
> be our sexy vampire?

> Brynn [9:13 A.M.]: I don't know.
> Did you ask Olivia?

TJ [9:13 A.M.]: I cannot speak words
in the presence of Olivia's sexiness.
You know this.

As the news spreads, it becomes wildly apparent that I never set up a structure for anyone to replace me if I became unable to continue as class president or head of the senior yearbook committee. It seems like an oversight given how often I'm out sick or canceling planning meetings at the last minute because I'm too bone-tired to haul my carcass anywhere but home.

It's only the beginning of October, but people are already coming unglued about how to find someone else to plan senior portraits and work on the senior gift. I spend most of the day crying in bouts and jags as I'm inundated with messages about everything from fundraising to whether I've been expelled. Someone with a username I don't recognize even has the audacity to ask me who I'm backing for prom queen.

Dad knocks on my door on Sunday afternoon, pushing it open slightly with one crutch. He leans against the wall, panting a bit. "Why did we think buying a two-story house was a good idea?" he murmurs to himself. He scans my room, and I have the decency to look embarrassed, snuggled up in two-day-old pajamas with my hair unwashed, my bedspread covered in a hailstorm of balled-up tissues. "I brought you some mental-health pancakes."

"I'm not really hungry."

Dad pulls off the drawstring bag on his back and removes a container of pancakes, leaning forward on his crutches to toss it over. "You have to eat something." He hands me a fork. "Here. I put on extra butter and that disgusting artificial syrup you like so much."

I take off the lid and hazard a sniff. "Thanks. Even if you are a total maple-syrup snob."

"Do you want to talk about it?"

I shake my head, dribbling a bit of syrup onto one side of my chin.

"Do you want me to accidentally fall asleep in the salon while you get a manicure-hair-foot-thing?"

Head shake, though the idea of getting my roots touched up is tempting.

"Do you want to come to my Cripples Vent on Zoom Because Human Society Is an Unending Nightmare support group?"

Head shake.

"Do you want me to leave you alone to brood in the dark like a sad Gengar?"

Head nod. "What's a Gengar?"

"One of the original Shadow Pokémon." Dad hovers in the doorway for just a moment. "I'm sorry about school.

About everything. Maybe tomorrow will be better."

"Maybe tomorrow," I echo, mustering what little, uncertain hope I can. For the first time in a long time, there's no concrete milestone in the distance to keep me moving forward. I try to think of what Pretend Brynn would do, but I quickly discover that in losing all the best parts of senior year, I seem to have lost all the best parts of myself as well.

Being suspended doesn't absolve me from doing work, and Monday morning, Mr. Waller's already modified one of my assignments. I sign on to see what he wants, secretly hoping that he converted my group project with Oliver into a solo one, but when I click on the notification for more detail, it's offering extra credit in exchange for reading a single page of the textbook. It's material from way at the end of the book, far beyond our current chapter.

My curiosity piqued, I scroll to the right section only to burst out crying again when I see that it's a page on self-care and self-love. On the list of things too wholesome for this world, it's puppies, Keanu Reeves, and Mr. Waller.

EYEBALLS
Please buy eye drops.
We're thirsty.

NOSE SKIN
And softer tissues while you're at it.

The boredom sets in once everyone else leaves and I find myself in an empty house again. I pace in circles, unsure of what to do with the free time I never dreamed of having, irritated by the squishy pulsing of the washing machine. It reminds me of quarantine in freshman year, the nights when one of us would snap and we'd all pile into the car just to drive around town and see something that wasn't nothing.

The faintest flicker of hope revives me when someone starts a petition to protest my suspension, but it dies with only a handful of signatures, one of which belongs to *Patrick Zeller*. Kayla makes an entire Discord group inviting almost fifty people to plan a walkout, but the excuses start pouring in almost immediately.

Ethan has a swim meet after school.

TJ can't miss student council this close to the Boo-Boo Blood Drive.

Francesca's mom is meeting with a lawyer to see if she can contest the school's ruling, so Francesca isn't allowed to talk about it.

Amber has to coordinate the spring sports calendar with photography club for yearbook.

Even after Kayla suggests multiple days, it doesn't

seem to work with anyone's schedules. I guess I shouldn't be surprised that my classmates are moving on without me now that I've turned over the keys to the proverbial kingdom, but I still wonder how the clubs are doing in my absence.

By Wednesday it occurs to me that I should do some homework to avoid falling behind in all my classes. Eliza keeps bringing home new assignments, but if I'm suspended until next week anyway, I just don't have the energy without the urgency.

The texts with questions about clubs and classes get less frequent as the week goes on with the notable exception of Oliver, who keeps checking in about our Life Skills project. I never thought I'd be able to resist reading a message from Oliver, but after a while, I let my silence be a response of its own. I just can't bring myself to care about income taxes and electric bills when this entire suspension is further proof that life is a game and only some people get the cheats.

By Thursday it occurs to me that I don't care about turning a few things in late.

By Friday, a whole week since I last sat in a classroom, it occurs to me that I don't care about school at all. What's the consequence of dropping a few letter grades? It's not like I'm expecting any academic accolades at the end of the year.

Plus there's no way to turn off the little status bar that says whether I'm online or not. Every time I log into school, the deluge of sympathy is relentless. Most of my classmates feel the need to tell me they're so sorry, texting or sending rambling emails through the online dashboards for our shared classes. I was hoping it would blow over and go back to normal by now—that maybe, somehow, I could go back to being normal too.

The rain comes on Saturday in such relentless droves that Eliza's race gets postponed. I hear her pacing the strip of hallway outside, venting. "How reliable is that weather report Coach Dee sent out? There's going to be so much chop." Her voice is so loud that I almost miss my phone buzzing.

Francesca [11:16 A.M.]: Wait until
you hear this

Brynn [11:17 A.M.]: What now?

Francesca [11:17 A.M.]: You know
how my mom was meeting with a
lawyer?? She's talked to seven of
them and none of them want shit
to do with us once they hear that

Pat's involved. WHAT DO WE EVEN
DO NOW

Brynn [11:18 A.M]: Give up?

I stew on it for hours, hating that you can do anything you want when you've got the right name and face
and bank balance. I've been cooped up so long that I
don't even notice how much time I've spent obsessively
fuming until I hear the opening melody of a song I don't
recognize.

It used to annoy me that noise from the music room
filters through the vent by my desk, but lately I enjoy listening to Dad's impromptu compositions as he invents
new ways to keep his students interested. At the very
least he's the only person I know who tries to adapt
Taylor Swift to trombone, rewrite BTS hits for piccolo,
or add a xylophone solo to the middle of a Nicki Minaj
track.

The odd missed note or bass beat is so common
before dinner that I notice immediately when it's cut
short. I listen for voices instead to see if someone inter-
rupted him, but I know that there's something amiss
when I hear the rap of knuckles on my door. It opens
slowly, spilling a spotlight across the carpet.

"Yeah?" I call, my voice croaking with disuse and

the rewards of a long-empty water bottle that I haven't wanted to venture downstairs to refill.

Mom steps halfway inside, her hand forming a claw around the knob. "Are you sitting here in the dark?"

"The sun's going down," I offer as an explanation, too embarrassed to admit that I hadn't really noticed between my focus on the music and the zebra night-light in the outlet by my closet. "Is Dad okay? I haven't heard any tuba farts in a while."

She smiles at the inside joke, a throwback to when Dad was learning brass instruments and every night sounded like a sad tugboat with indigestion was having an existential crisis in our basement. "I'm not sure. Can you . . . I have no idea what your father is talking about. He's not making any sense."

"I'll check it out." I know it isn't an emergency because Mom never hesitates to demand that we go to the doctor, which is perfectly fine unless she's doing it to me.

LEFT ANTERIOR CRUCIATE LIGAMENT
Hear me out. If you just stay in your room
forever, you never have to use the stairs
ever again.

ME
Tempting.

In the back corner of the living room, I spot a single foot sticking out of a pile of weighted blankets and fuzzy throws. I walk over quietly and nudge the bottom of Dad's foot with my toe. The pile of blankets yelps, "Ticklish!" in indignation, and the foot vanishes.

"Hey, Dad? Are you— Do you need anything?"

"There's too much temperature."

I bend over and lift the topmost blanket, a tiny Sherpa throw that my grandmother bought me for Christmas without realizing that the golden retriever on the package meant it was for dogs. "I can put a couple of these away."

"No, no," Dad protests. "I'm hot but not that kind of hot. My nerves. I'm freezing."

I add the Sherpa back to Blanket Mountain, wondering if I should go into the garage to bust out the big guns: the heated electric blankets that keep us both from disintegrating every winter. "Do you want some hot water?"

"I'm okay."

"Let me know if you want anything else."

I hear footsteps on the stairs and realize that Mom has inadvertently trapped me downstairs with Eliza. I wish there was some kind of signal that we're in a deep sisterly feud, like when Mom passive-aggressively puts the groom duck from their little wedding set in the corner of the kitchen facing the wall. "What's going on?" Eliza asks when she sees us awkwardly standing around.

"Your father's in Blanket Mountain," Mom explains, scrolling through recipes on her tablet with long flicks of her fingers. "I can't decide between burgers and meatballs. What do you think?"

Dad lifts the edge of a throw just long enough to say, "Burgers."

"The pile of blankets would like burgers," I relay in a louder voice.

Eliza doesn't even crack a smile, so there goes any opportunity to just ignore the awkwardness until it goes away. If she's expecting an apology from me, she's got another thing coming. I'm a Scorpio, and Halloween isn't too far off; my ability to hold a grudge grows stronger every day.

"What's going on with you two?" Mom asks, her words halting and hesitant, the edgy way a neighbor asks a firefighter about the inferno gobbling up a house two doors down.

"Nothing," we say in unison, each of us busying ourselves with anything else except each other. While Mom cooks, Eliza chops vegetables and moves sides to the table. I grab the dishes and place settings, careful of my shoulder now that I've decided I can go without the sling. We pass like two enemy bullets whizzing over neutral ground.

The truce lasts as long as it takes to extract Dad from his blanket fort and take our seats. Dad has barely finished his prayers before Eliza takes her gambit. "I have more homework for you. Basically all your teachers said you haven't done anything yet."

I impale a chunk of carrot, the tines of my fork screeching on the plate. "I'll do it this weekend."

"All of it?" she asks, her voice incredulous.

This is the difference between taking all advanced placement classes and taking all . . . not-advanced-placement classes. "What? It's not rocket surgery."

"That doesn't mean you should wait until the last minute," Eliza retorts. "What if you don't get the grades in before early decision?"

I slam my palms onto the table so hard the silverware rattles. "I'm not applying early decision, Eliza. We're not all you. I don't care about school."

Mom attempts to speak, but Eliza just talks louder. "The world cares about school, so maybe you should stop acting like you're literally too cool for school just because you're too lazy to do some math problems."

I have the unfortunate habit of crying when I'm angry, but this is beyond tears, beyond the stinging in my hands. I stare with unfocused eyes at absolutely nothing, the whine of the lights blending with the soft hum of the refrigerator. I draw in just enough air for six words,

seven syllables. "Maybe I should just drop out." There.
I said it.

MOUTH

Actually, I said it.

TONGUE

Bite me.

"What?" Mom flops out a hand in confusion, a single
bead of grease from her burger trickling down the side of
her pinky. "No, that's ridiculous. It's only September—"

"October," Dad interjects.

"—October. You have plenty of time to make up
whatever work you're missing."

Eliza nods along with such fervor that her hair comes
loose from the sloppy bun piled on top of her head.
"That's what I keep saying."

"Would you shut up?" I whisper, more of a plea than
an admonition.

"Don't tell your sister to shut up."

I stare at Mom, my eyes tracking hers as she tries to
elude making contact. "Maybe you should tell my sister
to mind her own business and stop acting like I'm not
literally an adult."

"You're only eighteen," Mom says.

"Literal. Adult. And I'm about to be nineteen. Literal adult plus one." I used to be self-conscious about getting held back in sixth grade when I was zonked on a bad combination of meds, but after the gigantic clusterfuck of online learning during quarantine, I'm not the only student who needed a do-over.

Dad's quiet sigh calls us back to order better than any gavel ever could. He massages his temple with the tips of two fingers, his eyes closed. "Why are you thinking about dropping out?"

"I don't even know if I want to go to college. If I do, it'll be community anyway. I can get my equivalency diploma and never have to go back to school." It sounds almost petty when I say it that way, but none of us have any illusions that I see high school as anything except a necessary check in a box. "Without yearbook and prom and our senior trip, what's the point? All the fun is gone. My friends will just do everything without me."

"You could try to join different activities," Eliza suggests. "You're not banned from everything. Just the senior stuff."

"Yeah, just everything I ever cared about."

Eliza, of course, can't just drop the subject. "But you can still go to homecoming. I'm going. I'm sure a bunch of seniors will still go."

"Homecoming is for jocks."

Mom looks unconvinced by my reasoning. "School isn't supposed to be fun. It's a stepping stone."

"But a stepping stone to where? I can't choose a career when I don't know if I'm going to be able to walk or type in ten years. I just want to experience everything now when it's in front of my face. Parties. Prom. Yearbook. Friends. Senior pranks. I don't want to be stuck sitting on the sidelines again." I turn to Dad, not quite able to meet his eyes as I ask, "You get it, don't you?"

He nods, his lower lip pinned between his teeth. "I can see where you're coming from."

"It's like you and the band and—"

"I don't regret a minute of that, though," Dad whispers, his eyes losing focus a moment as he goes wherever he goes when he remembers. "Life just took us in different directions."

I lean an elbow on the table, sliding closer. "They abandoned you when you asked for accommodations. That's not different directions. They're *assholes*."

Dad's eyes drift to the set of crossed drumsticks hanging on the wall, the permanent marker faded after too many afternoons in the sunlight. "Hey, I still got to be a rock star for a while. That's longer than most boneheaded kids with bad eyeliner and a drum kit in the garage."

"That's exactly my point, though. I'm tired of waiting to be included." Sure, Dad wasn't exactly topping

Billboard charts as part of some weird band that only got big in Scandinavia in a genre he calls "doom metal," but he should have had a chance to chase his fantasy as far as it would go. I bite my lip harder and harder, tilting my head back to keep the tears from cresting onto my cheeks. "I had to give up softball and high heels and roller coasters. I had to give up Alexis. Now I'm supposed to just give up my whole life?"

"Your life is always going to keep changing," Dad says. "It's hard to lose things, but you'll find a new baseline and new things that make you happy. You will find good people. I promise."

Everyone always says to dream big and shoot for the summit, but freefalling to rock bottom hurts a lot less if you never leave base camp. "I don't want new people. But now all my friends feel sorry for me, and I'm just going to have to stand around while they do everything fun? I'm not putting up with that. I'm done."

Dad holds up a hand to keep Eliza from interjecting. "You have to grieve, and I'm not going to tell you how to do that. It's personal." He points to his small collection of video games on a shelf in the corner. "I'm not going to tell you that screwing around on a guitar in the basement or playing Pokémon beats a sold-out show or hiking in Thailand, but it still makes me happy."

"School does not make me happy." I mimic holding

it in my hand and flinging it into the abyss. "This does not spark joy."

Dad muddles over my words while he helps himself to more fries and dips them in mustard like a freak.

"I will say that it hurts a little for you to be throwing away your education when I didn't have a choice about dropping out of law school the first time." Mom takes a bite of her burger, and I get the sense that she's not finished. "The whole economy crashed, and there was no way to keep going. That got taken away from me, and it was all *I* ever wanted."

"How do I have any choice?" I gesture to the law books and notebooks stacked on the counter, the coffee table, the top of the dryer. "At least you can go back now. You have time. I don't. And I don't want to waste the health I have left learning about *imaginary numbers* and how penicillin was invented."

More than that, I can't stand the thought of finishing this project with Oliver, fussing about fake jobs and budgets, all the trappings of a life we'll never have. People always talk about "the one that got away," but what about the one you dodged? The only reason he was with me is because he wanted Pretend Brynn, the girl whose body isn't a time bomb.

And as much as I want to believe that we could be like Mom and Dad, it isn't lost on me that they met before his health went this far downhill, before there was an avalanche of medical bills and the need for more and more care. Would Mom still sign up for this if she met him today, wrapped in a toga of blankets and fresh from a part-time job that barely pays above minimum wage?

"You do have time," Mom insists. "You're only eighteen. I know you think that feels grown-up, but you're still so young. You have years and years of an amazing life ahead of you no matter what happens."

"Just stop it." I push back from the table, almost falling over backward as the legs of the chair catch on the grout. "I don't expect you to get it, but that doesn't mean you can just gaslight me when you don't know what you're even talking about. I'm so young? My body is like seven hundred years old. You have no idea what the future is going to be like for me."

She doesn't understand how illness ages you, that youth might be a fountain for most, but some of us end up with dribbling faucets instead. It takes a mind that can't be measured in years to make the bargains demanded of us, eternally answering the same questions anytime we want to expend the tiniest bit of energy: *How much are you willing to suffer for it? How many days of your life are you prepared to wager?*

"You've been through a lot for your age," Mom

126

concedes, "but you still haven't been out in the real world. There are a lot of other things you aren't considering."

"Oh goody. This is just a fake world that I've been living in. That's great." I smack the top of the table as I stand. "When I get to the real world, will I get legs and eyes and organs that work right?" I stomp upstairs and dig around my room until I finally find my purse inside the laundry hamper. I trade my pajama pants for leggings and throw on an oversized sweatshirt.

"Where do you think you're going?" Mom stands at the table as she spots me at the foot of the stairs.

"I'm leaving!" I shout, ignoring my watch as it alerts me to my erratic heart rate. "Because I'm eighteen and I can." For a moment, I panic that Dad didn't return my car keys, but then I spot them dangling from the wrong hook. Before anyone can stop me, I throw open the front door and jog across the lawn to where my car is parked along the street.

HEART

Why are you running? Do you want to
pass out? This is how you pass out.

HEART

(animatedly)

I'M WORKING VERY HARD HERE!

Everyone always says that hearts are supposed to mean happiness and love, but with all this cardiac anarchy just from jogging twenty feet, I don't think mine got the message. I have, like, the Deadpool of hearts.

> HEART
> Happiness and love? That's only in picture
> books. If you want the sappy stuff, you'll
> have to talk to Hypothalamus. Sorry.

But I know better than to yearn for a storybook ending. I clamber into my car, folding myself into the seat and adjusting it to fit, wishing that all my mismatches could be so quickly solved. There are no happily-ever-afters for girls like me, the ones donning hospital gowns for the operating theater instead of princess gowns for the ball. I've had my chance to dress up and play pretend, but I knew going in that it wouldn't last forever.

All those memories I was so desperate to make while I could—falling in love, late-night movies, skipping school to hang out in Wawa parking lots—it's like packing in a hurry for a one-way trip. These are the good times, the memories I won't be able to make again when I'm older, stuck at home and left behind because I can't keep up. But what if I get to my destination and realize that the things I packed are too small, too tight, too itchy?

My great-aunt: *You just have to think positive. God has a plan, and He won't give you anything you can't handle.*

Alexis: *You're always panicking about your health when nothing is even wrong with you. You just want attention. I bet that knee brace isn't even real.*

Oliver: *I'm so glad none of us got sick. I can't imagine living like that.*

I've seen what it's like to show my heart. I've trusted people to love me, to make space for me even when I wasn't shaped the same as everyone else. In the end it was easier to just contort myself into what they wanted, a performance that has spanned countless stages. But I always knew the day would come to let the curtain fall, turn on the lights, and come back to the reality that I never quite belonged here.

Ten

I pull out onto the street, my destination a simple one: anywhere but here. I recognize that it's foolish to just drive with no direction when gas is this expensive, but I have a full tank in the car and I'm running on fumes myself, so I do it anyway.

Once I'm out of range of where my family can easily track me down, I pull into a half-empty lot in a shopping complex and park. It's early enough that people are still milling around the area or crowding the drive-thru lanes of the various nearby restaurants, but the sun has started to make its descent, throwing stripes of gold and white across my peripheral vision.

I contemplate where I want to go next and come up with fewer options than I'd like. How can I explain why dropping out seems like a good idea if none of my friends know the whole truth? It occurs to me then that there's not a single person who's just there for me by default, who doesn't need the prequel to my present.

I scan through the contacts in my phone, hoping I've missed someone. I skip over Amber and Francesca, and I'm almost to Kayla when I spot a name I haven't thought of in ages. My finger hovers over the call button, but I change to text instead, knowing she keeps strange hours. As if I have any right to talk.

Brynn [6:02 P.M.]: Hey, are you
around?

Tori [6:08 P.M.]: yeah at work
what's up

Tori's answer is just what I expected. I give her the short version of events, and it's so effortless to explain to someone who knows my family, my health. I shake my head when I notice the default picture of her on my phone. Of the entire population of planet Earth, Tori looks like the person least likely to be my first cousin.

She's tall to my short, with waist-length waves of hair that look a deep brown in low light and a reddish auburn in the sun. Her skin is a mass of dark freckles and tattoos, and I've never been fully convinced that the freckles aren't tattoos too.

And while she doesn't have the gene, she's seen enough of it from my aunt Sunny that she doesn't have the rosy stance Mom and Eliza seem to maintain. While they'll insist that I can do anything I set my mind to, Tori has no illusions that you can only pull so hard on your bootstraps before you fall on your own face.

> Brynn [6:07 P.M.]: Can I come see
> you at work?

> Tori [6:08 P.M.]: if you hurry we
> close at 9

> Brynn [6:08 P.M.]: Just stay open
> later? You're the boss.

> Tori [6:09 P.M.]: it's so obvious
> you don't have cats I'm
> definitely not the boss here

Enough time has elapsed since rush hour that I don't have much trouble with traffic, although the toll to cross the bridge is enough to hurt me in my soul. It's been years since I visited Tori for the grand opening of her business, a cat café called Beany Beans on the fringes of Center City.

I spot her car in one of the few spots behind the building and maneuver my small sedan in between her passenger door and the dumpster. It's a completely made-up parking space, and I can only open my door a fraction, but there are some perks to being a genetic contortionist.

The back door is propped open with a cat-shaped garden statue, so I slip inside, wrinkling my nose at the overwhelming scent of sugar, coffee, and an acrid smell that I delude myself into believing isn't litter box. I'm just about to call Tori's name when she emerges from the kitchen, a grumpy Maine coon—the original Beany Bean, "Beebee" for short—wrapped around her shoulders like a boa constrictor with a catnip addiction.

I reach out to give her a one-armed hug. "Hey."

"Oh my God." She slices one hand through the air, the motion halfway between a karate chop and a time-out. Her eyes bulge as she turns to fully face me. "You can't just sneak in the back and go like ambush hug mode. Happy to see you, but I think I shit my pants. Do you know what kind of weirdos come in here sometimes?"

"Yeah," her boyfriend, Zeke, yells from the kitchen. "They'll let anybody in this place."

"Sorry! I thought you saw me."

Tori toys with the end of Beebee's tail. "My vision is blocked by floof."

As we walk out to the public part of the café, I silently point between Tori and the kitchen, my eyebrows raised. She shrugs, earning an annoyed swat from Beebee. "We're back together for a little bit. I don't know. He needed a job, and I need employees who stop blowing up my four-hundred-dollar espresso machine."

"Makes sense."

Tori steps over to the gigantic chalkboard on the wall and picks up a piece of neon-pink chalk. I read through the rules while she makes a quick update in a slanting scrawl at the bottom.

1. NO OUTSIDE ANIMALS, INCLUDING YOUR CRABBY BOYFRIEND.
2. BE NICE TO THE WORKERS, OR WE'LL PUT CAT LITTER IN YOUR CUPCAKES. (THIS IS A JOKE, HEALTH INSPECTOR. LIGHTEN UP.)
3. WE WILL NOTICE IF YOU TRY TO LEAVE WITH A CAT.
4. TREAT THE STAFF LIKE I HAVE YOUR CREDIT CARD NUMBER AND WILL WRITE IT ON THE BATHROOM WALL IF YOU'RE RUDE.
5. NO SURPRISE HUGGING.

Tori beckons me over to a nearby set of lounge chairs and sets Beebee on a special crocheted pouf with yellow tassels before flopping sideways into a chair and resting her feet on the brick wall. "Make yourself comfortable. There's no one else here." She scans the empty booths and tables just to make sure. "Friday nights are kind of slow since we don't do dinner."

I sit down like a normal person, not wanting to scrape city grime all over the wall. "Thanks for letting me come over."

"Sounded like you needed to just blob. How's it going?"

"Been better." I bend forward, setting one elbow on my thigh and propping up my chin with my palm. "Been worse."

Tori makes a show of rolling her eyes. "That's so super specific and helpful, Brynn." She flaps an arm around the nearby table until she finds the tablet that doubles as their menu. She scrolls through, poking now and then at the screen. "You want pancakes? A pastry? Coffee? That weird raspberry-sorbet crap that Zeke eats?"

"Surprise me."

"That's a dangerous order," she mutters, poking with even greater fervor. "Do your parents know you're here?"

I stare off at a painting of a Siamese cat in an astronaut suit. "Why do you always ask me that?"

"Because if your parents are upset and they find out I'm involved, your dad will call my mom to complain and then *she* will complain at *me* until the year 2049." Tori holds up a finger to stop me as I attempt to speak. "I'm down for that because earplugs were invented in the year 1864, but I need to be prepared for it."

Sighing, I take out my phone and open up our family group chat, where there are already thirty unread messages from Mom and Eliza. "I'll tell them we're hanging out, but I'm not going to say where we are in case they decide to show up."

"Sounds serious," Tori says, glancing at the window like Mom and Dad are going to come parachuting out of the sky at any moment. "I assume you're here to vent it out, but if you just want to lurk and stuff cake into your face, that's cool too."

"Thanks." I hesitate a moment. "It didn't go so well when I brought it up at home, but I'm kind of thinking about maybe dropping out of high school."

"Oh."

I hazard a peek at her face, and it clearly wasn't what she was expecting me to say. "I figured if anyone would get it, you would. But maybe I was wrong."

Tori's stunned expression molds into a smile. "Sweetheart, I dropped out of Princeton's aerospace engineering program to open a cat café with the dudebro who sleeps on my couch sometimes. Do you really think I'm about to judge you for your life choices?"

"I'm not a dudebro," Zeke says as a way of announcing his presence, leaning down to set a circular tray of coffees and pastries on the ottoman that isn't currently occupied by Beebee. "I just like helicopters and cats. Turns out that's not a great career combo."

Tori pats him lovingly on the head. "That's what a dudebro would say, hon."

"My dad nicknamed our principal 'Dudebrowski.'"

She shoots me with a single finger gun. "That's why he's the cool uncle."

As much as Tori and Zeke's relationship is a saga of its own, his instincts are sound enough for him to realize that this conversation is for cousins only. Without a single word of small talk, he turns and leaves, reaching up to a shelf on the wall to rescue a trilling orange kitten that's decided it's too long of a leap to the next foothold.

"I've never been much of a cat person," I admit, which means they automatically flock to me in hoards. I fold my legs underneath me and tuck my feet against the armrests to avoid an overfriendly fur puff with legs and his curious, hairless friend that came over to investigate my shins. "The less I like them, the more they love me."

Tori snorts. "Seriously, though, when God made

cats, he was like, 'I wonder what'll happen if I put razor blades on the paws of tiny anarchists.' I'm grateful every day they don't raze this place to the ground."

"Sounds like an interesting life anyway." Before I know it, I'm pouring my heart out about the fight with Pat and Eliza's constant holier-than-thou attitude. Tori nods along, smiling and scowling at turns, always the sort of person to make you feel that she's ready to mutiny with you at a moment's notice.

That ebbs a bit as I attempt to articulate why the thought of going back to school is so pointless. "Going to school is exhausting. When I was having fun and doing all these clubs with my friends, it was worth it. But why am I going to waste all this energy when I could just get my equivalency diploma and take off until I get a job? Everyone is in my face about college. I don't see the big deal."

"It can help you figure out what want to do with your life for the super affordable price of $120,000!"

I take one of the chocolate mini muffins with cat sprinkles and slowly work my thumbnail around the pink foil wrapper. "I wanted to be an orthopedic surgeon."

Tori's lips press together in a wince. "Shit. I'm sorry."

"You're the only one besides my dad who listens to me about this stuff. I never even told my friends. Not after how middle school turned out."

"You haven't told anyone else? Even your, uh, that guy you were going out with before?"

"I thought it would come up somehow, but then it just seemed like too much to dump on him. He told me in health class that he wants kids. Doesn't that make us doomed anyway? I can't do this to a kid." I wave my hand over my body with a flourish.

"You don't know that you'll pass it for sure," Tori says, her voice taking on an uncharacteristically chiding tone. "My mom's got EDS. She obviously had me. It was a gamble she was willing to make."

But that's just it—it's a gamble, a genetic coin flip. There's no way to even the odds. "I just can't drag Oliver down with me. When the worst of COVID was over, he even said how lucky we were that we didn't get sick, how he couldn't imagine living like that. If he stays with me, he won't have to imagine it because he'll get a front-row seat. There's no unsubscribe button from this shitty body. It's not like I'm going to get better."

"A serious relationship is taking care of each other, even if you don't have health problems," Tori goes on. "But not everyone seems to realize that." She brings her hand down softly on Beebee's head, scratching absently behind her ears. When she turns away the light flashes across the wetness in her eyes.

"That's what I'm afraid of," I whisper. That one day,

after seventeen years of marriage and two kids, Oliver will come home and announce that I'm *too much*—and vanish. Uncle Steven tried to claim that he was overwhelmed by the kids, that if my aunt Sunny could barely cook or clean anymore, what was the point of even having a wife?

Tori wipes her nose with a cat-shaped doily. "You know what I think?"

I make a noise of acknowledgment in the back of my throat, something between a hum and a squeak.

"Worrying about probability is like letting a horoscope run your life," Tori says. "That's how I see it anyway." She spins the platter of desserts and pinches a chocolate chip cookie, breaking it into two pieces and offering me half. "All you can do is weigh the risk. I don't mean to sound like a jerk, but that's it."

"When you dropped out, what convinced you to do it?"

A pause stretches into pensiveness as Tori rakes her fingers through her hair, thinking. "I didn't even really plan it out. It just happened. Everyone was getting sick. COVID everywhere. We all had to go home, and for the first time it didn't feel like I was trapped on some treadmill of suck, moving toward something that didn't make me happy just because I'd gone too far by then to stop. I'd spent so much time trying to impress everyone and write a 'groundbreaking' dissertation and get a fancy-pants fellowship.

"And once I detoxed out of that, it just made me think that, like, man, there will always be someone to build a badass drone or make a better LiDAR sensor. I just didn't want to go back to that. I wanted to hang out with my cat and eat cupcakes." Tori sighs, picking at the reddened skin around her thumbnail. "But I was willing to say screw it and start over. Are you?"

I squeeze my eyes shut, feeling my heartbeat thumping in my eardrums, my brain, my still-tender shoulder. "I think so." I slither down in the chair until I'm staring at the exposed ductwork along the ceiling, watching a thick cobweb sway back and forth in the stream of air coming from one of the vents.

"That sounded convincing," Tori quips. "Well, you know what will help you think?"

"Sleep?"

"Sweeping!"

Eleven

"Tori's cousin, meet broom," Zeke says by way of instruction, handing me a broad-bristled shop broom. "It's best to hold your breath."

I watch the pile grow as I work the broom around the chairs, chasing up at least four different colors of cat hair. By the time I'm finished I have enough hair to make three kittens, and I send hero-worship vibes to my allergist for inventing a regimen that keeps me from becoming a human snot factory. "Is all this hair from one day?"

Zeke chuckles and sends a trash can on a rolling base spinning my way. "Believe it or not, that's not even a lot. You should see this place in the summer. It's like a carpet."

I shudder at the visual and follow Tori around,

searching for something else to do. More goes into closing a café than I thought. There's counting out the tip jar, putting away any food, washing the dishes, verifying that the ovens are off. It takes well over an hour before Zeke cuts the lights in the kitchen and comes out with a backpack and a sweatshirt slung over his arm.

Tori checks the clock and clucks her tongue. "Damn. We did that fast. Kind of nice having another set of hands around here."

"If you'd stop firing everyone, maybe we wouldn't have to do it all by ourselves," Zeke mutters, handing over her purse.

"Oh please. I'm not that bad."

Zeke lifts one eyebrow so far that it almost blends in with his hairline. "You've fired *me* three times."

"Yeah, but you deserved to be fired at least six times, so I really think I'm being charitable, honestly, if you ask me." Tori waves a rag at me. "If you're legit about calling it quits on school, you want a job?"

"Um, maybe? I haven't actually thought that far ahead yet." But much to my surprise, the prospect of having to start over unexpectedly almost seems enticing. Instead of wading through the ashes of almost three and a half years gone up in smoke, I could find a different path.

Tori holds out a couple of dollars from the tip jar. "I

feel bad not giving you some absolutely illegal under-the-table money."

I don't take it. "Consider it rent for absolutely illegally letting me sleep here."

"That's fair. I guess we better build you a bed." She scans the café, pausing on a set of square ottomans in colors so bright they're almost neon. "Those."

Zeke helps me carry the largest of them into the storage room while Tori kicks the smaller ones on wheels down the hallway like a terrible round of curling. "Are you sure you don't want to crash on my couch?" she calls out. "I can make Zeke sleep on the air mattress."

Zeke groans, and I don't think it's from the ottoman that goes careening into the back of his calf muscle. "I hate the air mattress."

"Oh, shush. You could pass out on a bed of nails."

"I don't want to risk staying at your place." When I texted Dad to tell him I was staying overnight with Tori, I conveniently neglected to mention that I wouldn't be going back to the house with her. "No offense. I just don't want Aunt Sunny reporting everything back to my dad."

Tori nods in understanding. The rumor mill in our family takes a while to get whirring, but once it's going, it'll churn you into dust. "Well, as long as there are no cats hiding in here already, you should be relatively safe from them crawling all over you while you sleep. Can't guarantee that it's a cat-free zone, though. There might be some in those boxes of paper towels. Yams *really* wants to show you his butthole, and Fred will try to put his mouth into your mouth. You've been warned."

I give her a quick hug, grabbing Zeke's left arm to make sure he feels included. "Thank you for not ratting me out. I owe you."

"Meh, you don't owe me. We're family." She grins at Zeke. "But if you *do* want to repay the favor, I won't say no if you want to babysit the cats at some point so that we can actually have a day off."

"I think I can manage that."

Tori makes me swear three times that I won't touch the stove or the espresso machine before they head home for the night. Without them the café seems quieter but not any less lively with four or five cats still roaming around clearly in view. I grab a key lime cupcake and a glass of water before heading to the storage room, dodging tiny paws and cat tails along the way.

I settle onto the ottomans, adjusting some of the various blankets and throws that Tori tossed in here as bedding. There's not even the slight possibility that I'll be able to sleep with so much roiling through my brain.

I've never seriously considered dropping out of

school before this, so I prop myself up into a sitting position against the wall and ask the great omniscient internet. Most of the articles are about how to prevent this exact scenario, but I eventually discover a few that are less biased. As I skim the arguments against dropping out, I read them all in Eliza's or Mom's voice.

Why does it always have to be about the future? Why can't I just prioritize the now because this is what I know for sure? It's like all the times we tried to plan a summer vacation and Dad or I ended up breaking something in the interim. Mom and Dad's anniversary hiking trip on the Appalachian Trail turned into a wine tour when Dad tore the cartilage in his hip trying to move timpani drums by himself. Meanwhile I thought my arms were going to fall off dragging my carcass around New York City on crutches with my foot in a boot.

METATARSALS
(in unison)
We're sorry! But that's what you get for
walking on a surface that wasn't completely
dry and level in exactly the spot we wanted.

ME
Oh my God. Why are you all so needy?

INTERMEDIATE PHALANGES
We don't want to be associated with the rest
of the foot bones. We believe we're quite
easy to get along with.

A few minutes later I stumble upon a message board where people have responded with their own experiences of dropping out of high school. I read through the original post, where an anonymous kindred spirit has already asked the question I truly need answered: *Do you regret it?*

The responses are mixed, but many people share their initial reasons, and it's validating to see it through their eyes as the smart choice, not just quitting. If they're online it's obvious that they didn't just evaporate because they took a diversion instead of the traditional route to a diploma.

And even though I understand that it's a terrible idea to make important life decisions at midnight—I can practically hear Mr. Waller's screams from here—I don't see many arguments in favor of going back to school. If I want to see Francesca or Amber or any of my other friends, we can always meet up somewhere else. Besides that there's just Oliver, and all I'm doing is cutting down our countdown until that final forever goodbye.

So without further fanfare or debate I follow my gut

and look up Mrs. Nguyen's email in the directory. As far as I can tell there's no consequence if I just stop showing up, but at least this leaves no ambiguity. I type out a simple message telling her that it's clear the school doesn't care about me or any of its so-called school values if it's going to stand behind a bully. It's so surreal to end my high-school career this way, sounding like a disgruntled restaurant patron complaining about soggy fries and mediocre service: *I won't be coming back.*

Twelve

The first thing I see when I wake up in a heap is a very disgruntled cat with half a left ear and three white feet. The second thing I see is a string of text messages from my family about how they're heading up to the lake for one of Eliza's fall championships, so they won't be there when I get home.

I hear the implication that I should head back today to get ready for school tomorrow, but it only makes me feel freer knowing that I have no schedule or obligations anymore. I can go home now or Tuesday or never.

Still, guilt crouches over me as I recall that I'd intended to go watch Eliza's race, even though there's nothing more boring than watching a regatta. Golf and bowling might be a close tie. One time we even cheered for the wrong boat simply because that school had the same colors.

I scroll to my outbox just to make sure my message to Mrs. Nguyen is still there, that it's even real at all. I read back through it, hoping she doesn't take it personally. And that's how I spot the email. I've been dodging Oliver's texts about the Life Skills project and leaving my voicemail full on purpose to keep him from leaving another terse message. But my willpower isn't strong enough to resist a subject line that simply says, *Brynn?*

I scan his bewildered email, hating that his writing skills make anything seem eloquent, as though this is some onstage drama and not just him berating me for being the slacker on the group project. *I've asked you again and again just to allow me a few moments of your time, even if it was just to tell me that you're okay. Is that too much to ask for? If you have too much going on and you need me to work on this project alone, then the least you could do is ask.*

All of my responses seem clunky and weak by comparison.

Brynn [8:26 A.M.]: I saw your email.
I'm sorry.

Oliver [8:31 A.M.]: You're sorry?

It's been over a week. This is
due tomorrow. When were you
planning on helping?

Brynn [8:33 A.M.]: I don't know. I've
been going through some shit.

It's such a flimsy excuse. It's not even that difficult of
a project, but I just couldn't make myself tune in for it.
The cupcake I ate for a late-night snack bubbles in my
stomach as I see who I might become if I only have eyes
for my own pain.

Oliver [8:35 A.M.]: I was trying to
give you some space, but now I
just feel like you're using me.

Brynn [8:36 A.M.]: I'm so sorry.
Is it too late?

Oliver [8:36 A.M.]: If you can meet me
basically now we can get it done.

Brynn [8:37 A.M.]: I'm visiting
my cousin in Philly, but I can
be there in like forty?

Oliver [8:39 A.M.]: The one with the
cats? I'll just meet you there if you
send me the name of the place.

Brynn [8:39 A.M.]: Are you
sure? The toll on the bridge is
like seven million dollars now.

Oliver [8:41 A.M.]: Yeah, I can take some
actual pictures in the city instead of
just using websites. And get a gyro.

The thought of finishing the project doesn't seem daunting anymore if it means that I can see him again. I don't like luring Oliver under false pretenses, but I didn't know the last time we were together was the last. I need to see him in person just once more before his face becomes a memory to fill old scrapbooks, an old scar on my heart to explain to new loves.

We'll have this one final day together, and then I'll tell him the truth—that the magnetizing pull he feels toward the stage and excitement and dark-haired children with chestnut eyes would simply tear me to pieces.

Brynn [8:46 A.M.]: Drive safe.
See you soon.

My finger hovers just above the screen as I watch it send and deliver. "Oh my God. What did I just do?"

THUMBS
We're not accountable for what you make
us type. This is a strict clause of the user
agreement.

Before I can fully process the significance of what's about to happen, there's a sharp knock at the door. I stand in a daze, checking that I'm decent before I answer. I work the handle with one hand while I cling to the edge of a shelf with the other, waiting for the wave of dizziness to pass as my circulation and heart rate have their little tango.

"Goood mooorning," Tori crows, looking for all the world like that's a bold-faced lie. She rubs at the bags under her eyes with one hand and slurps a bit of espresso from the tiny cup pinched between her fingers. "Sleep okay?"

"I just invited Oliver to come here," I deadpan. "Help."

"Whoa, whoa. Slow down." She slowly tilts her head back as she drains the rest of her drink, her eyes shutting briefly when it's empty. "Oof. That's bitter." She rolls her hand in the air. "You may continue panicking now."

I bend over, my subconscious rapidly calculating the odds that I throw up on Tori's Birkenstocks-and-ankle-socks combo. "What was . . . what thinking? Why . . . do?"

Tori pats me consolingly on the head and gestures for me to follow her toward the kitchen. "Do you want breakfast? I have spinach quiche and egg wraps."

"He's going to be here in like an hour." My attempts to slow my breathing turn into not breathing at all, leaving me somewhere between stunned blowfish and hyperventilating panic attack. I straighten suddenly and latch onto the sleeve of her oversized purple hoodie before she's out of reach. "What do I do? What do I do?"

"May I make a suggestion?" Tori drawls.

"Please."

She passes me a makeup bag with a toothbrush sticking out the top. "Brush your teeth. Your breath smells like a dumpster, my dude. And then eat something before you pass out."

"Do you have apple fritters?" I ask, sounding like a hopeful child asking for a favorite flavor of ice cream that isn't on the list.

Tori shoves just her head through the saloon door to the kitchen, yelling, "ZEKE! Do we still have apple pie in the freezer?" I don't hear his response, but she extricates herself with some difficulty and shrugs. "I'm going to pour apple pie filling over a bear claw and tell you it's an apple fritter. Now if this boy is coming here, I guess I should know something else about him besides his name, which I've also forgotten. So dish it out."

I follow her into the kitchen and sit on a bar-height stool stuck in between a countertop and a stainless-steel table. While Tori pours me a cup of coffee, I pour out my guts. "Well, his name is Oliver De Luca. He's a senior. We started dating just before the pandemic and broke up over the summer. He wants to be a playwright or a screenwriter. And I'm hopelessly, terribly in love with him."

Thirteen

It takes Oliver fifty-two minutes to get to the café, not that I'm checking so often that Tori sarcastically took an entire twelve-inch clock off the wall and propped it up on the table in front of me. I end up carrying the clock part of the way to the door to greet Oliver before the mental circuits click together and I set it on the edge of a table to hang up later.

I don't see his car on the street out front, but I spot him through the series of picture windows along the eastern wall. I'd know him anywhere, even a block away bundled up in a coat with a hood pulled around his ears. "He's almost here," I hiss to Tori, practically flinging myself onto the cash register.

She holds up a finger as she finishes making some

kind of blended iced drink in an unfortunate shade of purplish brown and passes it to the customer lingering by the far end of the counter. "Oh, sorry." I wince, leaning to see around the sign blocking my view. "I didn't see anybody standing there."

"I doubt they care. Welcome to the City of Brotherly Mind Your Own Damn Business." She says it with great affection, the same half-reverent way Dad treats this ancient pub by city hall that's so covered in glass frames and breakable knickknacks on the inside that I'm afraid to fart.

"I will never understand Philadelphia," I muse under my breath. "How do you care so much about football that the city has to grease the light posts to keep you from climbing them? Why do all the sports mascots look like Beetlejuice's stuffed animals?"

"Don't you come into our place of business and talk shit about the Phillie Phanatic," Zeke calls as he scurries by with bags of rolls and deli meat. "Or Gritty!"

Tori rolls her eyes. "I don't expect you to understand city pride. You live in disgusting New Jersey after all. Honestly, your town's only redeeming quality is that you at least call pork roll by the right name." She clicks a button on her watch to check the time. "Good. I'm glad it worked."

"Glad what worked?"

She jabs her finger at the door. "Distracting you until your 'friend' showed up."

I yelp and whip around with my back to the counter, hoping that I look nonchalant and mysterious as Oliver steps through the door, his eyes blinking in the low lighting of the foyer. My pose clearly doesn't have the desired effect because he gapes at me as he approaches, asking, "Oh. Hey. Did you hurt your back?"

Tori bursts out laughing and sidesteps closer to rescue me from the embarrassment. "Hi, I'm Tori. Brynn's cousin. And yes, we know we don't look anything like each other."

He offers to shake her hand, which clearly catches her off guard since she scrubs her hands on her apron about nine times before taking it. "I'm Oliver," he says. "Brynn's friend from school."

I lock eyes with Tori over his shoulder to telepathically communicate that I'm about to disintegrate and she should just pour me out of the dustpan at the end of the night. What he said isn't wrong, but I miss those days when we required no explanation, our familiarity giving us away even when we tried to hide it.

"Can I get you anything?" Tori offers, prying Beebee off the register and dropping her unceremoniously on the non-kitchen side of the counter. "On the house."

Medium Earl Grey, please. Slice of lemon if you have it.

"Medium Earl Grey, please. Slice of lemon if you have it." Oliver digs out his wallet, a tattered bifold of faux cognac-colored leather with his initials embossed in the corner that I bought him for his seventeenth birthday. "I don't mind paying."

Tori rings him up. "Not gonna argue with you. Thanks." While he signs the receipt, she gives me a furtive wave, beckoning me into the kitchen.

"I have to go help out real quick," I explain before hustling around the corner to the door. Some sixth sense keeps me from shoving through it, and I narrowly miss Zeke taking my forehead off with a tray of crepes. He twirls away, catching himself on the edge of a table and glowering at me. "You really are related to Tori."

I barely make it three steps into the kitchen before Tori accosts me. She turns an empty box of tea into a flimsy projectile, chucking it at me with all her might only for it to bounce harmlessly off my abdomen. "What is wrong with you?" she demands.

"Um. Many things. You'll have to be more specific."

She waves a teaspoon toward the front counter. "*That's* your ex-boyfriend."

". . . Yes."

Tori blows a low, deflated whistle over her bottom lip. "Just take whatever we talked about before and throw it out the window. You can't let someone like that go."

I gape at her in blatant confusion. "You've known him for, like, six seconds."

"He has a wool coat and trimmed fingernails." Tori pinches the bridge of her nose as though I'm rejecting the fact that the sky is blue. "He drinks Earl Grey and tips legal US tender instead of crypto insights. This is the jackpot of dudes, and he's obviously all about you."

I inch back before she finds any other beverage ingredients to fling at my head. "He's just here to work on a project. I'm telling you—it's so done between us."

"Only if you let it." Tori smacks the top of a prep table, her various rings clanging against the metal. "Only if you let it."

I make my escape when the timer for Oliver's tea goes off and rejoin him in line. Tori returns shortly after with a plastic mug, a lemon wedge speared onto a toothpick leaning against the thick outer rim. "Sorry. We can't have nice things because cats are assholes."

Oliver laughs, wrapping his hand around the mug to keep it from spilling. "Thanks." Another customer steps up behind us, so we slowly migrate to the dining area. "Where do you want to set up?" Oliver asks.

A few haggard-looking students in blue UPenn pullovers pore over tablets and tease the cats with feathers dangling from the end of a stick. They've covered a nearby table with textbooks and index cards, and it only further strengthens my aversion to spending thousands and depriving myself for years on the off chance that it'll all work out with a career worth the sacrifice.

I point subtly toward the other end of the café instead. "I was thinking over there, but on second thought that probably isn't going to work." The side with the lounge chairs is currently taken over by a group of parents and young children who have rearranged the lounge chairs into an even square around one of the heavy wooden card tables. "This probably sounds really weird, but do you want to go hang out in the storage room instead? It's a lot quieter."

"That works."

"I slept in there yesterday," I add, recognizing too late that that doesn't make it any less bizarre. "I got into a fight with my family. It's a long story."

If Oliver finds the setup in the storage room strange, he doesn't mention it. He sits on one of the ottomans, flipping over a paint-splattered ten-gallon bucket to use as a side table for his tea.

"I'm sorry for ghosting you on the project," I volunteer before we get started. I've been the productive partner in a crappy group project before, and there's nothing more frustrating than someone who just doesn't care. "I guess I just shut down after I got suspended."

"Well, we're here now," he says, gesturing vaguely

at the window despite the half-destroyed blinds covering it, the end of the cord shredded by countless claws. "Obviously, I want to move here for college, so it's actually good timing. It'll be fun." It's more of a statement than a promise, and the uncertainty in his voice strikes a sour chord with his inability to meet my eyes.

I'm not sure how to respond, and Oliver quickly resorts to using his tea the way I've seen adults use alcohol in delicate situations. He's all slow sips and short puffs of air across the top of his cup, watching his breath push the dark blend into ripples.

I didn't have the foresight to pack my laptop or school tablet, so I'm stuck with my phone. I attempt to log into the system to download the assignment sheet, but it's loading at a snail's pace. "Do you have the handout from Mr. Waller? I can't get it to pull up."

"I have it in here somewhere." Oliver sets his charcoal messenger bag on the floor and riffles through one of the compartments, producing a matching leather portfolio and company-branded binder.

I take deep breaths and silently count to ten, relaxing my shoulders and focusing on the fact that this is Oliver. Just Oliver. Once it was automatic for him to lower that shield of politeness when it was just the two of us, shedding his shell like a coat to be put away after getting home.

My gaze lands on his binder. "Do you own anything

without a logo on it?" I say, my tone teasing. "Or is your mom still wallpapering the entire house with Cricut?"

Oliver rolls his eyes, an encouraging sign that this cold kindness between us might yet wear away. "If I checked, I'm pretty sure it'll say De Luca Energy Consultants on my butt cheek."

Somewhat wryly, I hazard a joke that's both risky and risqué, emboldened by his laughter: "I mean, I've seen your butt. I think I would have noticed."

A butt joke is rarely the solution to one's problems, but in this case it works. We both laugh, albeit a bit shyly, and it's a necessary reminder that talking shouldn't be this challenging. There was a time when we used to talk for hours, my phone desperately clinging to the last vestiges of power as it consumed more than it could replenish. I'd fall asleep with my ear warm from the heat, seeing starbursts behind my eyes as I turned out the lights and waited to say good morning.

"Mom's been trying to do better about containing all of her work stuff in the office they built her in the basement. It was Dad's idea to keep her and my nonna from killing each other."

I almost forget sometimes that Oliver's family was only supposed to be here for freshman year, a short-term pit stop to help his grandmother fix up the house. But then COVID put the world on pause, and one year at

Pineland Prep stretched into two, three, four. "They're still bickering all the time?"

"It's getting better. Nonna just doesn't like that my mom works so much."

I know better than to poke that particular bear. Oliver's mom is brilliant, but when she couldn't even be there for our junior prom pictures, I wanted to find her and shake her until she realized that oil pipelines don't love her back.

Oliver passes me an assignment sheet. "Speaking of work, I have some notes." He takes out his Life Skills notebook and flips between two pages, humming faintly. It's a mass of smeared pencil, doodles, and narrow print that looks closer to hieroglyphics than a project outline.

"Your handwriting is so smudgy."

He holds up the side of his left hand where some of the skin is speckled with traces of green marker. "I'm left-handed. It's not fair."

I grin, wishing that I could record these moments for later when the small details inevitably begin to erode. It isn't just the contours of his features, sharper now than when we were still baby-faced freshmen hunched in front of webcams with our earbuds and styluses for digital school. It's also the flighty, almost ticklish sensation in my chest that I'll miss, the electric rush of simply being near.

I know that eventually I'll find someone else, but I

can't begin to hope that lightning will strike me twice no matter how long I stand in the storm.

"I've sorted a lot of this out already," Oliver mentions, tracing a box on his notebook with the tip of his finger. "We each have to make a profile thing about where we work, go to school, and stuff like that. Mr. Waller gave us this list of bills and utilities that we'll have to pay. We pick out the rest."

I read the assignment three full times before it starts to make any kind of sense. "So basically we have to make up our own personal budgets without screwing up our shared budget as roommates?"

"Yeah. Boy Sam and Jimmy got into this huge argument in class because Jimmy wants to spend all his money on renting a C8 Corvette, so they can only afford a cheap one-bedroom apartment unless Sam pays, like, eighty percent of the rent." Oliver produces the original handout. "Mr. Waller said we can just tape this on our poster boards and then fill in the rest with a collage. We need ten pictures. No stock photos allowed."

City/town: Philadelphia

Rent: $_____ from roommate 1, $_____ from roommate 2
Shared food and supplies: $_____ from roommate 1,
$_____ from roommate 2

Utilities: $220 from roommate 1, $220 from roommate 2

Cooking (percentage): ____% roommate 1, ____% roommate 2

Cleaning (percentage): ____% roommate 1, ____% roommate 2

Hint: Would you pay more expenses to avoid chores?

"You just decided that we live in Philadelphia?" I say in mock accusation.

Oliver unclips his car keys and holds his Drexel University key chain in the air. "Wishful thinking. I find out if I got in just before Christmas. I applied early decision."

"Oh, you did?" There was a time when I knew these things almost in real time, sometimes before Oliver's parents or his grandmother did, and the surprises between us were only our spontaneities. Bacon instead of sausage on a breakfast date. Choosing a horror movie over a blockbuster drama. "Good luck."

Roommate 1 occupation: playwright/set designer

Average monthly salary: $3,000

Car: $0, walk everywhere

Cell phone: $75

Entertainment: $100

Student loan: $250

Roommate 2 occupation:

_____

Average monthly salary:

Car:

Cell phone:

Entertainment:

Medical bill: $250

_____

I could understand the student loan payment, but I balk at the sight of a medical bill. "Wait, why do I have a medical bill?"

"Oh. Mr. Waller made us pick a wild card that either adds a debt or gives us another source of income," Oliver explains. "I think he borrowed the idea from Monopoly. Brandon's been obnoxious because he got six hundred dollars a month from an inheritance. I picked yours since you weren't there."

I let out an aggravated groan. I even have medical bills in my imaginary future. What does $250 even get you nowadays? A handshake? I'm filled with indignation before I remember that I am literally not enrolled in classes anymore. Or at least I won't be when Mrs. Nguyen checks her email tomorrow morning.

"I guess I should fill in my part." As long as I'm playing Pretend Brynn again, I don't see the harm in indulging a daydream, one where I don't have a double-helix chain wrapped around my ankle to hold me back. I fill in my lies and copy the rest from Oliver.

Roommate 2 occupation: medical resident

Average monthly salary: $5,000
Car: $0, walk everywhere
Cell phone: $75
Entertainment: $100
Medical bill: $250

Oliver tilts his head as he reads my upside-down additions. "You want to go to medical school? Since when?"

Only since I was five years old playing with my dad's blood-pressure cuff and bringing him Band-Aids without understanding that no number of colorful cartoon bandages would make him walk unaided ever again. "I'm not really going to do it. I'm just making something up."

"You'd be great at that." His entire demeanor glows with misplaced faith.

I wobble to my feet and search around for my hoodie. "Why don't we, um, go get some pictures and stuff? I know a place that I think you'll like."

I step out of the storage room and pivot immediately to the right to reach the back door. I hit the crash bar with the side of my forearm and step out into the crispness of the late morning. The day is more overcast than I expected, and I shiver as I get my bearings.

Oliver scrutinizes my hoodie as he walks over from depositing his cup in the dumpster. "Isn't that my sweatshirt?"

"You know what? I think it is." I've had it for so long that I forgot it was supposed to be his, a Christmas gift from his parents that had no hope of fitting properly. If it hadn't been so awkward watching his parents argue while Oliver tried to extricate his torso from the too-small hoodie, it might have been funny.

Oliver must be thinking the same thing because a moment later he adds, "I still don't know how my mom ever thought I was going to fit into a small. She must have bought it without asking my nonna."

"It's probably the nicest hoodie I have." The downside is that it weighs as much as three ordinary ones, but it's a small price to pay for not having to hide under Blanket Mountain every time I get chilly, which is always. "I wish I had more real clothes. I feel like all I wear are uniforms and pajama pants."

Oliver snorts. "You can come shop in my closet whenever you want. My mom still won't let us clear out any of our serious winter clothes. It makes me nervous that we're going to move again."

We start walking north, dodging broken chunks of

sidewalk and other pedestrians. "I thought she took a job here ages ago doing, like, electrical stuff?"

"She did, but companies keep calling and trying to get her to go back on the road to work on all their projects in the middle of nowhere," he mutters. "They say it's temporary, but I'll never get over that time we went to Minnesota 'for six weeks' and got stuck for ten months. A year in Ontario. Eighteen months in New Orleans. I'm just tired of it."

"What will you do if she takes one of these jobs?"

"My grandmother said I can stay." Oliver's shrug is one of resignation, not confusion. "I'm not leaving. No matter what."

I nod along, wishing those words could be about me.

Fourteen

When it became apparent that Eliza's skill at rowing was more than just having buff calf muscles and beginner's luck, my parents searched for advanced training programs all over the tristate area. But when it comes down to it, very few places love rowing as much as Philadelphia, which means that as much as I poke fun at Dad's childhood stomping ground, I'm not completely foreign to it.

Now rowing is like a code that's spoken exclusively in rivers and lakes with the odd city name thrown in. Cooper. Schuylkill. Oak Ridge. Maurice. "It's nice to be here without a time limit," I remark as we dodge skinny trees and weave around yesterday's puddles. "Usually we have to get back to the river to pick up Eliza before dark."

I know we're close as we pass by the Marriott that's built in a style I've always thought of as "architectural confusion." We skirt the cones for the valet parking, and I hurry Oliver along to make the light as we cross the street. He follows like a good-natured duckling, matching my pace and being mindful not to run into others.

I forget sometimes that he's lived in cities all over the continent, and compared to the pandemonium of New York City, I'm sure this is nothing. "We're here!" I announce with a flourish as we round a final corner.

Oliver peers up at the green-and-white awning. "Reading Terminal Market."

"You said you wanted a gyro. And this is probably where I'd get a lot of groceries for our fake apartment." I lead him inside, grateful for the lack of stairs. "The place with gyros is that way, but there are like ninety food options in here."

The bustle of the market is a pleasant buzz without the tediousness of a traditional grocery store or the frenetic pace of big-box stores. Signs lit and unlit dangle from the ceiling as we pass, advertising honey, candles, flowers, and postcards. I breathe in the blend of spices, almost tasting the air itself.

"This reminds me of a place we used to go to in Cleveland," Oliver says offhand in a tone that's more fascination than nostalgia. "It wasn't this big, but it had a lot of kiosks and food."

"It's usually busier," I add as Oliver eyes a fudge store and sniffs at a Thai restaurant as we pass, "but a couple of the vendors are closed on Sundays. The lines get so bad during the holidays that Dad calls it the Interminable Market."

We meander without a real direction, popping into stores as it suits us and snapping pictures of fruits and vegetables to justify our grocery budget. I'm allergic to half of what Oliver photographs, but for Pretend Brynn it doesn't matter.

"The internet says that a normal grocery budget is about four hundred dollars a month for two people," I mention as I take advantage of the sudden cellular connection. "But a lot of fresh stuff can be more expensive, so maybe it should be five hundred dollars just to stay on the safe side. That'll cover household supplies too."

Oliver fishes in his bag and scribbles the figure down on a scrap of paper. "That's two hundred fifty dollars each. Seems reasonable on my starving artist's budget."

"I'm sure I can loan you some cash for a cucumber every now and then if we're a few bucks off."

"Oh, thank you, Dr. Kwan. That's so generous of you."

As we pass by the next aisle one of the vendors is in

front of his display case with a tray of samples. Despite a neat white mustache, a crisp button-down shirt, and an almost grandfatherly aura, there's a whiff of mischief about him that reminds me of Dad. The man holds out his wares, an innocent array of crackers with some type of jam, and I'm confused by the mixed signals. "Free sample?"

Oliver clears his throat as I reach for one. "Uh, Brynn?"

"Yeah?" I pop the cracker into my mouth and chew.

"You know that's ghost pepper jam, right?"

I spit a pulverized lump of pinkish, mealy goo into my palm as Oliver and the vendor watch with bug eyes. "I'm sorry," the man says, pointing frantically to the sign advertising his hot-sauce-and-pepper stand. "It's all spicy!"

TONGUE
INCINERATION! INCINERATION!
INCINERATION!

SALIVARY GLANDS
DEPLOY DROOL!

BRAIN
WATER!

All of these directives arrive simultaneously, the panic making it impossible to sort priorities and demands. This culminates in me doubling over and then attempting to run away from my own mouth. My eyes become waterfalls, and I pinwheel my arms in a losing battle to stay upright as a new wave of fire streaks across my lips and throbs in between my teeth.

My hands clamp to my throat as scorching air blazes through my lungs. A couple of people shout as I smack into a piece of glass and slide to the floor, weeping.

"Here's some milk," Oliver says urgently, latching onto my ring finger as I paw in the air for the cup. My skin slides along cool ceramic, and he adjusts the handle until it's within my grip, supporting the bottom of the mug as I lean in.

It must be called hand-eye coordination for a reason because without being able to see the level of the liquid, I splash half of it onto my face, belatedly registering that it's milk and not water. The cold milk dribbles down my neck and into my collar, but the half a mouthful I manage to drink is blissful.

"Oh my God. Thank you." I send more milk cascading down my face, not even caring that my second-favorite bra now qualifies as a dairy product.

A laugh cuts through the haze of my suffering. I wave my arm at Oliver until, unseeing, I latch onto the strap of his messenger bag, forcing my charred vocal cords to speak the seven most critical words of my life: "Don't let anyone put this on TikTok."

He presses a handful of napkins into my palm. "You have milk leaking out of your nose."

"Please," I beg. "Defend my online honor."

"I am. Don't worry."

"And don't tell my dad. He'll judge me."

The heat gradually subsides over the next ten minutes, restoring most of my bodily functions to their normal working order—or at least their normal *disorder*. I can see enough to note that the glass I ran into is a deli's display counter. If having a rumpled, ghost-peppered teenage girl bleating next to your store is bad for business, none of the employees seem too perturbed.

If anything, I'm good advertising for the hot-sauce guy.

"You should say thank you to the coffee people," Oliver says as he steps inside to return their mug. "They donated the milk."

By now the milk has dried enough that it's not visible, but I can feel it sticking my hair together. "Thank you for rescuing me," I call from a distance, certain that I must smell by now. I want to wave, but if I stop physically holding my stomach, I cannot guarantee the results.

"I'm betting you're not that hungry," Oliver remarks

as we continue on and transition into one of the seating areas by a cluster of restaurants.

I usually love the gigantic poppy-seed bagels from the booth around the corner, but I'm pretty sure my taste buds are too seared for a solid meal with any kind of texture. "I'll just get some soup. Gyro place is over there." We split up, and the paranoid part of my mind contemplates whether Oliver is going to ditch me here for being so clueless and causing a scene.

Despite my ordeal with the ghost pepper, I haven't completely warmed up from outside, and soup is almost always a guaranteed source of salt to tamp down the dizziness. I order a small cup of matzo ball and a bottle of blue Gatorade. It's not the greatest combination of flavors, but thanks to my circulatory system acting like an unregulated water park, salt and electrolytes are what keep my blood moving.

Before Oliver can return I shake three extra dashes of salt into the soup and mush my jawbone into the right spot. The pain is taking up positions in the usual places, and I check the time, wondering how long Pretend Brynn will be able to keep up the ruse. On every date with Oliver, it's always a bit Cinderella, except instead of being the glamorous princess, I'm trying not to be the pumpkin at one minute after midnight.

Fifteen

Even though Oliver is hopefully finished with college by the ten-year date in the assignment, his wild-card expense is a student loan, so he suggests stopping by Drexel for a picture. I suspect that it's just an excuse to see the campus again and quell his growing nerves about early decision, but I don't mind.

After all, this is the last time we'll see each other for the sake of it, and I'd like for it to end on a high note, at least for him.

"It's like a half-hour walk."

Just kidding. I do mind. "Half an hour?" I gawp at him, perpetually astounded by the distances other people are willing to walk for the most frivolous purposes. "I'm actually not feeling up for a walk," I venture, keeping the details vague.

"We could rent bikes," Oliver suggests. "They're electric, so you barely have to pedal."

I trace his line of sight across the street to a set of green bikes secured to a rack. "Okay." As usual my resolve weakens after a single protest, and I begin the problem-solving phase of attempting to do an ordinary activity without dissolving into a tiny pile of crappy collagen and orthopedic hardware.

While Oliver argues with the QR code to download the bike app, I test the width of the bars, scowling at the rough texture of the handlebar grips. With the electric assist, there's a slight possibility that it won't be as grueling as I predict.

PELVIS
No. No. This is a terrible idea.

LEFT SHOULDER
I concur. Let's try literally any other method
of transportation.

RIGHT ANKLE
Except walking.

Can't the young man carry you? He looks
like he has good ankles.

It occurs to me then that I have an excuse already
that doesn't involve telling Oliver about my condition.
"Actually, on second thought, my arm still kind of hurts
from the pep rally. Do you think we could just call an
Uber?" It's almost reminiscent of that brief grace period
when the pandemic was still in play, when it was enough
for bosses or teachers or anyone really to just not feel
good without saying why.

"Sure," Oliver says, as though it's a done deal now
that I've outright settled on a specific solution. But as
pleased as I am by his immediate support, I remind
myself that this is always how others act when it's temporary, an injury or illness that can be easily explained
and assigned a fixed end date.

That wanes with time, drained by canceled plans
and unexpected changes. Supportive comments go ran-
cid, sounding more and more like accusations. *You'll
feel better if you just try not to think about it!* Sick friends
are such buzzkills, and at some point it's just less taxing
to have healthy friends who can get out of bed and go
to your birthday party without some lame excuse like
they're in the ER with kidney damage.

"They're only three minutes away," Oliver announces,

angling his phone to show me the map. We stand side by side, watching the little car icon move closer. Under his breath, Oliver recites the make, model, and color.

"Aren't you going to share our location with someone?" I ask when he doesn't do so on his own.

"Why?"

"I don't know." I give a nervous laugh, the notion seeming silly now that I need to justify it. "I'm always just afraid of disappearing into thin air because my driver is . . . a man. But half the time it beats walking by myself."

Oliver, ever earnest, blanches. "Wait a second." He passes his phone over and then scribbles an adjustment on his project notes. "I changed your transportation costs to one hundred dollars. Then you'll have a safer way home after night shift."

"That's probably a good idea," I reply, indulging him as he takes this project, like everything, a bit too seriously. I look around the city in the daylight, imagining it at nightfall or in the true dark of the early morning. Even if Pretend Brynn can run away from danger without having to worry about passing out, I'm not sure I'd ever feel entirely comfortable staying out late without a friend.

Oliver misreads my frustration. "I can pay for it if it's going to mess up your budget."

I pat him on the top of the shoulder. "It's okay, but thanks. It's not like it's real money."

A white Nissan sedan slows at the end of the street, crawling along the shoulder until there's another car parked in the way. Oliver flags it down, matching the data on his phone with the vehicle in front of us. "That's our ride."

We climb into the back seat, and I'm glad that Oliver has the energy to strike up the small talk. Our driver's name is Amanda, and I can't see much of her except for brown hair and a sliver of her tanned face in the rearview mirror.

"I won't need to stay at the school for long," Oliver says, leaning back. "Just a picture or two and then we can work on the rest."

"I was checking out apartments." I message him the link to a beautiful modern building that's freshly renovated. "This one's only two thousand dollars a month." I have no concept of square footage, so I skip that part. "Two bedrooms and a bathroom. Do you think we need two bathrooms?"

"Always get two bathrooms," Amanda interjects. Wisdom aside, there's a quality to her voice that suggests she's speaking from experience, and a quick glimpse at her driver picture on Oliver's phone confirms that she's older than she sounds.

It doesn't take long for me and Oliver to discover that we have opposing tastes on virtually every aspect of finding housing. I prefer white walls, grays, and stainless kitchens; Oliver wants the interior to look like a presidential library.

I almost chew my tongue off trying not to put down his more outlandish ideas, but I draw the line when he suggests renting on South Street. "No," I state firmly. "It'll be too loud."

"But there's a record store."

"How am I supposed to sleep after doing my important doctorly business?"

"How am I supposed to write without hedonism?"

"I literally don't even know what that means!"

Amanda chuckles to herself, shifting slightly in her seat at a red light to sneak a peek at us in the rearview mirror. "How long have y'all been together? It's cute."

I force a smile that's too much teeth. "Oh, we're not, like, together."

Amanda taps her fingertips on the steering wheel, her eyebrows raised up over the top of her sunglasses. "Have y'all told each other that?"

Amanda drops us off in front of an enormous, boxy structure that reminds me more of a European government building than a college. Oliver poses in the doorway while I snap a picture that doesn't quite capture the scale of the building. "Please accept me," he chants as he pats the bricks. "Please. Please."

We debate whether we're allowed inside and decide against it, opting to tour the outside of the campus instead. Given that the only college I've ever seen is the community one, Drexel is a city unto itself. Students mill around, a few sprawled out on the grass with laptops and textbooks.

Oliver moons over every detail like a smitten suitor. "Sorry for dragging you out here, but I just wanted to see it one more time before I get my decision. It's been a while since I came here with my dad for the tour."

"I don't mind. I've never been on a campus this big before." I can't stop myself from noticing the stairs and sloping patches of grass, the transitions between types of stone that are bound to get slick in the rain. It seems silly, but it's just one more reminder that unless it's painted bright blue with a little wheelchair stick figure, it isn't meant for people like me. "What did your dad say about it? Are they coming around?"

Oliver pauses to sit on a bench, scrutinizing the buildings rising around us. "My mom thinks I should double major in 'something practical' like engineering. I promised to sign up for one class in exchange for getting access to my college money."

"So she's holding you hostage." I settle in next to him, not quite touching.

He scrapes the toe of his leather chukka boot on the stone walkway, swinging it back and forth under the bench. "What else is new? She'll listen to what I want, but it doesn't matter. It's just more preaching about how she needs to make a little more, get one more contact, and then she'll have so much free time to spend with us.

"I didn't even tell her I was leaving today. I just told Nonna I wouldn't be home for dinner." Oliver takes his phone out and illuminates the screen. "You can see how worried she is. She probably hasn't even left her office yet."

"But it's Sunday."

"Business first." He smiles, but there's no mirth in it. "Tell me I was an unwanted surprise baby without telling me I was an unwanted surprise baby."

"I'm sorry."

"You know, it's about time for Dad to threaten to get divorced and then she'll become obsessed with him for a while." Oliver straightens and leans back, turning to face me. "At a certain point, when people keep showing you who they are, you have to believe them."

I don't know if that knife was half meant for me or not, but it lodges in my guts all the same. I drop my chin, staring at my lap instead of holding his gaze.

185

"Did you decide where you're applying yet?" he asks after it's clear my only response is to sit here, arms folded low over my stomach like that will stop the bleeding.

Like I always do, I dodge the question. "I'm still thinking about it." I've stopped telling anyone that I plan to go to community college, if at all. My teachers—even the substitutes—always find some way to disparage it, as though it's settling to not aim for a PhD from Princeton. "What made you pick Drexel?"

Oliver gives me an abbreviated summary of the campus, explaining the two-year housing guarantee and a few other particulars that I don't quite understand. "It's one of the only schools with a legit playwriting degree with internships and a student production company."

"That sounds perfect for you. It isn't all just about acting."

He types on his phone, clicking a link and scrolling. "They have a premed program." He speaks of it with such confidence that I can almost imagine this is real, a tour we're taking together before we matriculate in the fall.

In truth I don't know where I'll be after summer's end. I might be in community college. I might be in my living room. I might be just a stone's throw away, watching some race for Eliza's junior year. But I know I won't be here.

It just doesn't feel like goodbye yet.

I'm not ready.

But like any other tribute paid to the beast of this disorder, being ready has never mattered. I've watched it devour my mobility, my joys, my horizons. This time it will take my heart.

Sixteen

Maybe sitting down was a mistake. Sometimes it's better to just keep moving, capitalizing on all the inertia and momentum to carry me forward. Starting from a stop seems infinitely more draining.

I rub the backs of my thighs whenever there are enough people milling around for the motion to blend in. "Do you want to see anything else before we go?"

"I have no idea," Oliver admits. "There's so much."

On a whim we sneak into one of the smaller buildings to see what it's like, but there isn't much on the ground floor except for locked doors, an empty lecture hall, and a few nooks for studying. It's less frenetic than I envisioned a college of this size would be even on a weekend.

Regardless, it seems like more than enough fuel for

Oliver's wishful reveries. "I can't wait to go to college," he confesses as we tentatively open a side exit and emerge onto a landscaped crisscross of walkways. "I'll finally have some space. No gym class or dress codes. I'll be able to learn what I want."

"No horrible principals."

Oliver taps his messenger bag. "No 'fall projects' that are due in a week and a half."

"Oh, were we doing a project?" I ask in feigned confusion, grabbing his hand in a flash of daring. "I thought we were going to see your new production featured at your alma mater now that you're almost *thirty* and a very important . . . writer . . . person."

He nods along with a slight eye roll. "Why, yes, Dr. Kwan, you're absolutely right. We better go to the matinee since I'm so old now that I must be in bed by eight o'clock sharp."

When we reach the sidewalk on the periphery of the campus, Oliver takes out his notes about the assignment, and we lean our heads closer to read his nanoscopic handwriting. Entertainment is its own separate category on the budget, so it makes sense for us to find at least one example of something fun we like to do. "Maybe we're just boring," I speculate when we can't come up with a single idea. "Does napping count as entertainment?"

"I don't think so."

That seems unfair since it's my favorite life activity.

"Maybe there's something around here that looks interesting." Oliver rattles off a list of potential options, but none of them sound too enticing. With the college so close, there are tons of bars and clubs nearby to appeal to students, and part of me resents that it seems like every social activity centers around getting sloshed. All I need to do is read my pill bottles for a reminder of why that's never going to happen.

I join in the search, consulting various travel websites and listicles until I find an activity that I think we'll both enjoy. "There's the Museum of Secrets. Does that count as a weird museum?"

Oliver glances at me sidelong, only his eyes shifting until I'm framed in his peripheral vision. "You remembered."

"It's not every day that someone's hobby is finding weird museums." We intended to visit a few together, but then we lost one summer to lockdown, one to lack of transportation, and one to my own selfishness.

"It happened by accident. We'd move somewhere new for a little while, and the first weekend we made it a tradition to find something fun instead of just unpacking for the bazillionth time." He ticks some examples off on his fingers. "There's the Museum of Failure. The Museum of Illusions. The American Pickle Juice Museum."

"Pickle juice? That sounds so random."

"Some of them aren't full museums. It's just some guy's house or a shed with his collection of whatevers in it. Saltshakers or taxidermy squirrels."

FEET

We collect hospital socks. We have six
different colors with circles on the bottom
and four different colors with the ridges.

Oliver's voice quiets and turns wistful. "I never had a collection as a kid. You kind of slim down when you move all the time."

Oliver speaks of his travels with such disdain that it's a struggle not to romanticize it. When he describes such far-off places, I see only the beauty and freedom of it, the wonder in the wandering. So I say what I wish others would say to me, an unvarnished admission of the obvious: "I can't even imagine."

"That's why I was so surprised when I saw your room for the first time. It's not overflowing. I got used to everybody else having so much stuff around."

If only he knew the real reason my room was so spare on the few occasions he convinced me to hang out at my house instead of his. I was so anxious that he'd find something embarrassing that I took it all and shoved it into the closet. The last thing I needed was to send him running because he noticed that I sleep with a pregnancy pillow half the time.

There's a ripple in my consciousness that might be sound. I blink as fatigue begins to set its hooks in me. "Sorry, I was spacing out." I envision it almost as a fog rolling in, curling first at my ankles to get its grip no matter my attempts to shake it off. "Did you say something?"

"No. Are you feeling all right?" Oliver asks in the pointed manner of true concern.

"Yeah, I'm fine. I'm just tired from staying up late with Tori." And from researching how to drop out and get my life restarted, but he doesn't need to know that.

Oliver peers at me closer, his eyes sharp and piercing. "Are you sure?"

I internally cringe. This is how the well-meaning hovering starts, the suggestion that perhaps I've failed to see my own limits. And while I've walked myself off that cliff many times before, my eyes were open. "Yeah," I confirm again. "I'm sure."

When people can only see you as broken, they either want to put you in a box, packed away safely in paper and tissue in a special space just for you, or they want a refund for the utter waste of having invested in you at all.

* * *

At the museum ticket counter, the attendant is willing to sell me two tickets at a reduced student rate, but I decline the second. I'm not a student anymore; I'm not a doormat for the Zellers or a convenient sacrificial lamb for Principal Dombrowski. I pay the extra three dollars for admission and relish it.

Oliver snaps a picture of me standing beside a gigantic question mark painted on the wall in the lobby. We take a minute to set up the audio tour and orient ourselves on the folding maps.

The exhibits in the first gallery are somewhat anticlimactic for a museum with such a provocative name. "The Museum of Secrets," I say to Oliver in a goofy announcer's voice, waggling my fingers at him as though casting a spell. "Surprise! The secrets are bad conspiracy theories about John F. Kennedy and a misunderstanding of Dead Sea salt."

It gets marginally better as we continue deeper into the exhibits, and in spite of my criticisms I'm glad that we're able to check one thing off our old relationship bucket list, no matter how convoluted the route here. Oliver is a Ping-Pong ball whizzing between one display and the next, prodding buttons and reading signs to himself, his lips moving silently.

When I'm this worn down, asking my eyes to do anything except stay in my head is out of the question.

Luckily the museum offers a companion audio tour using these ancient remotes with a clicker on one end and a built-in speaker on the other. It faithfully follows along, reciting facts and quotes from stuffy medieval Europeans I don't recognize.

I get turned around in a gallery of acrylic paintings where all the artwork is meant to contain a secret message. There are instructions on multiple panels, but every time I click the remote it replies, "Uncover the hidden secret!"

Click.

Uncover the hidden secret!

Click.

Uncover the hidden secret!

Click.

Click.

Click.

And it bothers me. It bothers me that I can't have one damn thing that isn't curated for *special needs*, some shittier version of the experience that everyone else gets. I squeeze the receiver with such force that the back of the housing pops off, vomiting AAA batteries onto the floor, in unison with my thumb sliding out of joint because why wouldn't it?

I scramble to retrieve the batteries before they can roll under the cabinets. My right thumb is jammed in a worthless position, and my left hand lacks the proper motor skills. The result is that Oliver returns from checking out a case of diaries to find me hunched over like a malfunctioning human claw machine.

"What happened?" he asks, dropping effortlessly to a knee and collecting the batteries.

"The remote for the audio tour broke." I wrestle out of the lanyard and dangle it in the air for Oliver. He catches it and feeds the batteries into each slot, closing it with a snap. The light on the front illuminates, and the tinny voice begins speaking again.

"Thanks." I cut the audio and relegate the remote to serving as a heavy, garish necklace. If only all repairs could be so quick and painless.

RIGHT THUMB
Yeah, tell me about it. A little help here?

I refuse to participate in the puzzle gallery on principle, meeting Oliver on the other side, where there's a fourteen-minute video cycling on repeat about some Vermeer that had secretly been painted over in the middle. I'll sit through anything for a chance to sit in the first place, and I'm already in a twilight by the time the introduction is over. My eyelids open and close in lethargic blinks, and if the temperature weren't set to Arctic tundra, I doubt I would be able to resist the promise of a five-minute nap.

Oliver, meanwhile, is fascinated, perched on the edge of the bench and watching the screen with rapt attention. He doesn't notice me shrinking in my seat, relishing the break from our earlier pace.

"That's the big reveal?" I deadpan when the mini documentary explains that a portrait of Cupid was hidden behind a blank wall in *Girl Reading a Letter at an Open Window*. "That did not have to be fourteen minutes."

"I think it's interesting how they found it," Oliver offers as a positive, but it sounds like he's trying to convince a history teacher that class wasn't a bore.

I strike up an exaggerated pose with the museum pamphlet in front of my face. "Here's another painting for you. It's called *Girl Wanting to Know Why the Fuck This Museum Costs Sixteen Dollars*."

A barking laugh escapes him. "Oh, come on. Half the fun of going to a quirky museum is that it's usually awful. Do you really think that the American Pickle Juice Museum is the pinnacle of historical preservation?"

"I guess not," I concede.

"And be nice to Vermeer," Oliver adds. "It's bad enough that he died broke when his paintings are worth millions and millions of dollars now."

"I wonder how many incredible things we've missed out on because white men had a monopoly on doing, like, everything. Art, astronomy, medicine, you know." Vermeer wasn't the only one to take his talents to the grave, leaving behind a family in poverty.

If we hadn't kept so many people from opportunity, every major discovery could have happened just a few years sooner. Compounded over centuries, maybe the Ehlers-Danlos syndromes could have been managed with a pill or a shot by now. Maybe there could have been cures for at least some of the subtypes.

"You say it in the past tense, but it still happens just like that," Oliver spits with unrestrained vehemence. "Half the reason my mom started her own company is because she was sick of everyone treating her like it was her first day on the job. She always talks about this time that she finished overseeing some super difficult weld on a subsea pipeline that saved the company, like, five million dollars, and less than two hours later the VP asked her to get him a cup of coffee."

"Are those people still among the living?" I'd rather fight a Komodo dragon with chain saws for legs than incur the wrath of Oliver's mother. "Sorry, but your mom is sorta terrifying."

He smirks. "I think that's what she's going for."

We both startle as the surround sound kicks on again

197

to reveal a second short film. The doors close on a pre-programmed timer, and I don't want to be rude to the staff outside by leaving in the middle. Instead I scoot to the end of the bench and lean my head against the soft acoustic wall panel. Sleep eludes me, but even a few moments of rest can be a drop in a dry bucket.

The reward for sitting through the follow-up video—this one an exhaustive description of why Cupid mattered to Baroque painters—is reaching the hands-on area of the museum. "Now this is more my style," I remark as we enter. There are more messages hidden in artwork, the chance to add your secrets to a wall of sticky notes, and even an indoor maze that offers a daily prize to the first person to find the secret passageway.

Oliver picks up a paintbrush with rock-hard bristles covered in every conceivable color of paint. "I'm pretty sure this is meant for little kids."

I snort as I tally up how many times I've eaten popcorn for lunch and fallen asleep in the recliner in my Hello Kitty pajamas over the course of my lifetime. "And *I'm* pretty sure that I have the maturity level of a ten-year-old."

He's right that we're either too tall or too old for most of the activities, but the attraction by the exit to the gift shop is undeniably meant for adults. It's just two chairs facing each other across a table with a thick wall of glass in between. The outer walls of the booth are a semitransparent gray, giving it the overall appearance of a Catholic confessional crossed with an interrogation room.

"This exhibit is designed to let you share your secrets . . . without revealing the true meaning to the other person," Oliver reads from the instructions panel. "Write out your secret using the keyboard at the desk, and let our state-of-the-art technology transform your words into a personal art show. Your secret will always remain safe with us."

I wrap my arms around myself, unsure about the guarantee of confidentiality. "Do you want to try it?"

"Why not?" Oliver tests the door on his side and steps inside.

The glass is just opaque enough that I decide to give it a chance without stressing too much that the other guests in the museum will see. The chair is plain and unattached from the desk, which upon closer inspection contains an angled monitor that only I can see.

I pat underneath the desk until I find the keyboard tray. My fingers fall automatically into position, and I press a random key twice to illuminate the screen. The prompt is simple: *Look at the person across from you. Suppose that you could tell that person any secret without consequences. What would you say?*

I don't entirely trust the booth to work as designed, so I wait for Oliver to read through to the end. Our eyes meet for a brief moment before he bows his head to better see his monitor and begins typing. True to their word I get no hint of what he might be writing. For all I know he's inputting a fart joke to see what happens.

I sit back in surprise as the walls themselves illuminate, letters of all fonts and sizes scattered and mixed to the point of being unintelligible. Colors drip from the ceiling in cascades and swirls, the dark spaces between them forming a fluid abstraction. Images streak across the screen, and although I can discern what they are, there's no link between them.

I pick out the decorative edge of a poker chip, an ear, binoculars. But unless Oliver is planning a casino heist that I'm not aware of, it's too general to derive any overarching meaning. As disappointed as I am, this is exactly what the exhibit purported to be.

The lights and colors fade until the walls are the same hazy, smoky gray. I cautiously return my fingers to the keys. The program doesn't specify a word count, so I write out my whole secret and press enter.

Like before, the bare walls transmute into art, starting with nebulous tendrils of red and black, twisting into currents and flowing almost like a river. Letters fall and vanish without a single word standing out to me. I strain to see Oliver, but he's only another shape on the other side of the glass.

A pair of eyes appears, vanishing as hands materialize to cover them. I regret not recording this, but I also can't imagine that I'll ever be able to forget it. As the simulation ends there's an insistent beep and a flashing light from the desk. I glance at the monitor for a cue. *If you'd like to share your secret in real life, present the other person with your envelope. If not, please deposit your envelope in the shredder on your way out the door.*

I reach toward the flashing light and notice a thin slot just beneath it. I extend my hand just in time to catch a tiny envelope that barely spans the length of three fingers. I delicately fold back the flap and extract the paper inside. *I asked you here because I dropped out of school yesterday, and I wanted to see you one last time to say goodbye. I love you, but I'm sick. I'm falling apart piece by piece. And I think the only thing worse than having it happen in the first place is making you watch.*

"That wasn't what I was expecting," Oliver comments as we emerge from our respective sides of the booth.

"Me either." I giggle at the absurdity of my only conclusion. "The only thing I could guess about yours is that you were involved in a casino heist."

Bethany Mangle

Oliver sticks out his jaw. "You got me. My secret is that I'm a criminal mastermind."

"Oh please. You would make a terrible thief." If I trusted anyone to pull off a heist, it would be level-headed Francesca, whose temper never flares past lukewarm. At the sight of his indignation, I clarify, "You'd be sneaking into somewhere and get caught because you were humming the soundtrack to *Hamilton* under your breath."

Oliver, knowing when he's beaten, doesn't make another peep in his defense. "All right, but what about your secret? You throw books into the Underworld and then play peekaboo with them?"

It's not a half-bad description of what the computer came up with. "If I did throw books into the Underworld, it would be this year's entire reading list." Of all the books that have been written since 1847, I cannot fathom why Pineland Prep chose *Wuthering Heights* as its featured novel for senior English.

"It's not that bad," Oliver says in that way people often discount things that are absolutely that bad.

"I have read Burger King menus that are more interesting than *Wuthering Heights*."

I wait for Oliver to look away before stashing the tiny envelope in the pocket of my sweatshirt. I can't stop toying with it, pressing the pointed corners into the pads of my fingers or spinning it end over end as we pause in the lobby to regroup. Oliver skims the assignment sheet again, and part of me wants to film him and show Mr. Waller how hard he's working.

It's not that Oliver is by any means a slacker. He has better grades than I do, but I haven't seen him exhibit this much enthusiasm for a subject that wasn't creative writing or stage tech. "Why do you care so much about this project?"

Oliver glances up from his lists and scribbles, one shoulder bobbing in half a shrug. "I like being able to study what I want. It's boring when it's just the same old word problems and essays. And some of this might actually be useful in the future."

"True." Despite inventing half the details, I will presumably need to eat food and sleep somewhere. "What's left on the agenda?"

"We have to figure out how much rent will be and then fill in how we're going to divide cooking and cleaning."

Mom staunchly refuses to allow me to do any chores that could cause injury, and since that's practically everything, my experience is limited to sweeping and cleaning the microwave. "Can we just put fifty-fifty?"

"Fine by me."

Pretend Brynn will learn how to cook real food on YouTube. She'll set off the smoke alarm so often that the neighbors complain, but she'll eventually win them over with delicious cookies left on their doorsteps. Pretend Brynn will be able to bend over to get laundry out of the dryer without passing out in a pile of her sister's gross athletic socks. Pretend Brynn is a team player.

Yes, Pretend Brynn will do all kinds of marvelous, foolhardy things—she might even dare to fall in love.

Seventeen

Since I won't actually be turning in the project, I don't object to letting Oliver's priorities take precedence. "Are you sure *you* don't want to go anywhere?" he repeats as we determine where to head next.

"I'm good. I picked the museum, remember?" Plus we were together for years, which means that I can instantly sniff out that he wants to do something but doesn't want to be greedy. "Let me guess. You want to go check out a theater."

"I might."

"You're so predictable," I tease.

Oliver mimes an arrow piercing his heart. "That's the kiss of death for a writer." He shuffles a few feet for a better vantage point, gazing into the distance where

Drexel spills across the city. "No, let me never be that."

I pinch the spongy wool of his sleeve and reel him in from his daydream. "Come on, moody poet. You can be moody somewhere warmer."

"You're cold?" he asks, already fiddling with the buttons of his coat as he prepares to shed it.

"Stop. It's fine." As nicely as it fits Oliver, it would be too heavy for me. Much like Dad, I exist as the contradiction of too hot and too cold, oscillating between extremes from one second to the next. "And it's a good excuse to get coffee."

While I vanish into the next coffee shop to have an existential crisis choosing between hot cocoa and a pumpkin spice latte, Oliver correctly intuits that I want to take another car and reserves it before I return. "I can pay you back," I offer, scrambling to recall the password to send money from my phone.

"Don't worry about it. You got us the tickets."

"Those weren't much. Are you sure?"

"Of course I'm sure." Before, when we'd have this exact exchange, he'd end it with, "You're my girlfriend," as though to remind me that we didn't need to keep score. But that no longer applies, and the ghost of those words lingers between us as we climb into the car to cross the city once again.

"Which theater is this?" I ask, just for a change of

subject. We haven't broached the matter of what happened over the summer, and this late in the day, it might be better to let it go. There will be enough new wounds to leave us limping without picking at the scabs of the past.

"It's the Metropolitan Opera House," Oliver replies, without the usual torrent of accompanying details and historical facts. "The Met."

Ever since I transferred in ninth grade, the teachers have started the year with icebreaker exercises to introduce everyone, even though it's rare for new students to secure a slot with the school already at capacity. But no one ever has a solution for how to break the ice when you already know each other, that impenetrable kind of freeze that's meant to keep you from ever coming closer again.

"I thought the Metropolitan Opera was in New York City." As a rule, I'm clueless about the arts, but I must have absorbed some details from Dad if that's rattling around in my brain.

"There's actually one in Philadelphia, too."

"Oh." Oliver's graciousness when I don't entirely understand his passions is one of the many reasons I love him. Yes, his love for me may be negotiable; his respect is not. It's a refreshing change from the self-important boys I flirted with in middle school, who found every opportunity to mock me if I asked a question about how football works or misunderstood the rules of some video game.

Part of me wonders when this compulsion starts, the inability to just accept that we're not omniscient. I see it constantly in my appointments, where a doctor will make a ridiculous claim and refuse to accept evidence to the contrary. It's like that first doctor in the ER the day of the fight with Pat: *Ah, I see you have Dislocates Lots of Shit Disease, but it definitely can't be a dislocation.*

Does the posturing of our childhood continue on, poisoning our adult interactions as well? And if it does, what does that mean for the pretenders like me?

Our driver lets us out almost immediately in front of the theater. I'm startled by the relative tranquility of the neighborhood, as though we're visiting our local downtown and not a storied piece of history in a vibrant city. "I thought it would be busier around here," I remark, noting the construction going on up the street and the relative lack of pedestrians. I certainly didn't expect it to be across the street from a Dunkin'.

"It has to be busier at night," Oliver speculates, brows narrowed as he scans our surroundings, squinting against the brilliance of the sun overhead. But there's no sprawling arts district or edgy nightlife concealed behind the ordinary storefronts lining the street. The Met is just a beautiful outlier, a zebra among horses.

Regardless, Oliver's sense of awe is palpable. His muscles snap taut as he reins in his excitement, failing to look nonchalant as he almost backpedals in front of a Prius while trying to capture the full marquis on camera. The blare of the horn shocks him into alertness before I can lunge forward to save him. He scrambles back onto the curb, offering a two-handed gesture of apology to the driver and getting a one-fingered response in return.

"Oliver," I murmur in relief, smacking my hand over my eyes. "Please do not get run over. Your mom will make my skin into a tote bag."

The corners of his mouth droop into a wince. "Sorry. I swore there wasn't anyone there when I looked." He pauses for a beat. "And she wouldn't make your skin into a tote bag. She doesn't like tote bags."

I can't quite bring myself to laugh. "I figured she might, um, have a grudge about . . ." I wasn't close with Oliver's parents, and based on how they reacted to my presence, they fell somewhere in the middle between ambivalent and overly possessive of their son. Our dynamic shifted in milestones as the relationship stretched on, when it became clear that I wasn't merely a fleeting interest, but I doubt they're a fan of me after I ghosted Oliver over the summer.

"That was a joke," Oliver emphasizes, watching me pout as I sip at my cocoa.

This time I volunteer to be his photographer so that he can be in the frame. As I return his phone, he cups one hand against the glass door and peeks inside. "I don't think they're open. I wonder if they leave this unlocked for tickets." He tugs on the handle, earning only the deep thud of a latch catching.

"I'm sorry. Maybe we can find pictures of the inside online or something."

Without warning, one of the doors farther up the street pops open. An older woman steps out, balancing the door against the tip of her shoe. "If you're in line, it'll be a while," she barks. "The doors don't open until six thirty."

"Oh, we're not here for a show," Oliver replies, scurrying closer.

"So why are you here?" She sounds just curious enough for a follow-up question but perhaps not curious enough to care about the answer if we take too long to respond.

"We're doing a school project and talking about the theater."

"We'd love to be able to see the lobby!" I interject with precisely zero subtlety. "Please. He's obsessed."

The woman, Brenda by her name tag, appraises me

with a quick sweep of her eyes. I'm sure that I look and smell like a disaster, and I could probably use an entire lint roller and still have cat hair on my leggings. But somehow we must pass her test because she stands back with a sigh and ushers us inside.

"We didn't spend fifty-six million dollars on a renovation for you to take pictures of the lobby." Brenda jerks her chin toward a set of doors that I can only imagine leads to the theater itself. "You can check out the inside and the stage. Just don't make a mess." She gestures to a sign displaying the house rules. "No touching the equipment. No gum. No stickers. Bags stay here."

Oliver practically slams his messenger bag to the floor in his eagerness. "Thank you. Oh my God. Thank you. Can I go on the stage?"

Brenda lifts her shoulders in a loose shrug. "Knock yourself out. Just make sure you get out in the next twenty minutes before my boss gets here." She consults the slightly crooked clock on the wall above the exit. "And if she gets here early, I didn't let you in. You're delinquents who broke in the back door. Got it?"

Oliver nods so fervently that I'm waiting for his head to loll off. "Yes. Delinquents. Absolutely. Thank you."

She shoos him with a flick of her hand, and Oliver takes off like a shot, freezing a few paces away only to confirm that I'm still following. "Go," I tell him, laughing. "I'll catch up." I strike a slower pace as I pass the bar and the ticket office, admiring the gleaming white tile and the craftsmanship of the columns.

Even without the glitz and the glamor of an evening show, the structure alone is a monument in its own right. Yet despite the ubiquitous gold paint and the opulence of the chandeliers, it manages to seem elegant instead of overwrought. And as it loses the shine of its newness, the original wood seeping through the paint, it will age well—a patina on heirloom silver.

I reach the main doors to the hall, setting my heels against the heft of their weight as I crack one side just far enough to slip inside. In the near darkness, the heart of the theater is magnificent, the rows and boxes dressed in deep crimson and limned in white and gold—the arches like eyes above us.

Oliver emerges from the wings, and I watch him from the shadow of the doorway at the end of the aisle. He is nothing short of enraptured, bending to skim his fingertips over the wood. The motion reminds me of walking through an open field, fingers trailing in tall grasses just to connect for a fleeting instant.

Straightening, Oliver studies the emptiness sprawled out before him, transformed by the height and shadows of the stage into something untouchable and dreamlike and beyond the grasp of a girl with two feet on the ground. He continues into the center of the great space, his eyes panning the cavernous room in slow motion.

My smile breaks when I realize that he's looking for me. With all this beauty before him, he still only wants the ugliness of my deception. How many times must I star as the villain of our story before he at last divines that if I'm any part a Juliet, it's the poison on her lips?

I sigh and he spins on his heel, searching again at the sound. "I give up," Oliver admits to the dark. "Where are you hiding?"

"Right here." I've been hiding right here all along.

He cajoles, persuades, and almost begs until I agree to join him onstage. "Isn't this amazing?" He twirls a bit, his arms swinging into a low arc. "I mean, when I'm standing here, I swear that I can feel it. The magic. One day I'll have a show on these boards."

I let out a little puff of air that Oliver correctly interprets as a laugh. "What are you giggling about over there?" he asks.

I grin without intending. "You're just so . . . ," I trail off, smiling again. "It's like you never doubt for a second that everything is going to work out."

He turns to me, still breathless from his spinning. "What's so wrong with that? Don't you want to be extraordinary?"

"I think I could settle just fine for ordinary." I've seen

the price of being extraordinary, the way you're rendered down into a new specimen to be prodded by a handful of well-meaning medical students, all trying desperately to remember page 249 of that pathology textbook. Rare like a slab of red meat—bleeding.

Oliver waves his hand mindlessly through the air, cutting a crescent-shaped arc. "I don't know how to explain it. I just don't want my entire life to be a bunch of . . . double negatives."

"Double negatives?" I prompt, filling my usual role of getting Oliver's mind going. Most people have a train of thought. For Oliver, it's more like a stubborn cow wandering off and refusing to return to the rest of the herd without some prodding.

"Yeah. Double negatives. My life isn't *not* good. My odds of getting into Drexel aren't *not* bleak. I'm not *un*-lonely." His eyes drop at the end, flicking back at the last minute like an uppercut.

I've never detected more than the occasional whiff of discontentment from him before. "I thought you liked living at your grandmother's house. You were so happy when you found out you were staying."

"I liked getting to see my nonna. I liked knowing I'd be in one place for a while instead of getting lugged around the country like a lamp or a blender. I liked the neighborhood." Oliver pauses, shooting an inscrutable look over his shoulder before facing away again. To the empty stage, he mutters, "I liked you."

In this game between us, I make my fatal mistake.

Before I can remember that this is just pretend, I sweep around him in a single fluid step, face-to-face, so close now that I feel the whisper of his breath on my skin. I lean in, the smoothness of my cheek brushing against the roughness of his.

Oliver lifts his arms, and for a grim moment I think he's about to push me away—but he only presses one palm to the hollow between my shoulder blades, the other cradling my neck to hold me closer. He turns into my touch, his lips grazing a tortuous path to hover over mine.

I put aside our looming farewell and the knowledge that some loves may last for the ages, but ours will only last for today—and I kiss him like the wretched, besotted impostor I am.

Eighteen

We fit together as two hands folding into prayer.

The memories wash over me, and I've never yearned so much to linger in a mistake. I bend with the kiss like a dancer in a dip, hovering in the weightlessness of letting all my reservations go. The peace does not last long.

The walls between real and pretend, past and present, are crumbling, and I don't know what I can salvage from the rubble. I would stand here forever to see what we might build, but as romantic as it is to kiss on a darkened stage, I muster my willpower and break our embrace.

"What is it?" Oliver murmurs, refusing to let go as he brushes back errant wisps of my hair with his fingers.

"We're going to get Brenda fired."

Oliver heaves a sigh. "I don't want to go yet."

"We have to."

"A travesty." He kisses my forehead, his fingers winding down my forearm as he takes my hand. "But you're right. We have to go. I left my bag in the lobby."

"See?" I tease as I struggle to keep up on the stairs leading to ground level. "I told you. You'd make a terrible criminal mastermind leaving evidence all over the place like that."

Neither of us is sure about the exact time that Brenda's boss is due to arrive, so we move carefully, checking around corners and listening for voices on our way back out. A few lights are turned on that weren't before, but other than that, we slink across the lobby without issue and retrieve Oliver's messenger bag from the corner.

I ease the crash bar into the open position and hold it for Oliver. Once we're both through, I close the door as gently as I can, adding pressure with my hand from the outside to minimize the vibration as it secures. "Sneaking out was actually kind of fun." I giggle for half of the next block until the nervous energy wears off. "Look at me. Getting into fights. Breaking into theaters."

"Where should we make trouble next?" Oliver asks, peering around as though the city itself will produce an answer.

"Let's walk," I suggest, two words that have literally

217

never left my mouth in that combination before. "Maybe we'll find something interesting."

"Which way?"

I choose a random direction and point. "I don't know. There?" Truly, I would go anywhere to delay our final parting for even a second more. Because as long as we're together, then it isn't yet goodbye, and I won't have to think about that kiss and what it means.

But I think about it anyway. I suspect we both do as we continue on without speaking, our hands brushing like two passing pendulums with each stride we take.

My feet must have automatically led us west toward Boathouse Row because I soon spot the familiar skyline and foreboding towers of the Eastern State Penitentiary. An orange banner out front advertises a haunted festival and costume contest for Halloween, and I find the starkness jarring.

"Have you ever heard of a play called *Clyde's*?" Oliver asks, breaking the silence. It's old times again, when we spent lazy weekend afternoons snuggled on the futon in his bedroom, ignoring some movie that had caught our eye only minutes before. Oliver would tell me all there was to know about Hollywood and theater, and I'd fill him in on the secret goings-on at Pineland Prep.

I shake my head in response to his question. I never

had much of an interest in theater before I met Oliver, and after we broke up it was too painful a reminder of his presence.

"It's about a bunch of people who work at this truck stop after getting out of prison. My parents bought me tickets to the digital show for my birthday." I shiver as a spike of pain shoots through my leg, my muscles upset by the exertion. Oliver, misinterpreting it as the cold, quickens our pace a bit to get beyond the shadow of the walls.

"Did you like it?" I ask, clinging to the conversation to block out the growing ache.

"I loved it. It's by this playwright named Lynn Nottage; she's absolutely amazing."

> RIGHT HIP FLEXORS
> You need to sit down. This is too much
> walking.

> ME
> Weren't you just complaining about sitting
> earlier? Pretend Brynn doesn't have hip
> dysplasia or EDS. I don't have to listen to you.

> RIGHT HIP FLEXORS
> Well, *Pretend Brynn's* leg is about
> to fall off.

I zone in and out of the conversation as if tuning my consciousness to some far-off signal. The fog of fatigue is relentless, and I envision it as a rising cloud surrounding me, trailing my steps like the train of a white dress.

Just as I've almost reached my limit, Oliver lets out an audible gasp. "The steps from *Rocky*! That can be our last picture. It's perfect." He hums a dramatic montage as we approach, arriving in tandem with another group of tourists. "We can take it at the top. It's so dramatic and . . . *thematic*. I love it."

I stare up at the landing in the distance, and in my mind it's no different from the summit of K2. I stand there, transfixed, watching a child at least half my age chase a man at least twice my age up dozens and dozens of stairs. Two joggers crest the top and race down instead, their knees pumping, colorful shoes tapping a beat on the stone.

And all at once I remember why I'm here, the stairs rising before me like one lie stacked atop the next. "Oliver." I stop him before he can take off. "Can we talk?" I gesture to a fork in the path leading to the stairs. The branch to the right leads to a sculpture garden.

"Sure," Oliver replies, his unease palpable.

I find an empty bench tucked within a copse of

trees and pat the space beside me. Oliver sits on the very edge, spine straight and feet flat as though already poised to run away. I draw in a long breath. "I have something to tell you that I should have told you a long time ago."

I rack my memory for a reason, some decision point that brought me to this present. But I have no rationale to give him, no excuse that could possibly vindicate my betrayal. "And I guess I did tell you once today already, just not in any way that counted."

With a trembling hand, I reach into my pocket and retrieve the envelope from the museum. I meant to speak the words aloud, but as our history has proven to the utmost, I'm a coward. Instead I hold it out to him—a single truth to unravel all the lies, the years of half-truths and omissions.

"I don't want it," Oliver says, pushing the envelope away. "Whatever secret you have, I don't care. It doesn't change anything."

It would be so simple to take this as a gift. If I were like Dad and I believed that there's a plan for us all, I might even see it as providence. But I can't run away any longer from a reckoning that Dad foresaw when I first begged him not to send in my 504 plan for accommodations, to let me start in a new school as an ordinary girl: *It's your choice. But at most they'll only love you for half of who you are, and at worst they'll love you completely for everything you're not.*

I break open the envelope with the edge of my thumbnail and unfurl it in my palm. "Read it." I slide my hand into Oliver's, then let go, leaving the paper behind. "Please."

He kisses me once, chastely. "All right," he says, an undertone of sadness in the timbre of his voice. With reluctance he flattens the paper and begins. I wait for his reaction, expecting nothing but what I'm due.

"I don't understand," Oliver says, his face ashen. "You dropped out? And what do you mean, you're sick?"

"It's what my father has. Ehlers-Danlos syndrome." Oliver has spent enough time around our family to see the obvious at least. The home-compounded medicine in the refrigerator. The traveling wheelchair in the trunk of my car. The medical bracelets. "And I just don't want to waste any more time sitting in a school that doesn't give a shit about me when I could be starting my new life now while I still can." I cover his hand with mine, but he only flinches away. "Do you, um, do you have questions?"

"Do I have questions?" he shouts, and at first I mistake it for anger instead of what it truly is—fear. *"Do I have questions?"* Oliver lurches to his feet, pacing the seam between the grass and the concrete. "When did you find out you have it?"

"I was nine," I whisper. That's when it was official anyway. By my parents' account, Dad knew by the time I was a toddler, when I rolled instead of crawled and didn't walk for well over a year.

And just as abruptly, Oliver becomes another statue in the garden. I watch his muscles soften and his breathing slow. The truth drags him under and away as it repaints every memory between us with new understanding. And the Oliver who lived those joyful days with me is not the same one who breaks the surface.

Tears gather strength at the corners of his eyes. "Are you dying?" The words catch in his throat, turning hoarse. "Is that why you're telling me this now?"

"No," I whisper, my tears reflecting his. "It won't make my life shorter, but it does make it smaller. Every day it's a little smaller." Everyone says that they want the world for their loved ones, but what kind of world? Is a city not a world to someone who never leaves it? How much of a world is a bed? A mind in a broken body?

"Why didn't you tell me before?" He plants his feet and turns to face me, alternating between folding his arms and clasping his hands as though he's not sure what to do with them. "We were together for years. In all that time you couldn't have told me?"

"I didn't tell anyone," I say. "I still don't. It's not that simple."

Oliver stabs the tip of his index finger toward his sternum, his chest heaving forward to meet it in midair. "I'm not anyone."

Alexis's face breaks through the murk of my thoughts, her features childish to me now. "People always leave when they know, or they're not the same anymore. They want to fix you, or they resent you because you can't keep up with them."

Oliver rips the assignment sheet from his pocket like a smoking gun, not even reading it as he resumes pacing the same path. "I could have resented you for anything. You snore and then I can't sleep. You're messy and never clean up your stuff. That's love, Brynn. Resentment is part of love, and you just deal with it."

"It's not the same. Would you just let me explain?" I plead. "You think it wouldn't change how you look at me, but it would. It always does, any time I've ever told someone the truth."

"But we were in love. That's different. We were supposed to be a team. We were supposed to trust each other." He dashes away a tear with a swipe of his fist. "I loved you. I loved you right up until about forty-five seconds ago. Because if *you* loved *me*, you wouldn't have lied to me for all these years. You couldn't have."

I attempt to apologize, but Oliver throws up a hand. "No, no, no. You don't just get to apologize and make it all go away. Words have consequences, even the ones you don't say." He collapses onto the bench and reaches out, his envelope from the museum pinched between two fingers. "Here's my secret in return: I cheated on Mr. Waller's project. I traded Brandon for your name because I missed you and I wanted to know why you abandoned me. Are you even going to tell me that? And if you do, how can I believe it?"

"I had surgery," I whisper, recalling the days in the hospital, the pain, the maddening repetition of learning to walk again. "That's the truth. I didn't want you to see me like that, and I didn't want you to waste your whole summer sitting there with me. It wouldn't have been fair to you when you had all those shows you wanted to see, those trips you were planning for us."

"Is it fair to me now?" Oliver closes his eyes and leans his forehead against mine, our tears melding into one. His lips ghost over my skin, and I feel his words as much as I hear them. "I can't stay here. I'm sorry. Goodbye, Brynn."

I don't know what else to say because there is nothing else to say. This isn't a drama for the stage, where I can find an all-powerful sorcerer or unlock the magic words to reset the score. I did this to myself, and the thing that no one ever tells you about digging your own grave is that you're never meant to climb back out.

At the edge of the garden, just before he vanishes from sight, Oliver turns back one last time. "I could have loved you in sickness or in health, but I can't love a stranger."

Nineteen

Tori doesn't answer her cell phone. She does pick up the main line for the café, but she sounds thoroughly displeased about it. "Thank you for calling Beany Beans Cat Café, home of okay coffee and bad cat puns. How may I help you?"

"It's me." I sniffle, wiping my nose on my sleeve. All my clothes are disgusting by now anyway. "Oliver left, and I'm covered in milk and stuck at the Rocky Steps."

Static blasts against my ear as she huffs a laugh into the receiver. "That's a hell of a sentence. Hang on." There's some commotion on the other end of the line, and Tori's voice grows distant. "Don't you puff up at me, mister. I rescued your ass out of a dumpster. And *you* are supposed to eat the special pee food! Stop. Eating. The. Other. OW!"

There's a grating noise that might be her chasing a cat around a chair. "Sorry," she continues. "Dinner gets very political, and if they get too worked up, this whole place'll be covered with protest vomit."

"Can you come pick me up?" I add, just in case it isn't obvious.

"Yeah, I can leave in like ten minutes." Tori catches her breath for a moment. "Cats, dude. Why?"

I love her for not pelting me with questions despite her awkward execution of playing it cool. "Thanks. I'll see you when you get here."

Tori wouldn't let me drive home without taking a nap first, but at least she keeps up her policy of not badgering me for details. She fills two grocery bags to bursting with muffins, scones, and cookies. "Call me if you need the ingredients list," she says, pecking me on the cheek after we finish loading up the car. "Come back any time except next Saturday, okay?"

"That's oddly specific."

She bops me on the nose with her index finger. "Don't be nosy. Drive safe, or whatever counts as that in New Jersey. Text me when you get home."

"I will."

I'm numb to it for mile after mile, the scenes of this turbulent day replaying in my mind piecemeal. I make it over the bridge and through the suburbs, a short stint through nowhere with farms and fields on either side. I even drive the long way through town, past the sites of dinner dates or lazy afternoons, the errands I'd run with Oliver on the way home from school to spare his nonna a second trip.

It doesn't sink in yet that I won't get up tomorrow morning and put on Pineland Prep's hideous green plaid for another day of overpriced, undelivered private education. I won't get to see how Oliver's presentation turned out—it occurs to me now that we never chose between the town house with the bookshelves or the apartment with the balcony.

Will he tell everyone what happened, dividing loyalties among our closest friends? Are they even close friends when I've never truly thought of them as that, even Francesca relegated to the outskirts of arm's length? It's just like Oliver said. I'm a stranger, and I'm bound to lose them one way or another. They'll move away or get too busy or find better friends than me.

I attempt to call Francesca and explain, but first I'm babbling too much for her to understand and then she's too livid to care. "What do you mean, you dropped out?" she shrieks. "You already did it? You

229

didn't even tell me you were thinking about it!"

"It was a split-second decision. I'm sorry. I just—"

"But why? Because of Pat? Then he just wins. How does this possibly make it any better?"

I fumble around for the words and come up short. "I can't explain. It's complicated. But I wanted to tell you."

"No," she says. "No, no, this is so not okay. You don't just tell me after the fact when it's, like, done. You want to tell me? You should have told me you were thinking about it. We could have talked about it. This is *bullshit*."

"But it was my decision—" I know I've said the wrong thing as soon as I hear the sharp intake of breath from the other end of the line.

"Oh, so I don't matter at all? I don't deserve to be in your business *because we're best friends*?" Francesca growls in frustration. "You know, I'm not doing this right now. I'd say we could talk about it tomorrow, but you won't be there because you abandoned me. Great. Guess I'll see you never. Have a great fucking life." She hangs up before I can get in another word.

I pull into the driveway a few minutes later feeling completely unmoored. The smug satisfaction of dealing with my suspension by boycotting school forever has vanished in the wake of hurting Francesca. It was so validating to write that email to Mrs. Nguyen, but now that it's done, the permanence begins to sink in. With Pineland Prep's waiting list, I wouldn't be surprised to hear that my replacement is in class by Tuesday.

The administration won't even be sorry about it. That's the real kicker. They'd fall on the floor and cling to Eliza's bizarrely muscular ankles if she even alluded to going to another school, but I'm the unextraordinary Kwan, the donut you carry around for the sake of the wheel you really want.

Eliza hasn't noticed me yet, the garage door open to let in cool air while she gets in her weekend workout. I kill the engine and retrieve the bags of desserts from Tori's. The sound of the plastic must travel because Eliza turns at the noise and lowers the music with the spin of a dial on Dad's ancient sound system.

"About time." She pauses her fitness tracker with a stolid expression that I assume is supposed to convey disappointment. "You haven't texted in hours. Mom was getting worried."

"Can you please let me get into the house before you start trying to be my third parent?" I snap, picking a path through the maze of dumbbells and agility equipment. I open the door to the house from ground level, shoving the bags inside.

"Of course," Eliza snips behind me, her voice rising note by note. "Here comes the attitude."

I whirl around in the doorway, my left leg on one stair, my right leg in the house. "How about your attitude?" But before I can manage another word, the debt from today comes due and my knee buckles, sending me plummeting to the floor in a twisted heap.

Dad leaves his crutches and hobbles over. "Don't try to pick me up," I croak at him, "or we'll both die. Watch out for the food."

Eliza and Mom rush over to help, but I wave them away and slide the few remaining feet across the tile on my stomach. I pull myself to sitting, my back propped on what I vaguely register is the leg of the dining room table. The sharp corner digs into my spine, but I don't have the energy to move again.

Mom fetches me some water and an anti-inflammatory while Dad simply drops an entire guitar-shaped saltshaker into my lap. "Your graft okay?" he asks, indicating my knee.

"I think so." I pour some salt into my mouth and push it around with my tongue as it dissolves. "I just did a lot of walking today. It was stupid." I try to roll up my leggings from the bottom to see my knee, but the fabric won't stretch enough, which is never a good sign.

I strip them off from the top down instead. Most girls would be mortified if their fathers saw them in their underwear, but medicine and modesty are such opposing priorities that we don't care. Half the county hospitals have seen my bare ass at this point.

Dad joins me on the floor to examine my knee, bending and tugging and sitting on my foot in turns. The joint is already swollen to grotesque proportions, and I attempt to follow along with the tests, the Ehlers-Danlos syndrome version of a roll call.

ME

ACL?

ANTERIOR CRUCIATE LIGAMENT
Present but suffering.

ME
PCL, how you doin'?

POSTERIOR CRUCIATE LIGAMENT
I want a new human. This human sucks.

ME
Meniscuses?

MENISCI
We're holding it together. And it's *menisci*.

I pat Dad's knuckles as he continues fussing. "It's probably fine. I'll see if it still hurts tomorrow."

"I can write you a note for PE, but they started getting antsy last time about there being so many," he says. "We might have to get a formal doctor's note."

I'm not sure what comes over me, but I'm just too worn out to craft some grand announcement. I've run the tank down to fumes. "I dropped out of school." My parents melt into two muddled figures as tears well in my eyes. "But then Oliver asked to meet up for this project, and I said okay because I just wanted to say goodbye, and we kissed, and it got really confusing. And then I told him I've been lying to him, and he hates me, and now I don't know if I ruined my whole life."

And I know better than anyone that once something breaks, you can glue it and staple it and stitch it back together, but it won't ever be quite the same again.

Twenty

Dad maneuvers to his feet, his glasses slipping down his nose and fogging with every exhale. "Don't panic yet." I'm not sure if he's talking to me or himself. "We can talk it out."

Mom sucks in a breath but lets it out at a glance from Dad. "We can talk it out," she echoes, her voice pinched.

"Let's all relocate to the living room and see what we can do," Dad suggests, pausing to swipe some papers from the kitchen counter.

Eliza comes in a moment later, sipping her sports drink and toweling off her forehead.

"Why does Eliza have to be here?" I ask. "This has nothing to do with her."

"We go to the same school," she points out. "I may have some insights."

I groan and pour myself a glass of water first. "Fine." It's not even worth the effort of attempting to set boundaries with Eliza when she'll either gerrymander or outright invade to get her way regardless.

We disperse to our designated television-watching spots on the rare occasions that we can all agree on a movie. I spread out over the length of one recliner, sniffling, my limbs poking out like a confused starfish. Eliza sits neatly in the other, not even activating the footrest. Mom and Dad claim the couch.

"I brought food from Tori's by the way," I mention, pointing to the bags. In my experience, family meetings tend to be less contentious when we're all too busy eating to scream at one another, but no one moves.

"Where do we even start?" Dad mutters, scrubbing his glasses on the edge of his T-shirt.

"School," Mom replies. "That's the most important." She takes the documents from Dad and holds them in both hands as she turns to me. "We already know that you tried to drop out of school. Mrs. Nguyen copied us on the email with the paperwork."

I check my phone and see that she replied already. I wasn't expecting a response until Monday. I scan the first page of the attachment. It's just a simple declaration that

I agree for my scholarship to be returned to the financial aid fund.

Mom blows out another breath, and I can tell that she's trying not to explode. She releases her words in clumps as though that's all the calm she can manage at once. "Did you really . . . try to drop out of school . . . without even talking to us first?"

"We talked about it the other day."

She gestures toward the front door. "You stormed out in the middle of the conversation, so that hardly counts."

"Because all you wanted to do was act like I'm a little kid and try to make me look on the bright side. There isn't always a bright side."

"It isn't always doom and gloom either, though."

"I'm banned from all the cool stuff for the rest of the year. Why bother, then?"

"I only push you to look for a bright side because you're such a pessimist," Mom says. "It's like with your condition. There are support groups and all those online resources. You never want to try—"

"You just don't get it! I've tried it all, and that's not what I want." I keep in touch with a few other people who have EDS, but mutual misery isn't a solution for everything. "There's no cure, Mom. There's no care. I'm tired and in pain every single day of my entire life. Why won't you just let me be sad about it?"

"Because being depressed isn't good for you."

"It's not depression," I say, punctuating each word with a smack of my hand against my palm. "It's grieving. And instead of just letting me do what's right for me, you have to get in my face because it's not what you think you would do. But you have no idea what you'd do because you're not like me." I glance at Dad and make an amendment. "Us."

Dad doesn't move an inch, but his eyes look first to me, then to Mom. "I'm sorry, Jenna, but I think she has a point. You have to grieve. It's natural."

"It's not natural." Mom's face crumples, her fist slamming against the top of her knee. "It's not natural because I'm her mom and I'm supposed to be able to do something."

"You can't, though," I say as gently as possible.

She throws her head back, sucking in air in great gasps, tears falling in stripes along her skin. "I'm supposed to move heaven and earth for you, and I can't even move a quack doctor to get you pain medicine or move that worthless principal to undo your suspension."

Dad draws Mom into a hug. "I feel guilty sometimes too. I knew there was a fifty-fifty chance that I'd pass it. I took the risk anyway because I wanted a family. I wanted what everyone else got to have." He tries to meet my gaze, but I don't have the strength to hold it. "Do you blame me for that?"

"No." I shake my head over and over, tears winging in every direction. "I want to sometimes, but no." I wish I could tear open my heart to show him that while a rotten kernel of resentment is there, and I'm not proud of it, it's a speck compared to how much I love him. Oliver's words float through my mind unbidden: *I could have resented you for anything.*

"Maybe having kids was a selfish choice," Dad continues. "I don't think so, though. Because without this gene, we're not here at all."

"Isn't that what the world wants?" I ask bitterly. "Like, meh, it's really hard to put a ramp on this building and hire a sign language interpreter. Let's just have eugenics."

"I get why you're bitter." He steeples his fingers, all of them bending back too far in an unintentional reminder that Dad and I are cut from the same misprinted cloth. "And we can't force you to go back to school. You're an adult, and this is your decision. Just promise me that you're really going to think this through."

"I don't have any reason to go back. Oliver hates me—" My voice breaks into a rasp, and I gulp uselessly for air as tears careen down my cheeks. "Francesca is upset that I dropped out without telling her. Even the school doesn't want me. They want Eliza. No one cares if I just disappear."

I'm not as foolish as I was in middle school when I kept waiting for someone to text or call or ask why I wasn't in ninth grade with them. I transferred to Pineland, and aside from the occasional awkward run-in with a former classmate at the grocery store, it's like I just ceased to exist.

Eliza interrupts before Dad can speak. "I agree with Francesca. I don't understand why you would drop out without consulting me when we go to the same school. I'm more than able to help you with your homework if you have trouble catching up. None of your classes are that difficult."

Once again Eliza spectacularly misses the point. If my points were *rockets flying at her face and exploding as brightly as the literal sun*, she would choose that exact moment to bend over, tie her shoe, and miss the whole thing. "If only we could all be as smart as you."

"That's not what I'm saying. I'm trying to be nice."

"Are you? Because it sounds like you're saying that my classes aren't even that hard, so why can't I just suck it up?"

"You always put freakin' words in my mouth." Eliza throws up her hands, then piles her hair into a bun onto the top of her head, snapping three hair ties around in a series of rapid twirls. "You ever notice how Mom crams all her classes into years when you and Dad don't have surgery? You ever think that maybe I'm trying to get my license as fast as I can so that you don't have to drive anymore? We're trying to help, but you won't take any of it."

"You already said I'm stupid. I don't need you to guilt-trip—"

"I'm not guilt-tripping you. Oh my God."

"You literally just called me stupid, but okay, dork."

Mom and Dad are mirror images of each other, flopped onto opposite armrests on the couch, one hand massaging identical locations on their temples. It would almost be adorable if I weren't also positive they were regretting making two loudmouths like us.

Eliza gapes at me, shrieking, "Do not call me a whale penis!"

I squint at her, bewildered. Brain fog is real, but I'm pretty sure I wouldn't forget saying that. "What? I didn't call you a whale penis."

"A dork is a whale's reproductive organ," she hisses.

"Sorry that I'm not an expert on whale dicks. Did you learn that in Advanced Placement Whale Dicks for Self-Righteous Know-It-Alls?"

Dad raises his voice above our bickering. "That's enough from both of you. Just move on to a new topic."

This is my life now. *Dear diary, at 8:17 p.m., I*

got into a heated argument with my sister about whale penises. Suddenly, I burst out in an uncontrollable guffaw, remembering that all of this from the very beginning started with a disagreement about the Sammy the Shark costume and fish dicks. I've come full circle.

Incensed, Eliza stands and punts her empty Gatorade bottle so hard that it almost hits the ceiling fan. "I was trying to say that I could have helped you study if you weren't such a witch about everything!"

I stand too, grabbing her Gatorade bottle as it rolls by and torpedoing it into the corner. "Maybe if you didn't have to make *everything* about you all the time, I would have asked you for help. But you can't just support me in the way I actually need because you know better, right? You know everything."

"I make everything about me?" Eliza shouts back. "What about you? Having to be Miss Popular and Miss Perfect? Maybe Alexis was right. Maybe you do just want attention."

I bend over at the waist, covering my ears and letting out a scream. "I HATE YOU. I HATE YOU." I don't know if I'm talking to her or myself or Alexis or this whole fucking world that after 4.543 billion years is still survival of the fittest.

A rage unlike any power I've ever felt charges through my body. I don't feel the pain in my knee anymore; I don't feel anything except that bitter, desperate fury. I storm into the garage, shrieking, my hands tearing and destroying. "How's this for perfect?" I pull down the box of keepsakes and dump it on the floor.

I take out my old softball jersey and fling it unsatisfyingly into the air, watching it hover for a moment before falling at my feet. I take out the knee pillow I needed after surgery and rip away the plastic, my fingernails bending as I unzip the cover and rip out fistfuls of foam. "Are you paying attention, Eliza?" I pitch the chunks in every direction, and I'm still angry. So, so angry.

Mom sprints out and tries to wrestle a box of orthopedic equipment away from me. "Stop being ridiculous! What are you doing? Give me it!"

The box splits at the side and random medical supplies spill out onto the floor. "Why do you even keep all of this?" I shout at her, picking up armfuls of equipment that I wore as a child. "None of this fits anymore! Just throw it away! You won't just throw it away! They're not souvenirs!"

Mom lunges for some old wrap dangling from my arm, but I dodge her, running back into the house as I toss splints and braces in every direction. I leave a trail through the kitchen and the foyer, up the stairs, and onto the landing. "Guess this is my whole life now, right? Just medical bullshit all day, all the time."

I pant in ragged breaths as I continue into my room, pausing only a moment before I fling open my closet and start snatching my uniform shirts from their hangers. "No one at school cares if I come back, so I don't need these anymore," I yell to Mom as she leaps inside and gathers up the shirts as quickly as I can throw them down.

Eliza stomps in, her mouth agape. "What is wrong with you? You are acting like such a child."

"I'm just admitting the truth. I'll never be as smart and amazing as you are. I'm just a sad, attention-seeking dingbat compared to you. You're the most wonderful person in the world." I don't have to pretend to cry into my shirts because I'm literally sobbing now. I mop my face with a sweater. "'I've never seen such—such beautiful shirts before.'"

Mom and Eliza stare at me in confusion, and it only makes me cry harder. Oliver would have known the reference instantly because God forbid we read anything from this century in English. At the thought of him, I reach behind the door and pull out my junior prom crown. I bend it until it breaks diagonally down the center, the rhinestones and beads disappearing into the carpet. I render it into unrecognizable pieces. *Snap. Snap. Snap. Snap.*

Finally the wrath drains away, replaced once more

by the pain and fatigue that's never far. "Are you done?" Mom asks from the periphery of the blast radius. "You can't just explode like this because you're upset."

"Why not?" I mumble. "Why do I have to choose from your list of preferred feelings?"

"You trashed the house!"

I lack the words to justify why I did it, but I'm not sorry. "Because maybe Eliza was right. I do want attention. No one ever listens to what I want except Dad."

"Well, this is *not* the way you express yourself," Mom says, picking up a finger splint and brandishing it at me. "You don't get to have a tantrum because you didn't get your way."

"I never get my way around here. Are you kidding?" I throw out an arm toward the highway that leads to school. "You never let me do anything you think is the tiniest bit dangerous. You never let me talk about EDS without telling me to look on the bright side. I didn't even get a real vote on moving here or changing schools or anything. I'm just not that important to you, and it's finally starting to sink in. Because you damn well bet that if Eliza had been suspended, you would have burned the school down by now. But it's just me, so who cares?"

Mom huffs, perching one hand on her hip and placing the other over her heart. "That's not fair at all. You know that I have to think about my future too, and the Zellers could make it very hard for me. It's not just because it's you. I treat you and your sister equally according to your abilities."

"You just don't get it!" I exclaim, my shoulders rising as I lean my head back, expelling each breath in angry snorts.

"Get what?"

"I. Don't. Want. To. Live. Like. This. Anymore." I crush the heels of my palms against my eyes, the tears forcing through and cascading down my arms. My breath quickens until I nearly choke on it, breaking into a moan that crescendos to a screech.

I drop my hands in the silence that follows, turning my aching eyes to the doorway where Eliza is staring, her lip trembling. "Brynn? Are you okay?"

"No, I'm not okay. Do I look okay?" To no one or maybe to everyone, I whisper, "What's the point now? Why bother?" A numb forlornness settles over me. It's not that I don't want to be alive anymore—it's that I don't know how to live the life I have.

Eliza's cheeks gleam in the low light, and I can't decipher whether she's crying or it's a trick of my own tears. "You're scaring me."

"Yup. Seconding that." Dad pushes into the room from outside, squeezing past Eliza to reach Mom. "All right, I let you try your way. I need some father-daughter time now."

Eliza takes a tentative step back, but Mom doesn't move. "Don't you think we should talk tog—"

Dad's head whips around. "Jenna, you need to give us some space. I'm not asking."

"That's not—"

"MOM!" Eliza lurches forward and grabs the hem of Mom's shirt. "JUST DO IT." She curls an arm around Mom's waist and attempts to bodily pull her along.

When I'm finally alone with Dad, I collapse onto the foot of my bed. He takes a seat next to me and gently lifts me into a sitting position beside him. "Come on, little zebra. Time for the serious talk." He shifts uncomfortably for a moment, then holds up a piece of green plastic. "First of all, why is there a kazoo under my butt?"

I crack a smile, the levity catching me by surprise. "It was probably in my bag. They give them out at football games sometimes."

Dad scowls at it with obvious distaste and tosses it away from him like it's carrying an ancient hex. "They play kazoos in hell. I cannot imagine why anyone would give kazoos to three hundred teenagers."

"You should be happy," I joke, sniffling. "That's as musical as I get."

"Speaking of happy . . ." He trails off, shooting me a pointed look and tapping his finger against his temple. "What's going on in the old skull sponge?"

"I don't even know where that came from."

"Do you feel better or worse?"

I mull it over for a moment. "Actually I guess I do feel a little better."

"When you say you don't want to live like this anymore, what's that mean?" I'm not a very touchy-feely person even on the best of days, so Dad simply twists his foot until it bumps into my toes. "Because that's a pretty big statement there."

"I'm not, like, gonna . . . I still want to be here." I want to reassure him without downplaying the bleakness that I see in front of me. "I just want my life to be different than it is. That's why I dropped out. Everything sucks, so why waste my time? I mean, it's not too late to just start over, right?"

"It's never too late to start over. Sometimes you just wake up one day and tell yourself, 'Jason, you're a twenty-six-year-old man with a toddler to look after. You have got to stop wearing eyeliner and old jeans to job interviews.'" Dad grins somewhat sheepishly, his overlong hair and over-pierced ears the last remnants of his metal-band motif. "Actually I think maybe your mother was the one who said that."

"So you're not mad that I dropped out?"

"I don't like it," Dad replies, shrugging. "But it's not my life. People want different things. I can't even begin to guess whether this is going to work out for you, and it's not really my business either way. All I want is for you to want *something*. You can't just exist. That's not enough."

But maybe that's the problem. I've wanted so many impossible wants, becoming practically sick with them. I want to be a doctor, but I can't. I want to help people like me, but I can't. I want to play softball and ride horses and run as fast as I can for no reason. I want to marry Oliver in an extravagant, ridiculous dress and impractical shoes that cost too much money. I want to think about babies without thinking about pain, betrayal, loneliness—this.

I just *want*.

Dad must practically read my mind. "This condition is hard. It takes a lot out of you. And if you can't get to the exact thing you want, then you get as close as you can. You make concessions."

I shrug. He might as well tell me the color of the sky. "I'm tired of making concessions." It's not about the condition itself—it's about the conditions it puts on everything and everyone. They sit at the very heart of me, an addendum to all that I am: *You don't belong here. This world isn't made for you.*

"Is that your final answer, then?" Dad prompts. "You're done with school?"

"I just don't see any other choice." I don't have any reason to stay when I can just start working. Instead of

Algebra II, I can pick up a couple of shifts with Tori and
Zeke; every gym class can become the nap I really need.

Yet long after Dad leaves, as I lie awake into the latest hours of night, I can't quite find any peace in the prospect of moving on. It feels too much like a door is closing
behind me and I have no way of knowing whether it's letting me go or keeping me from ever coming back.

Twenty-One

Dad knows I'm awful about remembering to charge my phone, so I'm unsurprised to find a note taped to the railing outside my bedroom door in the morning:

> *I know you're at your limit. I support*
> *whatever you want to do. Someone*
> *is offering me thirty dollars an hour*
> *if I can teach them to "scream like*
> *Chino" (impossible) while "wrecking*
> *on drums," so I'm heading out early. If*
> *you call and I don't hear my phone, it's*
> *because I'm suffering. I love you. See*
> *you when I get home.*

I have no idea who Chino is or why he's screaming, but I can empathize. Dad must suspect that I'm sorting things out in my own way because all the random crap I threw yesterday is exactly where it fell, whether cast onto random furniture or strewn over the floor.

It's not that I expect anyone else to pick up after me. It's just that we all tend to be fastidious about keeping tripping hazards out of walkways, especially in the wider paths that fit Dad's wheelchair.

"Mom?" I call as I round the corner. "Eliza?"

There's no answer. I check the schedule on the refrigerator and see that Mom's on the early shift at the supermarket. Eliza's boatmates must have picked her up already. It's bizarre that so much of my life can change while they continue on with their usual routines. "This is my surprised face," I mutter to myself. It wouldn't be the same if it were Eliza in my stead. An insult to her would be existential; she'd poison us with it.

I track down the paperwork to formalize my withdrawal from Pineland Prep and set up on the stool at the kitchen counter where Mom usually does her homework. I sign and initial through all the pages, smacking the pen down on the counter when I'm done. "There."

I expected this moment to be more triumphant, to feel more like quitting for a cause instead of just giving up. Maybe it'll sink in when I deliver the originals to the office, pack up my locker, and leave for the last time. It isn't how I thought my high school career would go, but I'm used to the universe running me off the road like a vengeful driver with a bone to pick.

When I scoot my stool back, one of the back legs catches on something. I twist around to see what it is, recognizing it instantly by its color. It's the hot-pink knee brace I used to wear before my growth spurt, the sides covered in half-peeled stickers and little crystal gems from the nail section of the beauty supply store by our old apartment.

I pick it up and turn it in the light, running my fingernail over every familiar scratch. I loved this brace, even matching it with neon-pink shoelaces. I'm suddenly crushed with a yearning to go back to those days, to just keep my mouth shut and never bother Alexis in the first place.

In fact, it all started with this brace. It upset her that people would stare or ask invasive questions. At first she really was protecting me, but then it morphed into something darker. She started alluding to the fact that I was just showing off my brace to get special treatment from teachers and boys. I wore it under my clothes after that, then every other day, then not at all if I thought anyone could see.

People changed their attitudes toward me overnight.

I liked the confidence of blending in, the way it made strangers assume I could do anything instead of deciding at a glance that I couldn't. Alexis convinced me that love-able had a look, and I convinced myself that I wanted to be that girl.

Pretending seemed easiest, even if it made my body rebel against me. She was always happy to see me and spend time with me as long as I was willing to make a few teensy changes here and there. I let her dye my hair lighter for the first time, pick my makeup, choose my accessories. It felt like making compromises for one of the only friends I had.

But as I stand here now, surrounded by braces and splints and the debris of old dreams, I realize that my entire time at Pineland has just been another repeat of playing at perfect. Somehow, even years later, I'm still her little doll.

The thought throbs in my head as I recall how much I let Alexis blur and erase what she didn't want. All this time I thought I was drawing new lines for myself, but what if I'm just retracing old forms, the scars left behind by her portraiture?

I catch a glimpse of myself in the window, my reflection distorted and insubstantial in the morning light. Dark roots spread over the crown of my skull, bleeding into the lighter milky brown. It's almost the opposite of Oliver in warmer weather, when long days spent in the sun give his hair just the slightest hints of blond as though he's soaked up the very rays of summer to save for a rainy day. I rake my fingers through that inch of natural color, wishing I could make it replace the brown even faster.

Are people the same way? If I start over, will I become less and less of Pretend Brynn and more of who I might have been all along? I don't know how to move on, not just from all the things Pretend Brynn wanted but also all the things I've lost because I wasn't willing to hold on and fight.

I let Mom tell me that I couldn't play softball anymore.

I let Alexis convince me that my braces and crutches were ugly—and that I was ugly for needing them.

I let strangers scream at Dad in the grocery store, calling him a sheep for wearing a mask and telling us to go back to China.

I let Pat frame me when I should have been proud to stand up for my friends.

That's almost half my life of just going with the flow, but giving in to the strongest current doesn't mean it won't still drag you down and drown you. I think of Eliza's face last night, that stark fear as she saw how far adrift I've gone. I scared her, yes, but I rattled myself even more.

"I don't want to live like this anymore," I whisper to myself again. Dad's response echoes in my mind: *If you can't get to the exact thing you want, then you get as close as you can.*

Maybe it isn't making concessions to admit that some things aren't possible for me. I always thought of life as a slow-ticking clock, but with my illness, it felt like I was handed a time bomb instead. What if I've spent all this time trying to sprint for the lead when I could have slowed down and enjoyed the view?

Before I know it I'm going through my morning rituals, one eye on the literal clock as I get changed, take my meds, and pack some snacks for later. Unthinking, I put on my uniform, knowing that if I stop for even a second, I'll lose whatever spark inside is trying to sputter into flame. "Oh God, what am I doing?" I mutter as I rush to clean up the worst of the mess in case Dad beats me home.

LEGS
You're not doing anything unless you find
your car keys. We are *not* walking that far.

I crawl around until I find my keys stuck under the bag of pastries from Tori's. As I hurry outside and get in the car, I remember that I left the forms sitting on the counter. I mentally add them to the list of things to clean up when I get home. I don't think I'll need them now. Unless I will. But I probably won't. Probably.

I arrive at school slightly later than I usually do when I'm behind in the mornings, but it happens so often that the security guard just points me to the main office without even pausing her conversation with a parent who's signing in. I step over the threshold and immediately turn toward Mrs. Nguyen's desk. If she's surprised to see me, she doesn't show it. "Morning," I say, the word a bit loaded with anticipation.

"Morning," she chirps, scrubbing her glasses with the hem of her blouse. She eyes my uniform. "And welcome back?"

"I changed my mind."

"I was hoping you would." Mrs. Nguyen rolls back from her desk and beckons me closer. She glances around to make sure we're still alone before leaning forward conspiratorially. "I didn't tell the principal about your email, so this can just be our little secret."

"You didn't?"

She clucks her tongue. "I don't get paid to work on the weekend, and that's that. I only emailed *you* back because you're one of my favorites."

Well, at least someone in this school likes me.

"Thanks. I owe you one. Or, you know, thirty." My already impressive list of late arrivals doesn't even include all the times Mrs. Nguyen has let me sneak into class late without marking it down on the record.

"Thirty-one," she whispers conspiratorially, filling me out a late pass. She checks the clock. "It's still first period."

"Thank you so much," I say in a measured volume, not wanting to attract any undue attention to the situation. Internally I'm screeching with happiness that what could have been a permanent mistake functionally ended up being another piece of spam. "But actually I was hoping I could talk to Principal Dombrowski for a minute."

"Just have a seat by the door. I'll check to see if he's busy."

With how often I'm here to talk about the dress code, I might as well paint my name on one of these chairs. Before I can even sit, Dudebrowski's door opens and he gestures me inside with a pained expression that says he'd rather invite Dracula to cross his threshold.

I instinctively check for frays in my pants or loose threads on my sweater. For someone who's such a stickler on dress code, Dudebrowski could do with a mirror of his own. His black dress pants are hiked up too high, making his green Pineland Prep tie hang comically long. "Ms. Kwan. Pleasure to see you again."

"Is it?" I ask as I step inside, just to set the right tone. I quickly add, "I thought the pleasure was all mine." It hits me that I'm channeling Eliza's brand of impudence, a vicious jab followed by a benign comment to make you wonder if maybe you misunderstood. "Are you having a nice morning?"

My new tactic visibly throws off Dudebrowski, who plops into his chair and purses his thin lips. "Indeterminate. What can I do for you, Ms. Kwan? There's no need to check in with me before you go to class. Your suspension is complete."

"I want to appeal my suspension. How do I do that?"

"You don't," he replies. "This isn't a court system. You broke the rules, and we're within our rights to suspend you for that."

"But there's no proof." I wince at how flimsy that sounds. "If there's a lack of proof on both sides and witnesses on both sides, then how can you just choose one over the other? Can't I go to the board? They can overturn anything. Clear my record. Whatever." I've seen how quickly they quash even a hint of change from the status quo.

But I'm done with bullies, whether they wear suits or white coats or Pineland Prep lacrosse jerseys. I've seen where it leads if I let people take and take and take. I sink back in my seat and fold my arms to make it clear that I can be exceptionally annoying if I want to be. Before they had the leverage because I still had something to lose. How much lower can you push someone who's already at rock bottom?

Dudebrowski relents under the force of my stare. "I can make some calls, but I'll warn you that the board frowns upon this sort of thing."

The board frowns upon a lot of things.

"They were already involved with the original investigation," he continues, "so I don't know what you hope to accomplish."

"I'd still like to make an appeal."

Dudebrowski consults his blotter, the paper patterned with coffee rings. He traces his finger past the crossed-out boxes and taps on a square. "The next board meeting is tomorrow at two thirty. Otherwise the next one isn't until early November due to homecoming activities."

I nod, a ripple of nausea setting off my nerves. "I'll have something ready for tomorrow then." I stand slowly, feeling my heart rate spike and settle. "Thank you."

I wave goodbye to Mrs. Nguyen and step out into the hallway. I stare at the floor and watch my feet carry me forward, crossing from one tile to the next to the next on the way to Life Skills. As much as I might feel aggrieved by all that's happened, every story has its spin. And in Oliver's, I'm the worst kind of villain there is—the kind you love.

Twenty-Two

I've missed homeroom and half the period, but I don't think that's why everyone in Life Skills seems shocked by my presence. "Sorry," I say to Maria and Brandon as they freeze in the middle of their presentation. "I had to stop by the office."

I hand Mr. Waller my late slip, which he tosses in the trash without even reading. "I guess I have some outdated information," he volunteers, glancing in Oliver's direction. "I didn't think you'd be here . . . today." I hear the implied *. . . or ever.*

Oliver folds himself over a notebook and continues scribbling, not sparing me even a speck of his attention. Francesca at least shoots me a quizzical glance from the back of the room, her brows pressed flat.

I don't know what to say, so I just scurry to my seat and try not to interrupt more than I already have. "What were we talking about?" Maria whispers, consulting their collage. Brandon remembers a moment later and breaks back into a boisterous description of how he's going to be a veterinarian. "And I picked this profession because people are trash and dogs make you feel awesome."

Judging by Mr. Waller's grimace, I'm not sure that's the soul-searching justification he was hoping for when choosing our dream jobs. I doodle all over Mr. Dombrowski's portrait in the front of my agenda book, forcing myself not to look at Oliver while I wait for Mr. Waller to be distracted enough for me to pass a note back to Francesca. *I'm sorry. I'm an asshat buttface.* I draw a little stick figure with a butt-shaped hat and a butt for a head.

I'm pretty sure there are houseplants with better hand-eye coordination than me, so I smush the paper into a ball and drop it on the ground instead. We've had better luck with me kicking notes backward with my heel than Francesca has sending them forward. She once sent a note whizzing all the way to the front of the room and only persuaded Mr. Waller to return it unread by promptly dissolving into a human puddle.

I know this particular message is received when I hear a muffled giggle from the rows behind me. I don't think that means I'm fully forgiven, but it's a start. I smile and applaud politely as Brandon and Maria wrap up their presentation. I haven't seen Brandon since our trip to the office, but at least he seems to be on the mend. Then again, appearances can be deceiving.

Mr. Waller consults his watch. "Well, we do have time for one more." He hesitates with his hand extended toward the bag with our names in it. "In fairness, Brynn, your group is really up next. I drew your name earlier, but since you weren't here, I picked again."

Oliver's resulting sigh is so prolonged that even Mr. Waller looks uncomfortable.

Oh. Right. The project.

I follow Oliver back up to the front with great reluctance. He communicates only with gestures and single-word mumbles until we're roughly set up in a sensible manner with one of us on each side and the poster board in between. At least we don't have to look at each other.

"In the future I hope to be working as a playwright," Oliver says, an opening statement that surprises absolutely no one. "Since I'm planning to go to Drexel if I get in, I chose Philly for my city." He continues on like this, speaking only of his own affairs, as though even the fake roommate version of me doesn't register on his radar.

When it's my turn, I realize that I could just read from the poster, but now that Oliver knows the truth, what does it matter? "The first time I filled out my dream occupation and my salary and all that, it was a lie." I pause for a beat, searching for that galvanizing spark I felt this morning.

"I wrote that I want to be a doctor. And while that's true, it's never going to happen." I take a deep breath, and Francesca gives me an encouraging smile from the back of the room. She has no clue what I'm about to say, but here she is, cheering me on. I've taken a lot of missteps lately, but my choice in friends isn't one of them.

"I have a disability that I've never talked about before, and I wouldn't make it through clinicals or residency. Medicine isn't like in the TV shows where the doctors are all amazing and spending hours hunting down every possibility. In real life a lot of us with chronic illnesses get told we're fat, hypochondriac little girls who watch too many TikTok videos and want to feel special."

I point to my part of the worksheet on the collage. "When you're sick, no one wants to give you a chance or make any space for you. They used to say it was impossible for us to fit in, but when the whole world got sick with COVID, then our entire society made it happen for the majority. It was okay to call out sick. It was okay to need help. Why can't that just be all the time?"

I quote a few lines from the budget to stay even marginally on topic. "I know I'm rambling and that half of this doesn't even make sense, but my whole point is, Mr. Waller, that I can't do this project the same way that other people can. I can't stick to a budget if I'm suddenly unable to drive or I have to go to the ER unexpectedly for, oh, let me just make something up— getting punched in the face at a pep rally. And before anyone says to just go on disability, that pays less than minimum wage.

"So I know this isn't really the assignment, but my life and my future just don't fall into all these neat little categories. I'm tired of trying to squeeze into the tiniest space that's left for me. I'm tired of having my permanent record ruined because I don't have fancy lawyer parents who are rich enough to buy the school new locker rooms." Then again, I should have seen this coming from my first day. I've always been a lower-class outlier in this school that reeks of old money. "You know, I almost dropped out when I got suspended because it felt so hopeless. But now I'm filing an appeal with the board. At least then I can say I tried."

Brandon slams both fists onto his desk hard enough for the legs to briefly leave the floor. He stares at me, jaw clenched, his head nodding and nodding and nodding. "You're right," he says to no one in particular. "I worked so hard to get recruited by this school. And now my whole five-year plan, my whole life just gets blown up because someone swung at me? What if I can't get into veterinary school now?" He stands and slings his backpack over one shoulder, the main compartment still half-unzipped. "Can I go talk to the principal?"

"Now?" Mr. Waller says, his mouth opening and closing soundlessly. "Um, maybe this would be better for after class when you've had a chance to calm down."

"I don't want to calm down," Brandon snaps, gesturing to the door. "Can I?"

Mr. Waller sweeps his arm in an identical motion. "I won't stop you. Last I checked, this is Life Skills. Standing up for what you believe in is an important one." Unease ripples through the room as Brandon's heavy footsteps clap against the tile in the hallway. Side conversations break out, and I hear my name and Pat's over and over again.

"That's exactly it," I say. "That's the problem with this assignment. Life isn't just filling in the blanks of what you do and where you go and who does the dishes." Before the fight with Pat I thought everything felt so hard because there's no support for disabled people. But now I see that it's so much more insidious.

"We're all fighting our own demons, except that some people get a magic wand and some of us get a stick. And sometimes it seems like it's just easier to run away and hide wherever you can." I glance at Oliver, but his gaze is fixed firmly on a poster along the back wall. "But then you're not living anymore."

Mom and Dad wanted us to come to Pineland in the hopes that it would be better, yet it ended up just being more of the same. The world tries to chew up anyone who isn't in the lead, and most of the people in front are too afraid of stumbling to look back. I can't do anything to change the world, but maybe I can change this tiny little piece of it by showing Pat that I won't just go away.

I obviously didn't have much of a plan for my speech, so I'm not sure where to leave it. I turn back to Mr. Waller, shrugging. "That's it, I guess."

"Thank you, Brynn," he says, his tone oddly formal. "That was a very creative take on the assignment."

And that's a very creative way of saying I didn't follow the rubric at all.

Now that we're done, it's like all the nerves in my body resume firing at once, and I'm suddenly aware that I've been standing in front of an entire classroom ranting about life for ten minutes. Eyes crawl over my skin, feeling as tangible as any touch. A smattering of uncomfortable applause breaks out in the ensuing silence. Maybe that was the point of this whole monologue: I want people to feel uncomfortable. I want them to see just how much some of us have to bend to let one insult after another roll off our backs.

The length of the aisle seems to stretch into infinity, and I can't get my legs to take a single step forward. The slick poster board is slippery in my sweaty palms as I pinch my fingers tighter, feeling the crunch of the foam compressing. My heart rate alarm goes off, buzzing on my wrist.

"I have to . . ." I don't wait for Mr. Waller to respond. I rush from the room, overwhelmed by it all and needing a moment alone. I sit on the closest bench and lean my head against the wall, sighing. I told everyone. I did it. The emotions churn in my chest, tumbling from one extreme to the next.

But the halls around me remain utterly still, and I can't decide if the silence is peaceful or haunting. I thought that all the things Pretend Brynn perfected—the fake smile, the makeup, the laugh—were my armor, but now they feel like endless layers of costumes I have to shed to find my own skin.

I startle when the bell rings far earlier than I expected. Oliver is the second person out the door, the sole of his shoe squeaking on the tile as he pivots to his left and marches into the current of students flowing toward the gym. He doesn't spare me a look, a word.

I lean over, forearms balanced on my thighs, and ignore the lingering spikes of pain in my shoulder from holding up the poster. Two pairs of sneakers appear in my vision, followed by my backpack being set on the ground.

"Hey," Francesca says. "You left your bag."

"Thanks."

Amber and Francesca shuffle a bit when I don't say anything else, now standing sideways as though they're not sure whether to stay or go. "I kind of filled Amber in about everything," Francesca says quietly, tilting her head toward Mr. Waller's classroom. "I hope that's cool."

"Yeah. It's not a secret."

It's not a secret.

It's not a secret.

"I had zero clue that you're—that you're, um, disabled," Francesca says to the floor, her cheeks flushing as she parses the words. "You're one of my best friends. I feel like I should have known that about you."

Only Francesca could make my lies of omission seem like her failings. "It's not your fault. I didn't tell you. I didn't tell anyone." I glance between her and Amber. "I just thought no one would want to be my friend if they knew the truth. Is that ridiculous?"

She hums for a moment, thinking. "A little? We've been friends this whole time. We already like you."

It sounds so simple and obvious when it's put plainly like that. But Alexis used to like me too. Yet the more I asked her to make space for me, the more territorial she became. It wasn't enough to be there for her, to think of her as the sister I chose instead of the one I had. By the end I could only mention my health in bits and dollops without poisoning the recipe for her friendship.

"I'm not saying it's the same thing, but I understand a little," Francesca adds. "Coming out was really scary for me. That's part of the reason I transferred here from Catholic school. I get that sometimes you have to tell your secrets on your own terms."

"I just didn't want everyone to treat me differently," I confess, recalling all I did to keep everyone at arm's length. "Some of my friends from middle school . . . It's a long story. I've been a bad friend. I'm sorry."

"Yeah, you kind of suck," Amber jokes. "That's what I'm putting under your picture in the yearbook."

"Are we okay?"

Francesca flaps her hands at me insistently until I step forward into a hug, letting her rock me side to side for a few beats. "Yes, but you totally made me want to throw up yesterday at the thought of being stuck here without you. Don't you dare drop out."

Before the warning bell can ring, I give them the abridged version of my conversation with the principal this morning. "I think Kayla went too," Amber tells me. "I passed her and Brandon on my way here. They both looked pissed."

"I wonder if they'll come talk to the board with me. I have no idea what I'm doing."

"Well, about that—" Francesca cuts off midsentence, her eyes flicking to a space just over my shoulder. "Why is security coming toward us?" she says through gritted teeth, her lips barely moving.

I turn around just in time to see the guard from the front office beckoning me closer. "Brynn Kwan?" she asks. "The office would like a word."

Here's a word for you: *shit*.

Twenty-Three

"You can just come in now, Ms. Kwan," Principal Dombrowski calls as I try to take a seat outside his office, his exhausted tone sounding like he'd rather have breakfast with Hannibal Lecter than talk to me twice in one morning.

"Hi," I say awkwardly, feeling unprepared without knowing what this is about. I sit in the same chair as before, folding and unfolding my legs in a futile attempt to make the hard edge of the chair stop digging into my thighs.

Dudebrowski sighs again, the wrinkles along his forehead multiplying as he glowers at me. "Ms. Kwan, I know you're concerned about appealing your suspension, but sending your friends down here in some kind of protest isn't going to earn you any favors. I have a lot to do today that doesn't involve dealing with things above my pay grade."

"I didn't tell anyone to come here."

He ignores me and continues on with only a pause for breath. "I passed along your request for a meeting to the board, but they don't seem inclined toward leniency given your other violations for dress code, cursing, and unladylike behavior. If you don't want your suspension to become an expulsion, there might be other places that are better for your efforts than arguing against the board."

I narrow my eyes, bristling at the revelation that every time I'm in this office I'm being threatened. "So you're saying that I can either eat my suspension or risk getting expelled."

"When you enrolled you agreed to maintain a clean disciplinary record as a requirement of your scholarship," Dudebrowski explains, scanning the doorway to make sure no one else is waiting outside. "I'll tell you what I told Ms. Rivera and Mr. Mosley just a few minutes ago. The directors have the final say on what's an excessive number of infractions. If I were you, I wouldn't rock the boat."

"Is that a crew joke?"

He sighs again. "I'm glad your sense of humor remains intact, but I think your parents might take it a bit more seriously since they'll be the ones paying the penalties."

"Penalties?"

Dudebrowski spins in his chair and slides over to a four-drawer filing cabinet in the corner. He riffles through the folders and rolls back to hand me a weighty packet of papers held together with a binder clip. "Part seven discusses our standards of behavior for scholarship students."

I flip through the pages and skim it as quickly as I can, but it's written in such formal legal language that it might as well be another dialect. Maybe that's the point. "What's all this mean?"

"That section just says that the board has the right to assess financial penalties against scholarship students who fail to complete the year. It's meant for athletic scholarships to keep our athletes from leaving in the middle of the season to play for other schools. However, students who leave midyear for other reasons or get dismissed for disciplinary infractions are also technically subject to that clause."

"How much is the penalty?"

"Up to the full cost of tuition," Dudebrowski answers with obvious reluctance. He consults a paper pinned to the bulletin board on the wall beside him. "This year that comes to $19,522."

Panic sends every system into high alert. The fuzziness

of fatigue sharpens into hyperfocus as my chaotic nervous system dumps a tidal wave of neurotransmitters into my bloodstream. We don't have $19,522, and I'll be damned if I trust the board of directors to cut me a break out of the kindness of their hearts.

"Do you understand what I'm saying to you?" Dudebrowski asks, and for a moment his tone takes on a different type of urgency. "This isn't a can of worms you can close."

I nod, too stunned to manage more than that. I simply stand up and leave without another word, my throat aching as I fight to keep my tears from falling. It's so indescribably unfair to say that I can't leave without incurring a "penalty" while also making it intolerable to stay.

Plenty of my peers could afford to pay for another year's tuition without too much heartache, but not me. Mrs. Nguyen writes me a hall pass, and I hustle to Algebra II like my life depends on it—because it might. For me and Dad, $19,522 isn't just money we need for our living expenses. It's money we need for living at all.

This morning I thought I was untouchable. After all, how much lower can you push someone who's already at rock bottom? But now I see that they don't have to shove me down deeper when there's no way up and no way out.

Brynn [9:37 A.M.]: I told principal dudebro
that I wanted to appeal my suspension instead
of dropping out and kind of had a public
meltdown in mr wallers class and now the
school is mad and the board threatened me by
saying I'm on disciplinary warning and if they
want to they can kick me out of school and
make us repay my entire scholarship so help

[Missed call from Dad]

[Missed call from Dad]

[Missed call from Dad]

Dad [9:37 A.M.]: Call me right
now.

Brynn [9:37 A.M.]: I'm in class
texting you on the sneak

Mom [9:40 A.M.]: They told us
that was just for athletes. They
threatened you?

Brynn [9:40 A.M.]: what do

Dad [9:41 A.M.]: I'm calling the
office.

Eliza [9:45 A.M.]: . . .

Even though it just happened this morning, the news of
my presentation and three-student mutiny seems to pre-
cede me everywhere I go. Whispered conversations end
abruptly as I pass in the hallway, and people show way
more of their teeth when they smile at me in passing.

I don't know how to read it. Everyone's actions and
words are suddenly glazed over with a veneer of forced
politeness. Even my teachers seem dodgy. I can't tell if
they're treating me differently because they know I'm
disabled or because they're afraid I'll incite a riot in their
classroom. Maybe both.

I've missed so much class that I'm glad to be left alone
while I frantically attempt to catch up before the board
finds some way to weaponize my GPA, too. I didn't
actually do any of the homework that Eliza brought
home while I was suspended, so my previously lackluster
grades are now . . . lacking even more luster.

"I can send you my notes," TJ offers in American
History when he senses my distress. "I can't promise
they'll make any sense."

He slides his notebook across the table until it's easy

for both of us to read. I snap a picture with my tablet. "Thanks. Honestly I'll take whatever help I can get." Fortunately, this class has had a revolving stream of temporary substitutes who are unusually generous with their grading. "I wonder if they'll accept my work from last week if I turn it in as soon as I can."

"Probably. You can just wait until we change teachers and tell them you got permission. They'll never know."

"That's devious."

"No one suspects the farm boy," TJ replies, and it's true that there's something endearing about his terrible sunglasses tan and earnest smile.

Even so he only makes it about four more minutes before badgering me about the rumors just like I knew he would. "But really, I'm dying to know. Is it true that you're going to argue with the board?"

"I don't think I can. Dombrowski basically told me to drop it because the board can try to expel me for being a bad girl who shows her ankles in public and picks fights with upstanding students like Pat." I cut off abruptly as the teacher notices us. I pretend to be diligently taking notes for a moment before waiting for her to turn around again. "Do you know there's seriously a violation for unladylike behavior?"

TJ hums to himself. "Yeah, there's also one for ungentlemanly conduct. I got cited for having dirty fingernails." He holds up his agenda, where a condensed summary of the rules is printed in the opening pages. He flicks his wrist and pretends to chuck it at the ceiling. "Let's just fling this whole thing into the sun."

"Mood," I grumble, opening my own to share my mustachioed doodle of Dombrowski's staff picture. "They can also come after you for tuition if you leave or get kicked out, which is complete ass. How is that even fair?"

"What about any of this situation has been fair?" TJ deadpans. "Pineland Prep is not here to be fair. That's the whole point of the school."

With so much money potentially on the line, I'm itching to know whether Mom and Dad have any other ideas of how to respond. Part of me regrets my earlier bravado, and I can't help but wonder if the board would have been so interested in reclaiming my scholarship money if I'd just dropped out.

To make things worse, I run into Oliver more times in the hallway than I ever have before, even when we were intentionally trying to meet up in between classes. Every time he marches by, only acknowledging me with the slightest shake of his head that says *don't bother*.

I'm exhausted by the time I make it to the cafeteria. Well, I'm always exhausted, but this is different somehow. I don't like being boxed in, and I can sense the chaotic swirl of panic just below the surface, waiting to explode if just one more thing goes wrong.

It doesn't take long to figure out what that thing is. As soon as I grab my tray of chicken nuggets and start heading for our usual table, Pat throws out an arm and waves at me with such gusto that half the students turn around to watch. The buzz of conversation cuts out as he rises to his feet, not quite blocking my path.

"Hey, Brynn," Pat calls out, intentionally pitching his voice to carry as far as possible. "I heard about your 'disability.'" He puts the last word in air quotes. "We all know you're the dumb sister, but having to fake being special ed just to graduate is a whole new level."

Some people break out in laughter while others gasp and start to whisper to their friends. A few of the under-classmen are visibly horrified, but of course no one says a word. Pat's friends are the loudest, and even though I hate them all, I can't stop myself from reacting.

I eye my table like it's home base, seeing that Amber, Francesca, and Ethan are already waiting. My mind urges me to scurry over to my allies, but I'm tired of running away. I'm tired of letting people destroy me from the outside in.

The rage that's boiled in my chest for weeks detonates as all the fury and resentment pour forth. I lurch forward, preparing to swing my tray straight into his face and become the self-fulfilling prophecy the board has made me into—but a familiar voice stops me in my tracks.

"Ha. Ha." Eliza prances into the cafeteria, everyone's eyes turning to her as she makes a beeline for Pat. She pauses, somehow managing to look down her nose at him despite being six inches shorter. "Pat, your parents had to build an entire *locker room complex* for you to even get admitted to Pineland. That's how profoundly unremarkable you are. Sit down."

Eliza doesn't wait for him to respond. She brushes by as the laughter breaks out again, this time accompanied by a fair bit of heckling. Pat tries to retort, but Eliza's disinterest is so intense that if she hears him at all, it doesn't even register.

"That was some badass shit," Ethan gushes, staring at my sister with wide eyes.

Eliza takes a seat on the other side of the table where there's a slight gap between Amber and Ethan. "Thank you."

"What are you doing here?" I ask. "Besides kicking Pat's ass."

"Someone call that kid an ambulance," Amber mutters.

Ethan waves her off. "You don't need an ambulance. That was an ice-cold assassination."

Eliza acts like she isn't soaking up the praise, but I know that her relentless obsession with winning also applies to moments like these. She clears her throat, and I lean in to hear her answer to my question. "I got your text, and I just had a meeting with Principal Dombrowski. I told him that I've had offers from competing schools, so if the Kwans aren't welcome here, then maybe I have to consider my options."

"The Kwans? Like, you and me?" I ask, pointing to myself as though Eliza keeps one of our third cousins stashed in her locker or something.

She flings her head back in annoyance, tossing her ponytail. "Yes, obviously you, Brynn." She hesitates and lowers her voice until only I can hear. "You said I should be more supportive, so I'm supporting."

"But if we both leave, wouldn't that just be twice as much money?"

Eliza scoffs. "The board knows how much it'll lose by alienating all its athletes. Things have already been tense since the fight. They won't risk more people leaving because it'll hurt their reputation with their benefactors. Plus I could just work the cost of the penalty into negotiations with other schools. That's what Amanda did when she went to St. Mary's."

"It's true," Ethan agrees. "All their advertising depends on having the best student athletes. Not to be all full of myself, but we are pretty solid."

"It makes a lot of sense when you put it that way," I

say to both of them. Everything has become so muddled in my mind that I lost sight of how it all began. The administration backed Pat for his family's money, so it stands to reason that they'd switch sides if we can counter with an even bigger sum at stake.

"We might have a chance," Eliza muses, though her phrasing doesn't exactly inspire confidence. "Principal Dombrowski said—strictly off the record of course—that he can't alienate a major donor to the school when there's no proof that Pat is lying about you attacking him. However, if you can convince the directors to overturn your suspension, he can remove the other penalties as well."

"Sounds like he just wants to cover his ass," Ethan mutters.

When I don't immediately react, Eliza clarifies, "I'm telling you that you can have your old life back. Isn't that what you wanted?"

Is it?

Francesca inhales sharply and latches on to my bicep with both hands. "Pur-rom!" she exclaims, her enthusiasm making it into two syllables. "The board can save you. You have to try! You can still be queen!"

"Okay, so you think I should still go to the meeting tomorrow?" I ask Eliza, tempering my expectations. "Or do I just send them an email?"

"No, you don't just *send them an email*." Eliza points to the administration wing. "They meet in the big conference room. If you want to fight back, then you need to build a case."

I check the time on my phone. The meeting isn't even thirty hours away. "What if I can't come up with anything to say by tomorrow? It's still just my word against Pat's. I need some kind of new argument, right?"

"We can do it!" Francesca gives me a sideways half hug, tugging my arm as she sways back and forth. "I'm not going to let you get kicked out."

RIGHT SHOULDER
I'm about to get kicked out of this socket if she doesn't stop that.

I press my hand over hers. "That really hurts my shoulder."

Francesca whips her hands away so abruptly that she would have tottered backward off the bench if not for Amber's reflexes. She barely takes a moment to recover before repeating, "We can do it. We just need a plan that's a hundred percent completely amazeballs. And at least you won't have Pat's parents standing right there being douche-canoes. No wonder he's such a—"

"Weasel?" Ethan suggests.

She lets out a whimper and looks at him aghast. "Don't be mean to weasels. They're cute." She curls her fingers into pretend paws and mimes running. "They have such tiny legs."

"I have to go to class now," Eliza announces, pulling her legs back through the bench and standing. To me, she adds, "We can discuss the meeting tonight when I get home from practice."

"Thanks," I reply, the word seeming inadequate for what she's done. "Really, thank you."

She shrugs as though she's always had my back instead of making me look over my shoulder at every turn. "Don't worry about it."

I stifle a laugh as I see a few people unconsciously scoot away from Eliza as she heads for the door. Ethan taps a chicken nugget against the edge of his tray. "So what are you gonna do?"

Without Eliza there to make it seem simple, I can't focus enough to corral my priorities. My solution to not melting down over Oliver was to stop thinking about much of anything at all. "I guess I have to look up who's even on the board."

Amber lets out a hacking cough and sips at her apple juice.

"Actually," Francesca interjects, "my mom might totally definitely be one of the directors."

We all stare at her in unison. Since Pineland Prep is a private school—as they never let us forget—the board of directors has the final say on everything. It's like Francesca just casually admitted her mom is Speaker of the House. "When did that happen?" I ask. I swear that I've seen their names before, even though all their announcements are signed collectively.

"She ran for a seat to stop them from being so gross about stuff. You know. Mrs. Clem writing me up for saying 'queer' because she insists it's a slur when I'm a full flannel-wearing, U-Haul-ing pansexual over here. How no one can have a Black Lives Matter sticker, but Lisa's Confederate flag pin is totally just misunderstood American pride." Francesca takes a calming breath. "It's all just gross."

"U-Haul?" I ask, losing the thread a bit on her rant. "You're moving?"

Amber and Francesca burst out laughing, and I get the impression that I've missed some kind of joke. "I love you too," Amber says, planting a kiss on Francesca's cheek.

"Anyway, my point is that my mom can definitely give you some advice," Francesca says. "She only joined this year, but she's still been to a few meetings."

It just doesn't seem like enough time. "I mean, would she be able to meet up tonight? I feel like sooner is better because Dudebrowski said the next meeting isn't until after homecoming. Maybe I could ask my mom for help too." I mull it over, starting to see a plan take shape. "Or we can just hang out and let them scheme."

Francesca pulls out her phone and gestures for Amber to move closer. "Cover me. I'll see if I can get a text out." She types a few words and pauses. "Where would you want to meet?"

"My house?"

She lofts a brow without looking up from her phone. "Did you just . . . ask me if I want to come over?"

It's a line we've never crossed before. We meet at restaurants or coffee shops or Francesca's palace, but I've always been too nervous to have friends over. I make up excuses about Mom having an important test or exaggerate how much you can hear Dad practicing, but in reality I'm just a coward who was too afraid of what others might see.

"You don't have to if you don't want." I backtrack, unsure of how to read Francesca's reaction. Maybe I've pushed too hard.

"I'd love to come over." She gasps so suddenly that Amber and I both jump. "We could have a movie night sometime. A sleepover! Why have we never done anything fun together ever besides go shopping or eat pancakes or sit in my basement?"

"We could also check out my cousin's cat café. It's in Philly. I think you'd really like it."

Francesca's mouth falls open in a silent scream of excitement. "What kind of kitties are there? Can you just pick them up and carry them around with you?"

"Look what you've done," Amber mutters. "Now she'll be like this for days."

Twenty-Four

We manage to cobble together a loose plan over text messages and notes. Francesca's mom agreed to come over this evening to see what kind of argument we can put together. I invited Kayla and Brandon, but both declined, telling me that they're working on leads of their own. I guess we're all in this together.

I leave school in a daze, my imagination on overdrive as it spits out a thousand different possible outcomes. I cycle through all of Dad's techniques to make them stop, but the doom machine in my brain is stuck in on-mode as I pull out from the parking lot.

I find myself taking unplanned turns, my hands and eyes and feet colluding to kidnap me as I skip the entrance to the highway and head into the outskirts of the next town over. Yet deep down I know that I could never have stayed away for long.

If I'm going to battle to change so many other things, I can't refuse the kernel of hope in my heart that urges me to fight for Oliver too. If we're not meant to be, I want to be forsaken for who I am, not who I pretended to be.

When I get to Oliver's house, his SUV is already in the driveway next to a newer one of the same model. Summoning my courage, I slam my door to announce my arrival and trek across the yard to the front step. Once I might have opened it a fraction, sticking my head in and calling to see if it was okay to come in. I was welcome—a regular.

But I'm a different person now, so I merely press the bell and stand back to put my face in the frame of the camera. From inside I hear footsteps and voices, the stomping of feet as someone heads up the stairs just in front of the door.

Oliver appears in his bedroom window, his face tilted downward in my direction. I raise a hand a few inches in an uncertain wave. He doesn't move, just staring at me, his expression muddled by the reflection of the late afternoon.

When I see his palm press against the window, fingers splayed, I almost manage to convince myself that I could climb the tree next to his house and make it onto the roof. I wouldn't have to endure the awkwardness of seeing his mom and his grandmother. We could just be alone for a minute. People climb trees all the time in movies, right?

ALL BODY PARTS
(simultaneously)
Do you want to enter the afterlife? This is
how you enter the afterlife.

But this isn't a movie, and if my inability to effortlessly climb trees doesn't convince me of that, Oliver does when I realize that he isn't longingly pressing his palm to the window in his desperation to reach me. No, he was simply steadying himself as he reached for the pull string of the blinds.

The distance is too far to truly lock eyes, but we hold something close to contact as he lets the string slowly feed through his grip until the blinds fall between us.

I replay the scene about seventy thousand times in between leaving Oliver's house and making it home to wallow. Dad's already finished work for the day, and he patiently lets me word-vomit about Oliver. "Is it possible to die of embarrassment?" I groan, letting my forehead smack against the counter. "I can't believe I thought he was reaching out for me."

"I'm not gonna lie," Dad admits, wincing. "That is pretty cringe."

I mush my face even harder against the laminate countertop, tears trickling from my eyes and soaking into the curtain of hair around me. "Isn't it?"

Dad uses his grabber to retrieve the tissue box by the sink and deposit it in front of me. "I'm sorry. I hope he comes around soon."

I can't stop crying, though. At least not until Dad picks up a tissue and dangles it over my ear like a cat with a teaser toy. "Da-aad!" I bleat, laughing as I paw at the tissue. "You're so annoying!"

"There's a smile," he says, returning one of his own. "Would cereal make it better?"

"Sure. Cap'n Crunch still loves me."

"Oliver still loves you too," Dad insists, sending bowls and spoons spinning across the counter and rotating his wheelchair in place to get the pantry open. "He just needs to extract head from butt."

I pour us each a heaping serving of cereal, mine with too much milk and Dad's with just a dribble. "I don't know how you eat it that way. Don't the corners stab you in the mouth?"

"Yeah, but who wants to eat soggy cereal? It gets all mealy. I'd rather just have Suffer Crunch." He chews for a moment, the sound almost comically loud.

"Speaking of suffering, how was school? Eliza mentioned you were maybe sorting things out together with some friends?"

I roll my eyes at his thinly concealed delight over us actually getting along for once. "Yeah, Francesca's mom is supposed to come over tonight." It's then that I realize why the house is so spotless. "Oh no. Dad, I'm so sorry. I left this place a mess."

"That's okay," he says. "It wasn't actually that much stuff. Just a lot of trash."

"I should have asked if we could have company. I'm sure we can meet somewhere else if you just need to sleep."

"Nah, I'll live. I'll make it up tomorrow. I don't have anywhere to be in the morning. Plus I want to hear what's going on with this whole board fiasco."

I hate being the reason that Dad has to do less tomorrow to make up for today, but I don't push it. We've both made mistakes before, and it definitely isn't easy on days when we're both barely able to get out of bed. I just need to be better about thinking of him too instead of getting so wrapped up in my own world.

Maybe that's true of everyone to some extent. I've been selfish, always looking inward instead of truly investing in what was happening around me. I can't help but wonder how much I've missed by looking in the entirely wrong direction.

"Your mom's back." Dad's words break me free of my reverie as he hurries to put away the milk and cereal. I grab our bowls and rinse the crumbly, orange residue, hiding them in the dishwasher just as the door to the garage opens.

Mom is obsessed with having dinner together as a family. Dad blames a parenting seminar they took before I was born, but I think it probably has more to do with the fact that my grandparents eat on the couch and ignore each other. Either way she strongly discourages us from eating junk after school, so the rest of us tend to make snacking a covert operation.

Dad wipes his face one more time for good measure. "You're home late."

"I stopped at the college to get some books for this beatdown I'm giving the school board tomorrow," Mom says, heaving her bag after her and plopping it onto the table. She glances between us, then frowns at Dad's wheelchair. "Not a good day?"

"I was playing drums all morning," he clarifies, shrugging. "Good day for music. Bad day for leg. It balances out."

Mom grinds some coffee and fills a gigantic mug with *Live Laugh Lawsuit* printed on one side and the scales of justice on the other. She adds two Splendas and a splash of milk, hefting the jug once before putting it back in the fridge. "Where'd all the milk go?"

"I ate it," Dad blurts. "Drank it."

"Tell me next time so that I can bring some home from the store." She points at the embroidered shopping cart on her Smart Cart shirt. "God, I swear that's the only perk of still working at that place."

Dad sighs. "Well, I hear if you stop going, they stop sending money. At least they're paying for some of your tuition."

"Yeah. One class."

Guilt pools in my stomach, and it isn't about the milk. "I'm sorry about my tuition and the board. I didn't know they could, like, fine us. No one ever told me."

"It's okay," Mom says. "We didn't think it was relevant. They made it sound like it was a retention thing for athletes." She takes a long drink from her mug. "This whole thing sounds suspicious in general."

Dad nods. "It's so sketchy. And it's not your fault. It sounds like they're trying to pick and choose the rules because you won't toe the line." He briefly recounts his worthless phone call to the school, where they basically told him to deal with the board and leave them alone. "I just don't know why they'd risk antagonizing Eliza. Don't they realize she's terrifying?"

I almost tell them about how she stood up to Pat today, but something gives me pause. As much as Eliza enjoyed the limelight, I don't think that's why she did it.

Mom relocates to the table and begins spreading out her reference books. "I can be terrifying too."

"Oh, I know," Dad drawls. "I have to sit next to you when they do our taxes, remember?"

I spend the next couple of hours talking through the appeal with Mom and listening to her rationale about the best way to approach the situation. Her ideas for an argument are wishy-washy at best, and Dad has long since retreated to the couch to play video games.

It's almost comical listening to the two of them, Mom self-narrating her internet searches while Dad talks to his game. Most people might find the noise distracting, but we're so used to tuning out the noise of instruments and Eliza's never-ending video study group that it doesn't even register that much on my radar.

"We just need to find some weakness in the evidence they think they have."

"I only need one more ancient core! You couldn't have just dropped one? I hate you."

"That's hard because the board doesn't actually have any evidence."

"Why do I even want this helm? It looks like an ugly lampshade."

Part of me was waiting for Mom to try to talk me out of the appeal for Eliza's sake, but she's firmly committed, her brow set. "I was afraid that you wouldn't want me to fight with the board," I tell her as we take a brief break. "It's only eight months until graduation. I figured you'd just tell me to suck it up."

Mom sets down her pen and pushes her laptop to the side. "The only reason I didn't pick a fight before is because of the Zellers. They have so many connections here and at the college. It's sick. Your dad was worried about what might happen if they came after me too." She scrubs her face with her palm. "When I say it like that, it sounds awful."

"I just feel like you gave up on me." The epiphany rolls over me—flattens me. "You didn't care about my suspension because you don't think it'll matter for college. That's it, isn't it?"

"You've never wanted to go to the more competitive schools," Mom replies quietly. "Eliza's dream is to go—"

"—to Stanford. Yes, we all know. How can I not?" Hilariously she wants to go to school for public policy despite being the least diplomatic person I know. "With her backup plans of Harvard, Dartmouth, and Duke." I roll my eyes, smiling to show that I'm only slightly sour. "She's so smart. It makes me sick."

CONNECTIVE TISSUE
Technically, I make you sick.

ME
No one asked you. Shush.

"I shouldn't have let that keep me from sticking up for you," Mom says. "I'm sorry, but I'm here now. There's a big chance that the Zellers will show up tomorrow, but I'm not going to let them intimidate us. Maybe it isn't too late to fix this."

"Maybe. Thanks for helping either way." It's strange to be so grateful for something I usually can't escape. It's like wishing for more seawater in the middle of a shipwreck. But this time it's different. Instead of just imposing what she thinks I need, she listened when I asked.

Mom's lips twitch in the hint of a smile. "I'm glad to be able to do something. You never ask for help." My expression must give away my frustration because she adds, "You're just independent. That's never a bad thing."

I'm all the things I've had to become. That's true of anyone, I suppose. But I'd like to think that I've grown, not simply been carved and hewn by what others have cut away. My hand falls to the screws along the crest of my hip, and they bring comfort for once instead of hopelessness. I'm not afraid of the board; I've fought greater battles than this.

Still, I have to admit that it's bleaker than I expected. "It just seems so weird that private schools can do whatever they want. How are they not under the same laws as everyone else?"

"Money buys exceptions for all the things that shouldn't be for sale," Mom replies. "That's what my civil-liberties professor always says."

"It's true. But then what do we do?" I don't say it overtly, but my implication is clear that we're never going to outspend the Zellers or Pineland or anyone on the board.

"We try. That's all we can do. We try."

Twenty-Five

"I have to go pick up Eliza," Mom announces during the next lull in our research. "I might just get a pizza on the way back since Melissa and Francesca are coming by at seven."

"Actually I can go get Eliza and pick up the food if you order it."

Mom narrows her eyes. "Why?"

"I just want to talk to Eliza about some stuff that happened at school today."

"All right. That's fine. Saves me a trip." She pulls up the menu for our second-favorite pizza place, the one that's on the route home from the boathouse instead of in the opposite direction. "I'll get our usual. Jason, do you want mozzarella sticks?"

"Do you have to ask?" Dad shouts back.

I tug a non-Oliver sweatshirt over my head and pluck my keys from their hook. Mom appears in the hallway behind me. "Hey, you haven't had any pain meds, right?"

"Mom."

She holds up her hands in placation. "I'm just asking."

"I'm not answering that." I twist on my heel and pull open the door. "I'm just going to pretend you didn't ask."

I step outside and savor the small victory. It's hard for Mom to understand that I don't need her to micromanage my health, no matter how much she means well. After all the acrobatics I had to jump through for even the weakest painkillers, I wouldn't ride a bicycle if I thought it would risk getting them taken away.

As I drive, I think about how impossible it seems to shake the molds that society has impressed upon us. *Special-needs mom.* There's a part of me that still feels like I should have stayed hidden, locking myself in my room or skipping school whenever I needed a crutch or a brace that I couldn't conceal. But it's a smaller part now. It's a start.

I drive through the arts district and pause at a red light in the center of it. Patrons come and go, clutching carryout containers or swinging reusable shopping bags.

I remember when this road went dark, the doors barred and windows empty. The coronavirus snuck up on the world, and suddenly, disabled and chronically ill people were at the forefront of so many conversations. Everyone was afraid for us, afraid of us, and afraid to become us.

I rub my temple as though I can push the memories from my mind. Society might have moved on, but I haven't forgotten how little effort it would have taken to leave just the tiniest of spaces for us. Even Oliver . . . *I'm so glad none of us got sick. I can't imagine living like that.*

Eliza doesn't let me stew for long after I arrive, practically sprinting over and ripping the passenger door off. "What happened? What's wrong?"

"Nothing? I just said I'd come get you because Mom seemed tired." I don't add that I want to talk about Pat. It might seem too much like an ambush, and Eliza bites.

"Okay." She sticks her bag in the back seat and climbs in with a pair of spare socks balled up in her fist. "That was nice of you." There's only a hint of wariness to her voice. She rubs her arms and starts peeling off her wet socks as I wait in the line of cars trying to exit. "Sorry. My feet probably smell."

We creep our way forward, passing the row of boat trailers painted in Pineland colors. I cast around for something to say. "How was practice?"

"It was all right. A little contentious."

"Why's that?"

"Everyone is upset about Principal Dombrowski and how he treated Kayla and Brandon. We're all a little on edge about what's going to happen next." Eliza fixes her ponytail and turns up the heat. "Kayla isn't in my boat, but you know how it is. We stick together."

I don't know how it is, actually. I've never had a team at my back, an automatic family of sorts. But after today it's a lot easier to see that my actual family is willing to step up for me. "Thanks for what you said to Pat."

Eliza turns away, fidgeting with one of the draw-strings of her waterproof rowing jacket. "Don't worry about it. It was nothing."

"Nothing? Yeah, right. As Ethan said, that was a homicide."

"An assassination," she corrects, her lips tugging into a smile. "Though I doubt it'll be enough to convince people not to pick him for homecoming king. It's like the worse he is, the more people like him. It makes zero sense."

"I think people are just afraid of him. I know I'm not a jock, but I'm so tempted to show up at homecoming just to vote against him and be annoying until they throw me out."

"He'd just make up some new nonsense about you." Eliza continues staring out the window, wrapping the drawstring around her finger again and again. Most people wouldn't think anything of it, but I've never seen her antsy before. She isn't just an island; she's an iceberg.

I don't want to pry or sound like a presumptuous older sister, so it takes me almost until we get home to broach the subject. "Are you okay? You seem kind of jumpy."

Eliza's chin droops to her chest. "Not really."

"What's going on?"

"I don't have that many friends outside the team. Most of them have been in the same schools together since kindergarten." She presses her lips into a thin line, her eyes shining with tears. "Nobody asked me to home-coming, and everybody has a date already. No one ever asks me to homecoming, but I just thought maybe now that I'm at the top of the varsity roster . . ."

Now it's my turn to deflate. "Dammit. I had no idea." I never paid much attention to homecoming since only jocks go, not even considering that I sleep down the hallway from one. "I'm, like, the worst sister ever."

"You're not," Eliza says, unable to agree with me on even this. "I just wish we didn't fight all the time. Like, you scared the stuffing out of me last night. You were screaming."

"Sometimes I just feel like no one listens to me unless

I'm screaming. I don't need you and Mom meddling in my life all the time."

"But why is it meddling if we just want to help you? If you try to row a boat by yourself, you just go in a circle—"

"Eliza."

"—and it's not admitting you're a failure to say that you need a port to your starboard because—"

"Eliza."

"—it's not just about being fast and pulling off a great start and having an amazing power twenty. It's about having a sharp coxswain and that one person who remembers to bring half a milk jug to rainy practices and—"

"Eliza."

"—a stern who can keep a good stroke rate because we all have our own part and . . . and . . ."

"Eliza."

Her shoulders and her face slump in unison, the air whooshing from her lungs in a single slow exhale. "What?"

"I love you, but you're such a boat nerd, and I have no idea what the hell you're talking about. You open your mouth to talk about crew stuff, and it's just like . . . Sounds come out, but there's no meaning. I don't know what a weighing 'nuff crab catcher does, okay?"

She attempts to laugh while crying, resulting in a goopy, snotty mess. There aren't any tissues in here, so she settles for napkins from the glove box. "I can't believe you've got the entire team on the verge of revolt."

"Yeah, this might not go well. To be fair I made it like three entire years and change without getting semi–thrown out in disgrace. That's got to count for something, right?"

Eliza stares off at the ceiling, the fingers of her right hand twitching in the air like she's typing. "Well, actually, with nine months per school year, you're closer to eighty percent, which is a low C."

"So I'm only twenty percent disgraced."

"Something like that," Eliza replies, hazarding a smirk that proves she might not have *that* gene from Dad, but she's certainly inherited his knack for goofy facial expressions. "I'm coming to the meeting tomorrow."

"What about practice?"

"I can afford to miss one day."

I stare at her, waiting for the cracks to show. Our relationship has always been dysfunctional at worst, transactional at best, dating all the way back to trading my Snickers Nutcrackers for her Reese's Cups at Christmas.

But she doesn't take it back or make a demand. "Thanks. I don't even know what to say." I can't remember the last time it felt like we were on the same side. It maybe isn't the worst feeling ever.

"Well, you better figure out what to say before tomorrow because we don't have nineteen thousand dollars lying around and I really, really don't want to change schools." Eliza presses a hand to her heart. "Yes, I was bluffing when I pretended to be interested in other offers. I don't know if the principal could tell."

I pull into the driveway and head inside, still stunned that Eliza is willing to risk her coach's ire just to show up and support me. I walk into the kitchen and trip over my own feet when I spot Francesca and her mom in the living room.

Noticing my surprise, Francesca jumps up, saying, "Sorry, we're way early! Google said there was a big accident, but it must have cleared up before we got there."

"That's okay," I reply, holding my arms out in greeting. I'm not a huge fan of people in my space bubble, but Francesca's a hugger, and she's more than earned one for putting up with me. "I'm just glad you're here for evil scheming time."

Francesca's hugs last at least an epoch each, so I double-dip by waving hello to her mom behind her back. I've never been able to get a read on whether Francesca's mom likes me or not, but she clearly doesn't hate me if she's sitting on my couch. "Nice to see you again, Mrs. Hill."

"You too. It's been a while."

I finally turn my attention to Mom, who's been making fish faces at me since I walked in. "Sorry, what were you saying?" I ask.

This time she enunciates. "Where's the pizza?"

While Mom and Mrs. Hill discuss the particulars of how the board operates, Francesca and I take a detour back to the pizzeria to pick up dinner. Our food is a little doughy in all the wrong ways, but Dad revives it by being the only one of us who knows how to use the convection setting on the oven. "You live in an RV for eight months with a rock band and you learn how to reheat pizza," he says.

"My dad was in a metal band," I explain to a perplexed Mrs. Hill.

"Oh, that's interesting," she says, scrutinizing Dad for a moment. "That's not something you hear every day."

It's awkward to fit five of us in the kitchen, and that's before Eliza comes back downstairs to inevitably eavesdrop after her shower. Dad rearranges the stools by the counter, and we move the table out until we can all sit and see one another at the same time.

Mom's collection of reference books dominates most of the table once we're finished with dinner, but judging by her repeated sighing, it isn't going well. "There are just so many loopholes for private schools," she laments. "Where's the accountability from a legal standpoint?"

"There isn't any," Mrs. Hill replies. "That's why I joined the board. Otherwise there's no oversight whatsoever. You can file a parent complaint, but nothing ever comes of it."

"Do you have any friends on the board who are trying to change things?" Dad asks. "Any potential allies who might be sympathetic?"

Mrs. Hill searches for something on her phone. "I haven't gotten back anything concrete. I've been working on this for a while trying to get Francesca's in-school suspension overturned."

It isn't long before the conversation drifts into an area that Mom deems inappropriate for me to hear. "Why don't you show Francesca around?" she says gently.

To her credit, Francesca gushes over everywhere I do take her, even though I've been to her humongous house. "You know, it's kind of weird that I've never seen your room before," she remarks, peeking around as I try to remain unbothered by this sudden collision between worlds.

It helps that it doesn't look anything like my room. Dad cleaned up the rest of the downstairs, but this remains untouched. "It's not usually this messy. I had a meltdown and, um, you know, kind of threw things everywhere."

Francesca joggles her head back and forth, her lip jutting out a bit as she takes it all in. "Honestly, though? You totally deserved to have a meltdown. You've had a lot going on."

"Why are you so nice to me?" I ask, only half joking.

"Isn't that what friends do?"

"Not all of them." I pick up a few trinkets that I should have thrown away a long time ago and shove them into the trash can. "I had this one 'friend' in middle school who wasn't really my friend. She never actually thought about how she made me feel. And, like, whenever I tried to talk to her about being disabled, she just accused me of wanting attention."

"That's bullshit," Francesca says indignantly. "May both sides of her pillow be warm for no reason for the rest of forever."

I giggle in spite of it all. I never imagined I'd think of Alexis and laugh, but hearing Francesca's oddly specific curses always makes me smile. "Can you believe that I almost missed her sometimes?"

"Why would you even want friends like that?"

Francesca asks, her gentle tone making the question rhetorical if I want to dodge.

I can't escape it, though, and each answer that floats through my mind seems thinner and thinner than the next. "I don't know."

"I'm just glad that we're doing this together," she says. "I would lose it if I had to go in front of the board by myself. But with you it doesn't seem so bad."

"We should have fought back from the beginning," I muse, thinking back to that terrible meeting with the Zellers. It's more than hindsight being twenty-twenty. It's that I should have wanted more for myself and my friends. "What if we're too late?"

Ever the optimist, Francesca simply ignores the gloomy undertones of my question. "Better late than never."

Twenty-Six

As much as I would love to sleep in, skip school, and go straight to the board meeting, I'm at my limit for unexcused absences. I can't even get through breakfast without panicking. "What if they just expel us on the spot?" I speculate.

"They won't do that," Mom reassures me. "At the very least they have to hear us out. Now get going before you're late."

"Speed as fast as I can? Got it."

She pelts me with a granola bar as I gather my belongings and lay the formal Pineland jacket over one arm for later. "That's not what I said. And take a snack."

"Do you want me to come too?" Dad asks on my way past the living room. "I can call out for the afternoon."

I do want him there—I'll take any moral support I can get—but it's not fair to jeopardize his reputation at work. "No, that's okay. It sounds like Mom's got it figured out." Or at least I hope she has a plan because I sure as hell don't.

"In that case I'll be holding down the fort until it's time for tuba. Good luck. Keep me posted on what's going on."

"Thanks." My arms are too full to manage a hug, so I just blow him an air-kiss. "I love you. I'll try not to get expelled and lose all our money."

Dad stretches his legs out on the couch, his right hand making devil horns and rocking in the air. "I love you too. Have fun storming the castle."

There's so much energy in the hallway before the start of homeroom that I swear I must have forgotten about some kind of assembly. But when I really tune into what people are saying around me, I realize that it's all about the board meeting.

As we get through homeroom, Life Skills, and my morning dose of Oliver ignoring me, I start to get the creeping feeling that the buzz is just gossip, not actual support. I meet up with Brandon after class, his haggard appearance suggesting that he didn't get much sleep last night. "Have people been coming up and talking to you?"

He groans. "I couldn't even get in the damn door earlier without everyone getting in my face. They're all saying they know Pat lied, but when I asked if they're doing anything about it, they're like, 'Oh no, I don't want to get in trouble.' Then why are you even talking to me?"

I'd like to give people the benefit of the doubt, but it becomes increasingly more obnoxious throughout the day. Francesca has noticed it too. "Everyone just wants to be supportive," she theorizes at lunch.

"But only if it doesn't cost anything," Ethan adds.

"It's the thought that counts."

I scoff. "Is it, though?" After the pandemic I'm jaded when it comes to giving strangers the benefit of the doubt. For years it was a perverse window into the worst of humanity, people pouring out in droves to get brunch while my hometown hospital treated patients in the parking deck. "Thoughts don't change things. Thoughts don't change you."

I would know. I wasted so much time locked in my own head, convinced that I wanted to be there. It's frightening how cozy it can become, how easy it is to reject anything that doesn't fit neatly into that comfortable little nook in your mind.

Francesca doesn't argue, too focused on writing her statement to the board that she hasn't even touched her food. "Do you know what you're going to say later?"

"I emailed you what I was thinking, but I wrote it at, like, three o'clock in the morning. I don't think I can use a lot of it."

Amber and Ethan read over what we have so far, transforming our lunch period into an impromptu writing workshop. Francesca's mom wasn't sure if we'd be allowed to give individual statements or just a group one, but I hope it's the former. No one's fate should ever rest on my words except my own.

The stress builds to a nearly intolerable level, until I'm biting my lip and grinding my toes into the floor to keep from snapping at my classmates for gawping at me every other second. I might be a zebra, but I'm not a zoo animal, and I'm not here for anyone's entertainment.

I hold on to that resolve as I wait and wait for the final bell. It comes too slowly, my nerves frayed and frazzled by retracing all the moments that led me here. When class lets out I hurry to my car to get my jacket and then straight to the bathroom to fix my hair and makeup.

My heart and my hip have a contest to see which is more aggravated, so I eat a disgusting salt tablet and take a Tylenol on the way out to the lobby to meet Mom. "I think I burned myself out already," I murmur. "Please don't let me screw this up."

"I'll talk as much as I can," Mom promises. "But I

wasn't at the fight. They're definitely going to want to hear from you."

A tiny piece of me was hoping that Oliver would show up, but when we file into the conference area it's just Francesca, Brandon, and Kayla on our side of the room. Mrs. Hill is seated opposite, conferring with one of the other board members in hushed tones.

Eliza is technically a spectator, so she takes a seat on the outskirts of the room where a few of the extra chairs are already occupied by adults I assume are here for Kayla. She's the only one of us who's underage.

"This jacket is always so itchy," she mutters in greeting. "I can't believe I let Francesca talk me into wearing the itchy jacket."

"You think it's itchy too?" Since my list of allergies is longer than a CVS receipt, I always figured it was a personal problem. "I thought it was just me."

The remaining board members arrive within a few minutes, and the entire layout is far more intense than I anticipated. Somehow I envisioned that we'd be in a courtroom setting or some enormous amphitheater with podiums. It's disorienting to just be seated at an ordinary conference table, all of us so close together that I can smell individual perfumes.

The board members take turns introducing themselves, and I've already forgotten the first person's name by the time we get to the last. An older man with a narrow nose, thick glasses, and a navy blazer seems to be the leader of the bunch. He doesn't bother asking us to introduce ourselves. "Thank you for taking the time out of your schedules to discuss your concerns. We take all parent and student feedback seriously, and we uphold only the most stringent standards of—"

Navy Blazer stops talking abruptly as the door opens to admit Pat and his parents. Mrs. Zeller sets a folio down on the corner of the table and turns expectantly to the board. "Is there some reason we weren't informed of this meeting in a timely manner? I had to be notified by my son that there was some question regarding the unprovoked, violent attack he suffered while showing school spirit at the latest pep rally."

I'm ready to disintegrate and soak into the carpet, but Mom's smirk tells me that she's prepared even if I'm not. "This is just a preliminary investigation into student disciplinary action," Mrs. Hill clarifies. "There was no need for you to be notified at this stage. We're collecting information to determine whether the appeal will be allowed to move forward to the next stages."

"Isn't your daughter one of the students involved?" Mr. Zeller asks. "That's a clear conflict of interest."

Navy Blazer isn't having any of it. "Given the pride that this school takes in its legacy students, it's not feasible to remove board members from every circumstance that involves a blood relative. I myself have three grandchildren who go to this school."

The middle-aged man to his right nods along, his thick, brown hair smoothed back with too much hair gel. "You're welcome to stay and observe the meeting," he offers to the Zellers. "We're not making any decisions today. We still need to gather the facts to respond to the appeals, so you'll have plenty of time to tell your side of the story."

"They act like they were so concerned about an investigation and facts the first time," Francesca snaps under her breath.

Once the board members manage to get the Zellers to be quiet, it actually proceeds in some semblance of order. True to her word, Mom doesn't let Pat's parents get to her. She reads through her statement, pausing periodically for emphasis or to lock eyes with the board members. I can see all her speech and debate classes paying off, which is good since she almost talked herself hoarse last semester in her determination to get top grades.

I'm so used to seeing Mom as my mom that I was never fully able to imagine her as a lawyer until now. "There's a notable lack of evidence linking my daughter or any of her friends to the injuries displayed by Pat Zeller. He didn't report any injuries to security on the day of the event. He didn't go to the nurse. How exactly are you proving that my daughter was involved with enough certainty that you can suspend her and add it to her permanent record?"

"We have statements from several other students that they witnessed the fight just as Pat described it," Hair Gel points out.

"And we have several students here who say that's a lie," Mom counters.

This is the stalemate I saw coming, and it's barely taken us ten minutes to get here. "It is a lie," Kayla chimes in. "Pat was being his usual self about us using the Sammy the Shark costume. We were trying to work it out, and then he just hauled off and punched Brandon in the face. He tried to do it again and punched Brynn instead!"

Hair Gel remains impassive. "So your claim is that an upstanding student with no disciplinary record and a very generous history with this school randomly punched another student for no reason over a mascot costume."

"Generous donations and no disciplinary record," Mom repeats. "It's funny how those two qualities are so often correlated. I'd be really curious to know how many complaints have involved Pat Zeller without there being any actions taken. Isn't that the better measure of his behavior? Is that something I can request for you to consider?"

Francesca's mom agrees before any of the other members of the board can answer. "I'll look into that. That does seem like valuable information to have. I also think we could cast a wider net to see if there are more witnesses who aren't as directly linked to the incident. It's a pep rally. Someone had a phone out when this happened."

Maybe if everyone wasn't petrified of getting squashed for contradicting the official story, that person would come forward. Because I agree with her—there's no way a video of that fight isn't sitting in storage on a phone somewhere.

"If there's no evidence besides eyewitnesses who disagree with each other, I just don't see how it's fair that I have this suspension on my permanent record," Brandon says in the ensuing silence. "I haven't had anything on my record before this except a couple of lates and a detention or two for making a joke that a teacher didn't think was funny. I've never done anything super bad, so it's just not fair."

He closes his eyes and draws in a deep breath. I think there's more that he wants to say, but he only shakes his head, unable to get the words out. His fingers drift to his collar, scratching at the uncomfortable fabric.

I squint at his jacket, trying to condense my thoughts beyond the nebulous idea that I'm missing something important. Itchy jacket . . . collar . . . fabric . . .

"Itchy jacket!" I exclaim to myself, interrupting Navy Blazer and drawing confused looks from both sides of the table. "Can I see that statement that Pat gave Principal Dude-orrm-browksi?" I clear my throat, taking the paper from Hair Gel.

"Need to refresh yourself on the facts?" Mrs. Zeller calls from the spectator area.

I flip over to the back of the page, cursing internally as I search for one particular section that Dudebrowski read out loud when he summoned us to the office the very first time. "Here it is. It says that Pat was trying to discuss the crew team's 'disrespectful use' of the Sammy the Shark costume when things started to get heated." I turn to the Zellers, hoping one of them will take the bait. "Is that right?"

"It's in black and white right there," Mr. Zeller replies, and it's not lost on me that it's a total nonanswer.

"And then the next part says that Pat was on his way to the locker room to return his homecoming regalia. Is that also true?"

"That's why it's in the official statement," Mr. Zeller snaps. "Is there a point you're making here? We're not debating the contents of my son's statement."

I quirk my head a bit, smiling so hard that it aches. "Aren't we, though? Because the funny part about that homecoming regalia is that it's made to be worn in the cold weather. Outdoor pep rally, right? Football games? That's why it's made of this thick, heavy fabric that looks like it's got to be annoying to wear because it has this gigantic fur collar that goes all the way up to your throat."

Francesca gets where I'm going before anyone else. She gasps, her mouth hanging open as she blinks at me. "SO YOU COULDN'T HAVE SCRATCHED PAT! BECAUSE—BECAUSE—"

"—because Pat was wearing a prince costume that looks like it has ninety pounds of fabric over his chest!" I finish with a flourish, resisting the urge to fling the statement at the Zellers. "Unless we took the time to rip his robe off first, it's impossible for fingernails to have made it through there to scratch him." I hold up my fingers for emphasis. "Look at my nails. Make it make sense."

One by one, the board members turn to the Zellers. While they're distracted, Brandon pulls my hand from the air and moves it in a dunking motion, whispering, "Mic. Drop."

"Well, Mrs. Zeller, you wanted to have your day today," Navy Blazer says. "It looks like you're going to get it." To us, he adds, "Thank you for your insights. We're going to continue investigating, and we'll reconvene at a later date to have a formal vote on your appeal. At this point we'd like to discuss things with the Zellers in private."

Kayla practically backflips out of her chair in her eagerness to get to the door. We leave in something close to orderly fashion, our faces rigid with forced seriousness. But the moment we reach the lobby we break out into celebration.

Brandon latches on to Kayla and swings her in the air, both of them laughing with relief.

"Did you see their faces?" Francesca asks, sharing a rare moment with Eliza. "They couldn't believe it."

"Oh my God." With such a weight lifted, I'm almost dizzy from the sudden change. "I wish they were recording that. I would watch that over and over and over."

"We should go get ice cream or something to celebrate," Mom suggests as we all calm down enough to start heading outside. "My treat obviously." To just me and Eliza, she adds, "It's certainly cheaper than nineteen thousand dollars."

Francesca stops abruptly at the head of the stairs. She twirls on her heel. "Um, actually, Brynn, I don't think you're going to want ice cream."

"I literally always want ice cream."

But then the group disperses enough for me to see beyond them to the person waiting at the bottom of the stairs.

"Oliver."

Twenty-Seven

Everyone is quick to depart, giving me some privacy with Oliver. There are still athletes heading off to practice and students working on club projects, so we tuck ourselves away in the parking lot, sitting on the open hatch of Oliver's SUV.

"I wasn't sure you were ever going to talk to me again," I admit after a lengthy stretch of silence. "It's not like I wouldn't have deserved it."

"I'm still just so angry," he breathes, unable to even look at me. "I shared everything with you. I was all in. And to find out that you were hiding so much from me . . . How am I supposed to get over that?"

He looks so forlorn that I almost want to leave and spare him the turmoil. His complexion is ashen instead of glowing, his eyes shadowed and glassy with pain. I reach out, ghosting my fingertips over the curve of his cheek. "I haven't seen you this way since freshman year, since the world was ending."

Oliver catches my hand and presses his lips to my skin. "My world *is* ending."

"I'm sorry." It's such a useless, throwaway phrase most of the time, but I mean it with all of my soul. "I let my fear hold me back from loving you the way you deserved. But I also needed to do this in my own time. It doesn't change how I feel about you. That part was always real."

His eyes flit to mine, and he brings our hands to rest in the open space between us. "I don't know how to start over. I don't know how to separate out what's real."

"All I can do is tell you the truth," I say. "It's not like I wanted to lie to you. But I remember how you acted during COVID, when all those people were getting sick and realizing just how bad it could be. You said you couldn't imagine living like that. How was I supposed to feel? Sickness is part of my life. And if you love me, then it's part of yours, too."

Oliver sighs, his feet dangling an inch from the pavement. He swings them back and forth, and I've always loved how he's slow to answer and slow to anger until he knows exactly what he wants to say. "I said that out of ignorance. Or empathy. It wasn't supposed to be about you."

"But it's not empathy to say that you can't imagine living with an illness," I explain. "That's pity. That's something else. It makes our lives seem so dark and sad and not worth living. And up until recently, maybe I would have agreed with you."

I gesture at the front steps of the school. "I guess the bright side of all this with Pat is that I had to look at my life and what I want it to be. I thought it was a dead end, but that was only because I talked myself out of living. I had to come to terms with it.

"It was always me when we were together. It just wasn't all of who I am." Like it or not, I have to admit that Dad was right—without the gene, the sickness, the pain, we wouldn't be here in the first place. It's part of who I am, and even if it's the worst of me, pretending it isn't there means that I'll never quite be whole. "And I do love you, Oliver. I've always loved you. I just never felt like I could keep you."

He turns to me at that, leading me closer. This kiss is different from any we've ever shared. It's soft and desperate and new. "I don't know why you would think that," he murmurs, our heads bowed together, hands clasped. "I've always been playing for keeps."

* * *

Over the next few days we return to long-gone habits, the little games we played when we were just faces on computer screens and voices on two ends of a phone line. Oliver takes it as a challenge, trying relentlessly to reconcile the Brynn of my past and who I am in the present.

"I tried to look up some information about EDS," he confesses one night as we stay up late talking about nothing, our phones barely charged enough to keep a connection. "There are so many types. I'm trying to understand."

"It's hypermobile Ehlers-Danlos syndrome, or hEDS for short." I type the full name out in a text to show him the spelling. "There's a mistake in one of our genes, but no one's pinned down which one just yet. It's a mutation of connective tissue, except instead of becoming something awesome like Mutant Ninja Turtles, we just get loose joints, velvety skin, and foot lumps."

"I never know when I should laugh. It's not funny, but the way you talk about it?"

"It's cliché, but sometimes laughter really is good medicine. Plus I don't know how I feel about being compared to a reptile who lives in a sewer." I trail off. "We're more like really bad X-Men who fall down a lot."

I yelp as my door bursts open to reveal Eliza in a regatta T-shirt and a pair of Pineland gym shorts.

"You're very sickeningly, disgustingly cute with Oliver, but would you *please shut up*?"

"I have to go," I say into the phone. "Eliza's going to kill me if I wake her up again."

She holds out a finger in warning. "I mean it. If you even think about getting on the phone again tonight, I am stealing it and dumping it into the middle of Lake Lenape."

Yet even after we hang up, Oliver resumes quizzing me over text message in a years-long game of 21 Questions that's exceeded its name by so much that we've lost count. I fall asleep answering the easier questions and wake up to more.

Oliver [6:03 A.M.]: Is blue really
your favorite color?

Brynn [6:04 A.M.]: Maybe it
was when you asked last time?
I don't really have one now.

He even texts me from the parking lot when he beats me to school.

Oliver [7:04 A.M.]: Cats or dogs?

Brynn [7:06 A.M.]: Dogs

Oliver [7:06 A.M.]: Storms or snow?

I read it at a red light and roll my eyes in six laps around my sockets. That is *such* an Oliver question.

Brynn [7:07 A.M.]: Neither
because they both hurt? I
guess snow. Cocoa and snow.

Oliver [7:08 A.M.]: Dark chocolate
or milk?

Brynn [7:09 A.M.]: Dark

But not all of his questions are completely absurd. When I check my phone just before dismissal, there's something far more serious waiting to be answered.

Oliver [2:09 P.M.]: Homecoming?*
(*not actually homecoming)

Brynn [2:09 P.M.]: Yes?

I find him waiting by my car, clutching the world's deadest, floppiest bouquet of chrysanthemums. He winces at the sight of me, holding out the flowers. "One,

I thought you were right behind me, so the timing was supposed to be better. Two, I did not realize it was going to get so hot today, and I have regrets about leaving these in my car."

"They're perfect anyway," I say, kissing him in between laughs. "I'll dry them. What do you have in mind for our not-actually-homecoming?"

Ever since the jocks took over homecoming, there have always been variants each year for what everyone else wants to do. Some students get creative with it, hosting "poemcoming" trips to slam poetry clubs or overnight camping trips in the state forests. Historically, Oliver and I have always gone to the beach, but I don't want to presume that we're still sticking to old lines.

"I thought you'd want to go with Francesca," Oliver says. "She suggested Wildwood this year instead of Ocean City."

"Yeah, she's been spamming me pictures of Oktober the Oktopus. Apparently it's Oktoberfest down there this weekend." I start walking toward my car to put away the flowers. "At first I thought she was after beer, but she says she's just in it for the pretzels."

Oliver chuckles. "Why does that not surprise me at all?"

"She's been so stressed waiting to hear back from the board." It's not like I'm exactly enjoying the wait, but it doesn't hurt as much as I thought it would to be without my clubs. I have more time to spend with Oliver and Francesca, more time to nap in the afternoons before I have to dive into homework. "She's going to hit the ceiling if Pat still wins homecoming king."

"It wouldn't surprise me if he did," Oliver says, echoing the thought that's been rattling around my brain now that the candidates are campaigning in full force.

As the days go by, I care less and less about having the social pulse on Pineland. These days I'm more infamous than popular, and I no longer find it worth the risk to poke around the rumor mill. But that doesn't mean I'm completely oblivious. "Oh, that's Ethan. I have to ditch you for a minute. Sorry."

I shoot Ethan a text message telling him to stay put. He turns in a circle at the edge of the parking lot, still not seeing me until I'm practically under his left foot. "Hey, there you are," he says. "What's up?"

"You haven't mentioned whether you're going to homecoming."

"I'm going. I just haven't planned it out yet." He scrutinizes me. "Why? You want to crash and make Pat's life miserable?"

"I'm pretty sure his life is already miserable with the way he acts. But no, I was actually trying to see if you have a date yet. My sister is kind of upset that no one asked her." Given Ethan's enamored expression after he watched Eliza verbally drop-kick Pat in the cafeteria, maybe it'll work out.

Ethan's eyebrows disappear under the shaggy mop of sandy hair that he grows outside of swim season. "I'll ask her," he blurts. "She's a total badass. Do you think she'll say yes? Will you talk to her for me?"

"I'm not going to make it *that* easy on you," I joke. "She likes sunflowers, dark green, and, um, boats. You can . . . talk about . . . water."

Ethan gnaws at his lower lip. "I better ask her today. We don't have a lot of time to plan." He fishes his cell phone out of his pocket. "Is she on Insta?"

I pretend to beat him with his own phone. "You. Are. Not. Asking. Out. My. Sister. On. Insta. Gram."

"Okay. Okay!" Ethan runs in a circle to evade me, laughing. "I'll ask her tomorrow! Don't break my phone! It's new!"

Eliza wants to play hard to get, but she only makes it a few hours before she caves and agrees to go with Ethan. She spends the next day and a half fretting about whether they match and how they'll ever find a boutonniere this late. I'm happy for her, though. Ethan is her polar opposite, and somehow it works.

Oliver and I decided against dressing up for Wildwood,

so I don't mind when Mom ditches us to take pictures of Eliza at Ethan's house. This might end up turning into something more than just being dates to a single dance.

I know we'll be walking along the pier, so I sit to put on my leg brace, the one that runs from my foot to my thigh. I plan to start small, phasing in the mobility aids I should have been using all this time. Looking back on all the pain I endured at Pineland without them, it seems so indescribably foolish that I didn't just use them sooner.

"You know what I'm looking forward to?" Oliver aims for a cute wink and misses so spectacularly that it ends up being adorable anyway. "A kiss at the top of the Ferris wheel. I always see that in movies, but I haven't gone on one since I was a kid."

I almost mumble something noncommittal before I catch myself. I've hidden my health for so long that I almost forgot what it's like to ask someone to meet me halfway. "I actually have, like, really bad vertigo. I can't even stand close to the railing on the second floor of the mall."

"Oh." Oliver's cheeks redden in splotches. "We can, uh, eat schnitzel. Do you like schnitzel?"

Dad sidles behind Oliver and bops him on the shoulder with the flat of his palm as he heads into the kitchen. "Very smooth."

"I'm sorry." Oliver draws in a steadying breath. "I don't know why that made me panic."

"It happens all the time." I stand and kick my right toe against my left heel to seat the foot plate of my orthotic, gesturing to the brace for emphasis. "People don't know what to say when you talk about health problems."

"Let me try again." Oliver combs a single lock of hair with his fingers once, twice. "Okay. So. You get vertigo. That means we shouldn't do anything at heights. I'm sure we'll find something else when we get there."

"I do like schnitzel, for the record," I say, smiling as I sling my purse over my shoulder and slip my arm into my crutch. "You have the whole drive to think up somewhere else for our epic kiss."

"Well, I would never suggest something cliché like— oh, I don't know—kissing at the top of the Ferris wheel. No, no, I have a much better idea. You see, we'll sneak away from the others for a bit, just the two of us." He leads me to his car and helps me load my things in the back seat, all the while speaking in that low voice he always uses when he pulls me into his daydreams.

"Maybe we'll come back with sand caked on our feet and windblown hair. . . .

"Or maybe we'll have full bellies and greasy napkins hidden in our pockets. . . .

"Or maybe we'll be carrying cheap stuffed animals and arcade prizes. . . ."

As we drive beyond the streets that feel like home, he gifts me with maybe after maybe. It's so different from the dates he used to describe, when his words would build adventures so detailed and untouchable that I couldn't quite place myself there. But now, even if the sand is too difficult to walk in or the greasy food turns my stomach, there are choices. Possibilities.

And in this moment I realize that this world doesn't leave much space for people like me, and no matter how much I fight, perhaps it never will. The villains don't always get their due, and instead of riding off into the sunset, I might have to limp my way there instead. But maybe Oliver, the boy who dreams of fantastical worlds and terrible third-act betrayals, can be a shelter in the storm of my disaffection—a home, a haven, a sanctuary to rest for the battles ahead.

"And when people ask where we went, I'll say, 'Nowhere special. . . .'

"Because it's not about the place or what we do there. . . .

"It's about you—unconditionally, you."

FADE OUT.

Acknowledgments

My eternal gratitude to my agent, Jennifer Wills, who has put in countless hours listening to me panic that maybe I don't know how to write a book after all. And to my editor, Nicole Fiorica, who always knows what I *meant* to say instead of what I actually typed at two o'clock in the morning after my fourth cup of coffee.

From the Simon & Schuster team, Aster Hung and Debra Sfetsios-Conover owe my neighbor an apology because I literally screamed when I saw this gorgeous cover. I'm in your debt. My thanks also go out to Eugene Lee, Elizabeth Blake-Linn, and Kaitlyn San Miguel.

All my love to my family—adopted, by marriage, and found. To Mom, Dad, Nana, and Andrew, you've put up with my weird writerly habits for over thirty years. That takes dedication. Mia, I'm sorry for making fun of your cat, but he deserved it. To Howard, Dottie, Katie, Rob, JR, Regan, Andrew, Erin, Andie, and Charlee, your support has meant so much to me as I've chased my dream of being an author.

Thank you to Jeanene Ciemancky, Caitlin Colvin, Sara Colvin, Zach Colvin, Mike Evans, Michelle Mohrweis, and Bethany Ruccolo for being the best friends I could ever have asked for. Special mention to Meghan Eyler since I somehow spelled your name wrong in Prepped's acknowledgments and still feel bad about it.

An entire paragraph of Anika—because I said I would. I must also include you, Callie, because I fear that a cursed onion ring will find me if I don't.

To my dogs, Remi and Potato, thank you for all the snuggles and love while I'm working, even though you try to eat my writing snacks when you think I'm not paying attention.

Lastly, I couldn't have done this without my husband.

James, you don't hesitate to pick me up an iced latte, drive me to surgery 700 miles away, or read terrible first drafts of my books, so I guess I'll renew your spouse subscription for another ten years. I love you, nerd.